MAZE OF MYSTERY

Who had stolen the sapphire necklace? Was
the thief really Lady Phillida, the poor little
rich girl who accused Marianna Wyndham of
the crime? Or Mademoiselle de Vere, the
demure French mistress who needed money so
badly and came into it so unexpectedly? Or
perhaps Betsy, the model maid with a secret
love life?

Even more pressing a question, why had the
brilliant and handsome Lord George
Barrington come to Marianna's aid? Was this
scandalously unconventional gentleman out to
prove her innocence—or to steal it?

Miss Marianna Wyndham had to find out the
truth—or face the consequences. . . .

EMILY HENDRICKSON lives at Lake Tahoe,
Nevada, with her retired airplane-pilot husband. Of all
the many places she has traveled to around the world,
England is her favorite and a natural choice as a setting
for her novels. Although writing claims most of her
time, she enjoys gardening, watercolors, and sewing
for her granddaughters as well as the occasional trip
with her husband.

Miss Wyndham's Escapade

by
Emily Hendrickson

A SIGNET BOOK

SIGNET
Published by the Penguin Group
Penguin Books USA Inc., 375 Hudson Street, New York, New York 10014, U.S.A.
Penguin Books Ltd, 27 Wrights Lane, London W8 5TZ, England
Penguin Books Australia Ltd. Ringwood, Victoria, Australia
Penguin Books Canada Ltd, 2801 John Street Markham, Ontario, Canada L3R 184
Penguin Books (N.Z.) Ltd, 182-190 Wairau Road, Auckland 10, New Zealand

Penguin Books Ltd, Registered Offices: Harmondsworth, Middlesex, England

First published by Signet, an imprint of New American Library, a division of Penguin
Books USA Inc.

First Printing, September, 1990
10 9 8 7 6 5 4 3 2 1

1

Marianna contemplated the choppy expanse of the North Sea as she slowly strolled along the damp, shell-crusted sand. The water off the Yorkshire coast looked cold, relentless, and unforgiving—and dead, as dead as she felt inside. She stopped at the far end of the beach where the pale sand turned to hard shale. She had been told the shore dropped off quite rapidly here. The waves rolled in to slap against the shifting sand, with foaming fingers beckoning, coaxing.

She sighed, angrily brushing a tear from her cheek that had the temerity to sneak from her eye. Glancing back, she could see the distant form of her maid, sitting huddled in a sheltered spot amid spiked clumps of green sedge. Daisy most likely thought her mistress had turned a bit daft after being sent home in disgrace.

Certainly it was enough to drive any woman to desperation. She returned her attention to the sea once again. She might slip and tumble from a rock into the icy water. If she did, it would be declared an accident, would it not? Although her mother said not a word and her father generously offered her a home, she knew her shame sat heavily on their shoulders. They were decent, respectable people. Her father was truly the knight and her mother always the gracious lady. Had times not turned against them, Marianna would have been the pampered daughter of the house. She'd have made her come-out in London just as they had planned since she was a young girl.

If only she had not gone to that miserable school, Miss Chudleigh's Academy for Young Ladies. That was where her troubles had started. That, and the depression in the price of wool, were behind her dilemma. Her dearest papa had invested unwisely, and that loss was due largely to the unforeseen changes because of that blasted war with the French. She kicked savagely at a piece of shale, succeeding only in hurting her toe.

"I'm innocent," she fiercely declared to the kittiwake that bobbed up and down on the waves. Clenching her hands into impotent fists, she glared at the bird. He neatly gathered a meal in his pale-yellow bill, then gracefully flew off, unconcerned with the angry young woman who stood on the shore.

A movement beneath the ebb and flow of the water off-shore caught her attention. There was something out there: large, silent, stealthy. Her troubles forgotten for the moment, she stared in horrified fascination as an enormous coppery creature with a hump in its back rose to the surface, then came toward her. It was impossible to run. Her feet clung to the damp shale as though glued.

The body was sleek, not scaly like the dragons in the fairy-tale books. It was a weird, frightening sight. Then she saw that what had seemed to be staring eyes at first glance were narrow windows of an odd sort. There was a peculiar little curved pipe that rotated about on the hump of the thing—or was it perhaps some manner of machine? Marianna watched, frozen, her heart thumping madly, as the strange-looking object seemed to direct the pipe end toward her. She stood her ground, the thought flashing through her mind that, were the thing to consume her, it would surely solve her family's latest trouble.

Then, with amazing rapidity, the object bobbed to the surface. Marianna observed bubbles foam up about what seemed to be a large copper-surfaced boat—a most peculiar boat, to be sure. The top of the hump flipped open and a man's head emerged.

Her gasp was unheard by the man who gazed across the water. He first stared at her, then searched the shore. When he disappeared from view, she wondered what would be next. After seeing this apparition rise from the sea, nothing would have surprised her at this point.

When Marianna found her feet could once again move, she began a slow, backward retreat. Fascination was all well and good, but hadn't she ought to alert someone to the presence of this vessel?

Before she could suit her actions to her thoughts, the man appeared once again and began to climb from the boat. Marianna paused to look again. There was a familiarity about that man. She watched as he plunged into the sea and swam ashore. He emerged from the surf, a primitive, compelling figure.

Water streamed from the tall, most masculine body clad in a now-transparent white shirt and indecently clinging nankeen breeches. She discreetly fastened her gaze upon his face. She knew that face! He winced as a piece of shale bit into the bottom of one bare foot. Wind ruffled his chestnut hair, drying it into a tangled mess.

"Hello, there," he called. "I wonder if you might be of help?" He strode cautiously across the shale until he faced her from a distance of a few feet. The breeze tore at his shirt, then plastered it more closely to his broad chest. Marianna found the sight of chestnut hair curling beneath the damp cambric more than a little intriguing.

His voice was as she remembered, deep and pleasant, with a hint of Yorkshire about it. He was more handsome, if such a thing were possible. Her eyes narrowed in amusement, her own troubles dismissed for the moment. He did not remember her in the least. Had she altered so much, then? She dipped a proper curtsy.

"I do not know what you wish, but perhaps we might be of assistance when I learn what you require, Lord Barringer," she said with just a little tartness creeping into her voice. She was aware that he had in the past a tendency to exert his excellent memory only for his scientific projects. However, it was humbling to know she had changed beyond all recognition to one who had known her so well.

He glanced about, obviously wondering who the other person might be. Seeming to catch sight of the maid, now hesitantly approaching, he nodded. "I need help in pulling my diving boat ashore. Would you be so kind to call some men?" He glanced down to his bare feet, hardly fitting for a trek over rough grasses and the rocky lane to the nearest village. He looked out to the vessel, where another man peered from the hump, then turned back to her, frowning. "Do I know you?"

Marianna almost laughed at his look of puzzlement. He hadn't changed in that respect, still wrapped up in his projects as his sister had written. That she knew he was titled had at last sunk into his brain. A stranger couldn't possibly tell that from his sodden attire.

"We have met in the past," she admitted. His sister had once complained to Marianna that her brother, George, was so single-minded, it was a wonder he remembered his own name, let alone the day, month, or year.

George Mayne, Viscount Barringer, surveyed the young woman before him with none of the haughtiness of a good many of his fellow peers. Truth be told, George hadn't bothered to use his title very much in the past, only when it got him something he dearly wanted. Pleasing his father about the dratted business of his title usage meant he now used it all of the time. Since his father indulged George's explorations into the realm of science, it was the least a good son could do for such a generous father.

He ran an impatient hand through his damp hair, wondering where he might have met the woman. He didn't go about much, too preoccupied with his current project, whatever it might be at the moment. Since his sister, Samantha, had married, it seemed he removed himself from company even more of the time.

Running a swift, analytical gaze over the woman, he could see she clearly was not a schoolroom miss. Her composure revealed that, if not her shapely form, so nicely revealed by the persistent wind. Focusing his full attention on her, he rapidly studied what he found. She possessed a tall, slender figure and a pair of very speaking sea-green eyes. The green sprigged thing she wore became her well. That fine-boned face, surrounded by a wealth of curling golden hair, did strike a familiar chord somewhere in his memory. Her speech declared her of the gentry, and he began to search his mind, mentally tabulating all the women he knew. There were not many to review in that list. He frowned, then his face cleared and he snapped his fingers.

"Wyndham. Sir John's daughter. Marianna." It was a statement from the man of science. He had sought a fact and found it. Never mind the "fact" was a lovely young woman who ought not be off by herself on this lonely beach so close to a dangerous tide. He ignored the wisp of a maid. She was too far off to be of any help. Why, he could scoop up the willowy Miss Wyndham and carry her off with him with no problem at all. Didn't she realize the perilous nature of her situation?

Then he recalled she'd been a friend of his madcap sister, Samantha. Not wild, though. As he recalled, when Miss Wyndham had been present, she'd been a calming influence. Why wasn't she married by now as Samantha had?

Hadn't his Aunt Lavinia said something about her coming back from a school? Some scandal, as he recalled more clearly. His eyes sought Miss Wyndham's in question. She certainly hadn't the look of an improper female about her. How could she be involved in anything like a scandal?

Drawing in an annoyed breath, Marianna nodded. His eyes revealed more than he suspected. He had remembered something about her, and she supposed it had to do with the crime of which she was accused. She turned away, resigned to the snub of a cut direct. Without looking back at him, she called over her shoulder, "I shall send someone directly when I reach the village, sir."

George raised his hand in futile appeal. She hadn't met his gaze. What had happened just now? One moment she had looked at him with an appealing glimmer of amusement in her lovely eyes; then, the next, she had turned, and now fled across the sands. He watched until she disappeared from view, then he plunged into the water and returned to his diving boat. He grasped the anchor rope that dangled from the bow and began to swim toward shore, trying to tow the boat.

"Save your strength, Barringer. No hope you'll make the beach. The odds are too great against you."

Treading the swells of the sea, George looked up at the conning tower where his best friend, Alex, peered at him from dry safety. "You could join me," he said, knowing full well how Alex disliked a cold swim. He agreed with his friend's assessment and motioned toward the anchor.

Alex dropped anchor, but George had doubts as to how well it would hold. He decided to return to the shore. Even he found the North Sea too cold after a bit. He stood on the sand, allowing the wind and sun to dry him off.

"Your young lady must have found help," Alex called out. He waved a hand toward the south.

George turned to discover several men trudging across the sands. They were sturdy, plainly dressed countrymen.

In no time at all the men had joined in beaching the fair-sized diving boat. It was a sturdy craft, well capable of holding six people below. While the others stood around examining it, George entered his boat. He shortly returned dressed in clean clothes and polished boots.

The lot of them retired to the Gull and Herring for a pint and to talk about the strange boat that had come to shore. George found himself and his crew of three the object of scrutiny and shrewd questioning. The locals knew his father and of himself by reputation, he supposed. It was some time before he could free his small group from the curious men in the congenial surroundings of the village inn.

The crew returned to the beach to check on the boat. One of the men, the lanky redheaded Tom Crowdon, offered to keep watch. George agreed, mentally noting to add to the man's pay. The other men, Bill and Joe, straggled back to find a room at the Gull and Herring for the night.

Barringer and Alex stood up on a grassy dune to survey the scene along the beach. The lowering sun cast shadows across the water, the subtle shadings lending a muted peace to the turbulent sea. The shorter of the two men spoke.

"Who was she, Barringer? The lovely lass who came to our rescue? Did she know you? She didn't fly away at the sight of you, at any rate." Sir Alexander Dent wondered if his friend had paid all that much attention to the lovely young woman who had stood on the beach. She had looked to be of the gentry. Such a lithesome, tantalizing girl so suitably covered in a demure muslin. Those blond curls that the wind had tossed about her head had seemed to capture the sun, like a halo of shimmering light. Why hadn't she worn a bonnet, as most proper ladies might?

"Sir John's daughter." George muttered the words in an abstracted baritone.

"That really doesn't tell me a whole lot, old man," Alex said, ruefully acknowledging his friend had turned his mind to his project. When that happened, the rest of the world ceased to exist for him.

In that assessment, Alex, for once, was wrong. George was still thinking about the lovely Marianna Wyndham. What was it Aunt Lavinia had told him about the scandal? How could anyone like a daughter of the respectable Sir John be involved in such a thing? She looked so innocent, as fresh and pure as the first snowdrop of spring in that green sprigged gown she wore. His memories of their childhood play were fond, if vague. But she had been a good child, ever ready for a romp. He had liked her.

"I believe she's innocent, Alex." George stooped over to tug up a long stem of grass, which he proceeded to chew. He thoughtfully narrowed his eyes as he attacked the problem presented with a scientist's critical examination.

Intrigued by these odd words, Alex prompted, "Of what, old man?" There were a goodly number of ways those words might be taken, and knowing Barringer, it was best not to make any assumptions.

George motioned his friend to join him in a walk back to the village, where he fully intended to locate transport. His mind demanded immediate answers to the question of Miss Wyndham's strange behavior.

Alex was more than a bit curious. This was the first time in his knowledge that Barringer had looked twice at a young woman. Especially in that searching, studied manner that revealed a deep interest to those who knew him well.

There had been more than one woman who had been attracted to the sensual good looks of his friend. Tall, lean, yet broad of shoulder, with that distant aspect about him that appeared to challenge the belles, Barringer seemed unaware of his appeal. Alex doubted if he gave women much thought other than an occasional good-natured tumble of a country maid when the mood struck.

An obliging ostler at the Gull and Herring brought forth two horses of respectable pedigree for the gentlemen's ride. Alex followed Barringer's lead with a rising stirring of excitement. He had felt this sort of thing when the army had crossed the Bidossoa into France. Anticipation of something to come.

The ride to Mayne Court took but two hours via a twisting route Alex would have been hard-pressed to duplicate. It was unexceptional as to the view from the road. At one point George slowed his mount to survey a pleasant estate. The house was of neat brick with lovely gardens to one side. At a questioning look from Alex, Barringer simply said, "The Wyndham place." He had spurred his horse and the two men had continued until Mayne Court appeared in view.

The house, built of small, finely pointed bricks, was a fine example of Baroque architecture. The bright-red contrasted beautifully with the weathered stone of the window frames and door surrounds. An elaborately scrolled pediment displaying carved stone horses decorated the entrance. Barringer ignored all this, jumping down, then tossing the reins of his mount to the groom who rushed toward them from the direction of the stables.

Alex dismounted, thoughtfully handing his reins over as well. Following Barringer up the broad steps and in the door, he found himself being greeted by Barringer's most curious-looking aunt. Alex had heard about her. He repressed a smile as he bowed formally over her hand. What an odd creature she was, to be sure. Wispy white hair escaped from a white lacy cap, while a white shawl was draped haphazardly over a jaconet gown, also of white. She looked like a very substantial ghost except for two patches of red on her cheeks.

"I knew you'd be coming back tonight. Saw it in my cup this morning." She caught sight of the puzzled expression of George's guest and explained, "I read the tea leaves, my dear boy. They are never wrong for me."

George tucked his aunt's hand close to him and ambled in the direction of the drawing room. This elegant ground-floor salon was where Aunt Lavinia held court from time to time. "What is on this evening's schedule?" he inquired with rare interest.

"I've invited the Wyndhams over for dinner and an evening visit. Since Marianna came home a few weeks ago, they have scarcely been out. I mean to see that stop. The chit is as innocent as a newborn babe. She would no more steal than I would," Aunt Lavinia declared with a righteous air.

George seated his aunt on her favorite chair near the window, then gave her a frowning look. That was not the best comparison she might have made, considering her penchant for adopting objects that did not belong to her while out and about. Although, he had to admit, since his sister married, Aunt had done nothing out of line—as far as he knew.

"I'm pleased to know your charity, Aunt. Miss Marianna . . . you feel she will come?" His question was posed with studied casualness.

Only Sir Alex caught the naughty gleam in Aunt Lavinia's eyes before she dropped her gaze to the delicate white fan in her lap. "Of course. It is most important that the gel be received in the best of homes. How utterly preposterous that anyone accuse her of stealing jewelry. She is hardly the sort to covet jewels not her own. Sir John saw to it she owned a lovely string of pearls before the cutback in trade reduced his fortune." Aunt Lavinia sighed over the distress of her dear neighbors.

"I met her earlier today. I must confess she does not look the type to be filching jewelry. Where is this supposed to have happened?" George inquired with a continued casualness destroyed by his purposeful line of questions.

"Dear Marianna was reduced to the position of a junior teacher at the school she had attended for some years. Her father's reverses, don't you know." Aunt Lavinia shook her head in sad reflection. "The darling girl has been accused of stealing a sapphire necklace from one of the schoolgirls. Silly chit ought not have had such a valuable with her. They could never prove a thing, of course. The headmistress accepted the word of the stupid young miss and another teacher. Marianna was dismissed merely because of the shadow of disgrace.''

"That is quite terrible," George said, thinking of the young woman he'd seen earlier. She had noticed something in his expression that revealed he knew of her circumstances, he felt sure of that. She had turned away from him then. Had she expected to be snubbed? "What utter rubbish."

Turning to Alex after reaching a quick decision, George declared, "I believe we must do something about this poor girl."

"I say, old fellow, it's a smashing notion, but I do not see how it is to be accomplished. What could you possibly do?" Sir Alex was fascinated by the change in his friend. Barringer doing something about a young lady's distress? Charging to the rescue, so to speak? Alex's gaze slipped to Aunt Lavinia. Here he met the satisfied eyes of a genuine schemer. The old lady was up to something.

"When she arrives with her parents, I intend to discuss the problem with her," George declared, rubbing his hand over his chin in a reflective gesture. "I am certain that if we analyze this business, we can see a solution." He turned to see the butler standing just inside the door. "Peters, would you be so good as to order up a couple of baths for Sir Alex and me? That saltwater swim has left me feeling dashed crusty. We wish to be presentable when Aunt's guests arrive for dinner. I suppose we dine early, as usual?" Turning to his friend, he added, "Alex, you will have to tell your stomach to adjust to country hours."

"My stomach has never been overly fussy about the dinner hour. As long as I get fed." He grinned engagingly at his friend, then bowed over Aunt Lavinia's hand before departing the room with Barringer.

Peters paused before leaving to issue instructions regarding the baths.

"I believe I shall have tea," Lady Lavinia said, smiling with glee at the long-time retainer with the air of a fellow conspirator.

One of the footmen entered shortly with a silver tray holding the necessary components for Lady Lavinia's requested tea. She stirred the contents of the pot, faintly resembling a witch at her brew. She poured, drank hurriedly, then began her tea-leaf-reading ritual. Rotating the cup for the final twist, she turned it over to study the interior. Hmm. The shark told her that danger lurked close by, since the shape was close to the handle. A noise at the entrance forced her to set the cup aside. She rose reluctantly, hating to postpone the reading, yet she smiled with pleasure at the sight of her good friends.

"Irene, my dear, and Sir John. How good to see you. And Marianna. I am so glad you have come." She said nothing regarding the scandal. She had discussed it with Irene, Lady Wyndham, exhaustively. She had persuaded Irene that there must have been a conspiracy afoot, a solution her friend had been only too eager to accept.

Glancing at the cup on the table, Lady Wyndham said, "I fear we have disturbed your reading."

"Actually, it was for someone else. Or something else." Lavinia darted a hasty glance at Marianna before giving her friend a meaningful look. "Perhaps Marianna would give me the pleasure of reading her cup? There is ample tea."

"Oh, I do not know . . ." said the young woman with no little hesitation. She was not all that sure she wished to partake in what she considered a pagan rite, and she was not thirsty in the least. Yet Lady Lavinia was quite respectable, or near enough so.

Succumbing to her curiosity, Marianna joined Lady Lavinia in the sofa, then followed the careful instructions, sitting back to await the verdict.

"Oh, dear," Aunt Lavinia murmured.

"What is it?" asked Marianna anxiously, leaning over to peer into the cup, quite forgetting she had been reluctant at first.

"The drops of tea remaining in the bottom of your cup show a sad situation indeed. Tears, you know." Lavinia then brightened, continuing, "But the shell close to the handle tells me that the injustice you fight against will soon have a good outcome. Good news, luck, and money are on the way. There is a boat as well. I believe you are to travel, my dear." She beamed a satisfied smile at the young woman.

There was a stir at the door. George, Lord Barringer,

followed closely by Sir Alexander Dent, entered the drawing room. They bowed with perfect civility to Sir John and Lady Wyndham, then turned to Marianna.

"We meet again," George said. "I trust you met with no difficulty in your return to your home?" He stood before Marianna with a casual, unaffected grace, his usual pensive air dispelled.

She blushed slightly and shook her head. Finding the voice she thought she had lost, she replied in a soft tone, "None whatsoever, thank you, sir." Pleating the soft peach muslin gown she wore, she wondered why she should suddenly feel ill at ease with a family friend. The memory of that damp cambric shirt and water-plastered breeches that had clung so enticingly to his form rose in her mind, and she thought she knew why. Barringer had stirred unfamiliar feelings inside her. The sort that had made her heart beat fast, her mouth go dry, and an ache begin in her middle.

"I was discussing your situation with Aunt before you came." He ignored her look of distress. "I decided we must, as good neighbors, do something to help."

Sir John had overheard this remark, spoken so close to where he sat. "How do you propose to prove that she is innocent when they refuse to accept anything but the jewels? If she finds the sapphires, they will say she knew where they were all along. If she does not find them, she is still guilty in their eyes. My poor girl." He bestowed an anguished look on his only daughter. "I can think of nothing that we might do to help her."

Marianna felt angry and humiliated that she should be discussed in such a way, yet she sensed they meant well. A feeling of injustice burned within her.

"It is obvious," George declared with the air of one who has that rare ability to see to the heart of a matter. "Someone else must locate the sapphires for her." He glanced around the group to see if the others agreed with him.

"What a capital idea, George. But who can accomplish such a difficult task?" inquired his aunt with a sly little smile hidden behind her favorite fan.

George glanced at his aunt, then at the lovely Marianna. "I shall. But I will need your help, Miss Wyndham."

"I believe that as our families are old friends and you have known her for donkey's years, you can dispense with the formalities, George. First names are such a nice way of conversing." Lavinia looked at her friend, Lady Wyndham, to see a mutual gleam surface momentarily. "What do you propose, George, dear?" Lavinia didn't believe in wasting precious moments.

"Time is of the essence. The sooner we tackle this nasty accusation, the better. We shall take my diving boat down the coast to wherever it can be closest to her old school." He looked to Marianna to supply the location.

"Miss Chudleigh chose to situate the school in Lowestoft. 'Tis a small town, but it has much traffic, and gentry send their children from quite a distance. I suspect one reason she selected Lowestoft is that costs are much cheaper there." There was a hint of bitterness about Marianna's mouth that soon faded as she looked about the circle of friends and parents. How comforting to think she had a champion, though he did not resemble her notion of Saint George in the least. There was nothing saintly about his appearance.

"Excellent from our point of view," George said, quite pleased his scheme would work.

"And is your diving boat called a dragon?" Marianna said, thinking that if he was to be her champion, his boat might as well have a companion name.

Sir Alex caught her meaning at once. "George and his dragon? Oh, I say, very good, Miss Wyndham. Very good." He grinned at her with great charm, a bit sorry she had eyes only for George. But then, he always felt more at ease with young women who didn't appear on the hunt for a husband.

"Call me Marianna, please. If you are to be a part of the rescue of my good name, we will become quite close, I expect. Although I am not certain about traveling on that boat." She looked to George for the answer to this query.

"Oh, it is fast and quite safe," Aunt Lavinia declared. "I

believe I'd best go along, to provide a character witness, don't you think? And chaperone as well, of course. I shall be able to testify I have known Marianna since she was an infant, her family as well. I daresay that as the sister of the Earl of Cranswick, prominent personage in the government, my word shall not be ignored.'' She tilted up her nose in a haughty manner, then winked at Marianna.

That young woman gave a soft laugh. How glad she was that she hadn't slipped off a rock this morning. Of a sudden, the world had taken on a happier glow. Turning her eyes to the person who offered to solve her dilemma, she sighed. This scheme did not promise to be the easiest path. She could foresee a difficulty or two along the way, not the least of which was that she was attracted to George and he . . . Well, George, Viscount Barringer, was a hopeless case.

Every woman in the area had long given up on him. Marianna would ignore him the best she could. The important thing was to recover those sapphires and prove her innocence. Until then, she was beyond the pale for anyone.

2

"Tell me about this diving boat of yours, George," said Marianna as she confidingly placed her hand on his arm. She supposed George was like other men, flattered at interest in what absorbed them. Yet she was truly curious of his strange craft. Samantha had told her all about the flying machine that led to Sam's marriage to the estimable Marquess of Laverstock. And now to consider that George had turned his attention from the sky above to the sea below was quite fascinating.

They strolled along behind the others into the dining room. George felt an unfamiliar surge of emotion, though he couldn't put a name to what it might be. Rather, he concentrated on explaining the concept and background of his unusual boat to a gratifyingly rapt listener.

"You see, the theory of diving boats has been around for many years. Why, an early mention of the idea is found in the 1500s. A chap named Van Drebbel actually built a submersible boat and 'tis said he had King James as a brief passenger."

"Amazing." Marianna gracefully slid onto her chair at the dining table, most intrigued by George's account.

"Later," George continued after seating himself at her side, "a Frenchman named de Son tried to build one, but it never did submerge completely, although it was considered a great wonder in its day." He helped himself to a portion of turbot, then added a spoon of potatoes before resuming his explanation. "An English fellow—name of Wilkins, as I recall—also proposed a submarine vessel, an ark, I think he named it. Never built one, though."

George indicated a preference of wine, then saw to it that

the lady at his side was properly served before resuming his discourse. "Then this Fulton came along a few years back. He is an American chap who actually built a submersible boat that worked. Only thing was that our war department did everything they could to keep it under wraps." George speared a piece of excellent beef as though it might be the unfortunate gentleman who had spirited the information of Fulton's boat into hiding.

"Surely they wished to keep such a boat from the hands of the French," Marianna said reasonably.

"He had offered the plans to them first; Napoleon knew all about it. I had the information directly from Lord Hawksbury. I found Benjamin West knew Fulton as well, but West was of little help to me in my search for the actual plans. I ran into quite a few brick walls." George remembered to eat and forked a morsel of potato in his mouth.

"Then, however did you succeed? For I can see you have done very well in your quest." Marianna flashed him an admiring smile while managing to consume an excellent tidbit.

"It took every bit of pull my father had to locate what information I could get. You see, the men at the ministry put the information on Fulton in private files rather than the official files. When they left, the files were either destroyed or taken with them."

"So, what happened?" Marianna found his tale intriguing. Who could believe such a complicated deal regarding a mere boat?

"Fulton had finally persuaded the French government to build him a diving boat. They tested it at sea and blew up a vessel so completely that nothing was left of her. Well, it seems that, in spite of this success, Napoleon lost interest in the craft." His scorn for the shortsighted Napoleon was mingled with thanks that the Corsican had been so foolish.

"How fortunate for us," said the perceptive Marianna.

George gave her an approving look. Really, the girl was most intelligent.

Across the table, Lady Wyndham exchanged glances with Lady Lavinia. It was truly a joy to see her dear girl put aside her troubles for a while. Knowing the viscount, it was doubtful that anything might come of the interest. He was so absorbed in his scientific projects it was a wonder he remembered to eat. But it served a purpose for the evening. It was well Marianna possessed a sensible heart. There would be no false expectations.

"I take it that Fulton offered the plans to our government after a bit of skillful negotiation, and you have managed to ferret out enough details to develop your own diving boat?" Marianna said, deciding to lead the conversation to the present time.

"Well said," George replied. Marianna really had become a most remarkable woman. "Your powers of observation do you credit." Her grasp of the situation was far above the usual. In his experience, women were either bored to death in a few minutes of his conversation, or merely continued to flirt, not listening to a word he said. Marianna was different.

"When Fulton left this country for America, it is believed the submersible-boat plans remained behind, locked up in someone's private library. No matter. I went to everyone who knew anything about it and wrote down their descriptions. From that I was able to design my own boat. Fortunately there are excellent shipbuilders right in Scarborough." He considered the meat on his plate and consumed a few more bites before returning to his current topic of interest.

"I thought Papa said they built mostly whaling ships?" Marianna wished to let him know she was informed as to the local area. But she knew full well that George was quite wrapped up in his project. She was grateful that his present concern was one that would keep her from dwelling on her dilemma for a brief time.

"True," George replied. "I found just the right firm I needed for my project." He caught a couple of words from the other end of the table and glanced at his aunt.

Aunt Lavinia spoke. "You are of a mind, I take it, Sir John?" She didn't bother to query Lady Wyndham. She knew what her answer would be.

"How do you propose to go about this, George?" Sir John replied by way of an answer. His hazel eyes fairly snapped beneath those frosted brows and hair. Lean and fit, he looked capable of taking on the threat to his daughter single-handedly. Only when he moved about did he reveal a hesitancy in his left leg, the result of a hunting accident.

Immediately aware of the subject, George said, "I shall leave one of my men here and take Aunt Lavinia and Marianna along in his stead. I might request you to perform a task or two if you don't mind." George glanced at Marianna, but found no demur. He seemed to take for granted that his aunt would be able to perform the slight jobs he might require.

"How long will it take to travel there?" Lady Wyndham asked, finally accepting that something was actually going to be done to help her dear girl.

"I shall know that after checking my maps. We travel with the currents, and they are well marked. Since there is no need to submerge, we can go faster by using the sail." George took note of Lady Wyndham, another sensible woman, it seemed. That augured well for the trip. If Marianna took after her mama, there was not likely to be vapors and such nonsense on the journey. He couldn't abide missish females.

"I fail to see why you don't just take a plain old boat," Sir Alex said, teasing his friend a bit.

George gave him a derisive look. "Because this is the only boat I have at present, and—who knows?—it may prove useful." He believed in being prepared for any eventuality. One never knew what curious development might occur. He relished the very idea of the novel and the unusual.

Seeing that everyone had finished eating—even her dear nephew had consumed more than usual—Lady Lavinia suggested they move the discussion to the drawing room, where they might have their tea and discuss the expedition. "All must be planned with care, you see," she explained to Lady Wyndham, who nodded in return. The two older women exchanged meaningful glances while making their way from the table.

George said nothing about the abandonment of the customary sharing of port and conversation by the gentlemen. Rather, he focused on the project ahead. That a lovely young woman was an integral part of that project appeared not to have penetrated too deeply, Sir Alex decided as he watched his good, if absent-minded, friend. Not that there was a thing wrong with dedication, mind you, for little in this world was accomplished without such devotion to the task at hand. But at times George went overboard. He hadn't always been this way. Before he plunged into this scientific business, he'd been the best of fellows. He'd been a curious sort all his life, always poking about and into things. But lately . . . Alex shook his head, trailing behind the others, watching the various expressions, musing about possibilities.

Once in the drawing room, the group drifted into two distinct parts. Marianna gladly joined her mother and Lady Lavinia on the sofa before the fireplace while George strolled over to be with Sir Alex and Sir John over by the windows.

The viscount found himself at odds with this arrangement, but could find no reason to alter it. He had found Marianna Wyndham to be a very superior young woman and missed her place at his side. However, he soon turned his powers of concentration to the proposed expedition, setting aside his thoughts of Marianna with surprising reluctance.

After some time spent discussing the eventualities of the proposed trip, Peters brought in the tea tray loaded not only with the delicate Wedgwood china, but with an assortment of tasty cakes and biscuits. A footman followed with the tray bearing the very large teapot plus the pots of hot water and milk along with the dish holding thin slivers of lemon.

Marianne observed that the silver pots were shining and that the biscuits and cakes appeared to be first-rate. Signs of a well-regulated household. How fortunate that George had his aunt to manage things for him. With his mother dead these many years and his father in London, deeply involved in government affairs, should Lady Lavinia ever decide to move away to more pleasant climbs, George would be left in dire straits. And in need of a good woman at his side, a voice added. She admitted to herself that she could think of far worse fates at the moment.

The gentlemen joined the women near the sofa, accepting the teacups and delicious cakes with pleasure. If Sir John might have wished for the conversation at the table and the good port George's father had laid down, he certainly gave no indication.

"Well, Viscount," said Lady Wyndham, always the one to use a correct title, "I am gratified of the service you do us in assisting the restoration of our daughter's good name. We shall be ever in your debt." She nodded ever so slightly in emphasis.

George reflected that Lady Wyndham was undoubtedly the most ladylike woman he had confronted in some time—other than his own dear aunt, that is. Lady Wyndham possessed that fine degree of aristocratic, dignified, yet feminine grace of the true gentlewoman. He was also not slow to note that her daughter showed herself to be in a fair way to emulating her mother in these qualities.

"Should he succeed," Marianna added softly, who was by no means convinced that the handsome but pensive George would be able to clear her name, no matter how brilliant he might be.

Sir Alex was amused, but not George. Though those words might have been softly spoken, both men had heard them. George gave her a glacial look. Perhaps she was not as intelligent as he first thought.

Unaware of his aunt's earlier reading for Marianna, he said rather stiffly, "Why do you not prevail upon Aunt Lavinia to read the leaves in our cups before setting out on our journey?" He was cognizant that Sir John and Lady Wyndham were not overly enthusiastic about Lavinia's unusual talent, but felt the reading to be useful.

Marianna glanced at George, surprised that he would have reacted to her gentle comment, but glad that he had. It was good to know his mien could be pierced.

Lady Wyndham patted her friend on the arm. "I should like to be the first," she said, hoping to offset her daughter's unguarded remark by this action.

Lavinia smiled, quite accustomed to skeptics. After her predictions had all come true in the *May Queen* affair with Samantha, word had spread and she was seeing less disbelief lately.

After reminding Lady Wyndham of what she might have forgotten since last she had joined in this ritual, the gentlewoman slowly swirled the tea around in the cup in a counterclockwise direction, using her left hand. After this, she turned the cup over, keeping the handle toward her, then handed it to Lavinia to read.

"I see lace, elegant lace, in your cup," Lavinia announced with great satisfaction. "That is a lucky sign, a sure indication that things will improve soon."

In spite of not actually believing in such nonsense, Lady Wyndham felt strangely comforted by the words.

"Would you be so kind?" Sir Alex stepped forward, cup ready for his reading.

"Naturally," said Lavinia, liking this particular friend of her nephew's very much. She studied the interior of his cup, then smiled up at him. "There is a ship, which tells me your journey will be lucky for you. The rocket reveals a happy event to come." Lavinia decided to conceal that said event was to be a passionate one. Alex might not appreciate such news in the present company. "But this eye on the other side warns you had best keep vigilance."

"Hmm, that is not unusual when I'm with George. A man needs to keep both eyes open, for George, here, often has his fastened on a book," Alex said with a decided twinkle in his brown eyes.

"Or a project?" Marianna inserted in a daring comment.

"But," continued Alex, ignoring that little aside, "why consider it a warning and not an instruction? Are we facing danger, then?"

Lady Wyndham gave a tiny cry of alarm and Marianna sighed with disgust. Really, men were not very bright when it came to knowledge of the female mind. Should her mother acquire the notion there might be danger in the air, Marianna would be confined to the Wyndham estate. She suddenly felt a strong desire to make this expedition. And not just to clear her good name.

"I do not see how there can be much danger, dear lady,"

said her husband. "After all, it is merely an academy for young ladies, is it not?" He looked to the others for reassurance. "There is nothing else?"

"Of course, Mama," soothed Marianna. "There is absolutely nothing to fear. George's diving boat will surely get us there in safety, and as to the rest, I feel certain there is no worry."

Mollified, Lady Wyndham relaxed a trifle, although it was difficult to detect. She had been rigorously trained by means of a backboard in the importance of proper posture. Once instilled, this learning remained for life.

Lavinia accepted Sir John's cup in what she felt was a conciliatory gesture. A glance at the pattern revealed brought a smile to her lips. "An ivy leaf, Sir John. How fortunate you are. Why, it means you have reliable friends. Could anything be better?" She gave him a playful glance, then smiled at his dear wife, the nicest of friends.

"A good wife and daughter . . . and perhaps a favorable price for wool?" While he said the latter with humor, all knew it to be the truth.

Clearing his throat, George stepped forward with his cup, giving Marianna an annoyed look. Perhaps he ought to have second thoughts about bringing that young woman along? Yet, she was vital to exploring the town and area near the school. And, after all, how much could she do to alter the course of his serene life? He was quite content as he was now, with his aunt capably looking after his needs and overseeing Mayne Court with devoted care.

A strangled sound from his aunt brought his attention back to her. She seemed mildly upset.

"I see a windmill, George. This is a tricky venture. It will probably work out, but it will require a deal of hard work before success comes." She squinted her eyes to see a little clearer.

Sir Alex moved a branch of candles closer for better viewing. He was amused that while one might assume George to be disdainful, he was most intent on what his aunt had to say.

Lavinia gave Sir Alex a grateful look, then continued. "I believe that is a rabbit's foot I see near the handle. 'Tis good luck, you know. Your gamble, whatever it might be, ought to pay off handsomely." Aunt Lavinia beamed an encouraging smile at George. "There also seems to be something else represented. I think it is a weathercock, which tells of indecision. That would not be too unusual. Decisiveness, dear George, is what is called for at a time like this."

"Well, that is not so very bad, is it? What about you, Marianna?" George bestowed a lofty stare at his guest. Really, it was annoying to feel so ambiguous about a young woman, so torn in two ways.

Her heart plunging oddly, Marianna gave George a defiant look. She leaned forward, smiling to reassure Lady Lavinia. "A second reading, milady?"

"I could read yours again, Marianna," said Aunt Lavinia, who felt compelled to make a second attempt. Those tears the first time, you know.

Marianna had never figured out how Lady Lavinia could make sense out of what seemed to be odd blobs and bits of soggy tea leaves, but was far too polite to give voice to her thoughts. Rather, she sat courteously as she waited while the good if somewhat eccentric lady peered into the teacup once again.

Aunt Lavinia's readings probably accounted for the china at Mayne Court. It seemed new and was a delicate design, with cups that were plain on the inside. A pattern would definitely interfere with the readings. Aunt Lavinia had much to do with the ordering of the estate, what with George having his nose in projects of late. Marianna wondered what he would do once it came time for him to choose a wife and produce the required heir to inherit Mayne Court and the considerable fortune his prudent father had amassed, plus what had been inherited. That was a subject best brushed aside. Even with her name cleared, the daughter of a nearly impoverished neighboring knight would not be on the short list of candidates for viscountess.

Lady Lavinia studied the interior of the cup for a few moments, then gave Marianna a troubled look. "Near to the handle I see a vulture. This tells me of the recent loss and theft. It also reveals jealousy and spite from someone close to you." Lavinia returned her gaze to the cup while feeling a disturbing rise in concern. "The open umbrella tells us you will get help,

and the small lighthouse indicates to me that the trouble can
be averted, but that hidden dangers will be revealed.'' She set
the cup down on its saucer with a tiny clink that echoed throughout the room.

This pronouncement was followed by a shocked silence. And
not one of the group was more shocked than Marianna.

While faint, her stunned gasp had been caught by George.
''Have you thought of something? Perhaps a clue?''

She slowly shook her head, not desiring to reveal what wild
notions had raced through her mind upon hearing Aunt Lavinia's
words. Her mind fastened upon some of the phrases: ''will get
help'' and ''trouble can be averted'' had registered, but what
stood out were the other two—''jealousy and spite from someone
close'' and ''hidden dangers.''

''Oh, dear,'' Lady Wyndham murmured, obviously much distressed again. It was evident the good lady was of a mind to
forbid the journey.

Sir John, wise man that he was, took matters in hand. ''We
must risk this chance to clear Marianna's name of the evil deed
imputed to her. I trust George and his friend Sir Alexander to
do all that is necessary to protect our beloved daughter from
harm.'' He placed a comforting hand on his dear wife's
shoulder.

Wordlessly the couple exchanged a look, which, while
troubled, seemed to bring final reassurance to Lady Wyndham.
She nodded, then dropped her gaze to her lap, where her restless
fingers had mangled a dainty handkerchief into shreds.

''You undoubtedly have the right of it, Sir John,'' his wife
said with all the formality of her generation.

Idly staring at Marianna's cup, Lady Lavinia frowned, then
stated. ''Those jewels are somewhere near a body of water. I
can feel it quite strongly.'' She turned her gaze to George, her
face plainly revealing her curiosity. She was rarely given to such
statements—just out of the blue, so to speak.

This statement was also followed by a deep silence. Sir Alex
dropped onto a chair near the sofa, watching the faces of the
others with keen eyes.

George appeared to be much struck by his aunt's words. He slowly paced back and forth before the fireplace, hand rubbing his chin. A few minutes went by, then he paused, staring first at his friend. Assured at what he saw on Alex's countenance, George spoke. "There is no doubt we must return to where the accusation was made. Do you not agree, Marianna?" He turned to her, eagerly awaiting her reply. He couldn't have begun to explain the urgency he felt, nor the compulsion that drove him to right this wrong done to his neighbor.

She was warmed by his concern and the undecipherable look in his sherry-brown eyes. The candles created tiny golden flames in the sherry, bringing to mind the heat of the sun on a late-autumn day. Suddenly she decided that she would like to make that short list for his viscountess.

George Mayne, Viscount Barringer, was a good, kind man to become so involved in her troubles. He was also handsome. And as far as Marianna was concerned, he also was a reincarnation of Saint George at the moment, coming to her rescue in such a dashing, positive manner. That he would use what she thought of as his dragon to assist her, instead of slaying it on her behalf, mattered little. Marianna had a protector in the old-fashioned sense of the word. And she felt cosseted and wondrously feminine and very aware of her womanly powers. She believed they would succeed. Now if only George did as well . . .

"I believe George is correct," Marianna said. "Whatever clues there may be to the mystery surrounding the disappearance of those sapphires will undoubtedly be found at the academy. I left in such a rush I had no opportunity to do any sleuthing about the place. Although I do not see how it can be accomplished at this point. While the girls are still at school, I am forbidden entry there. What good may we accomplish once we come on the scene? How do you propose to ferret the truth of the matter and bring the jewels to light?"

She gave him a trusting look and was disappointed to see he was so deep in thought that he totally missed her admiration.

"Can you tell us anything that might help? Is there any one

person who might benefit from the theft?'' Sir Alex queried.

Marianna gave the group a grim little smile. "Nearly everyone in the academy. The girls are allotted very small amounts of pin money, the rest remains with Miss Chudleigh. No one ever seems to have sufficient money for wants. And please understand that the teachers are not only underpaid but overworked. Miss Chudleigh appears to be similar to what I have heard of other headmistresses. She is strict and tightfisted, doling out sums in dribbles, always with reluctance. I imagine she feels she must set aside as much as possible for her future retirement. It results in a few teachers who are shockingly ill-informed about their subjects, the remainder left feeling most put-upon.''

"I fear it is all too common in our schools today,'' George murmured, thinking of his days at Eton. Those who were well-tutored and able to speak up acquired the classical education deemed necessary. All others remained in ignorance of mathematics, the physical sciences, even their mother tongue. He knew many boys who had had little skill in writing and whose spelling might be called creative at best. It seemed to George that his school still clung to the Middle Ages of its founder, Henry VI. The entire staff had been required to put down one student rebellion. His only respite from the severe discipline had been playing cricket.

Oxford had been slightly better. He had attained proficiency in mathematics. Though not required to attend lectures due to his title, he had, and consequently he had absorbed some knowledge. Sons of the nobility were exempted from any examinations for their degrees. He had learned more following his departure from the institution than while there. He suspected there was a parallel in the young ladies' academy, though undoubtedly without the violence he and his schoolmates experienced, excused on the grounds that it served to prepare them for what the world was really like.

"I expect we will have to find some manner to reinstate Marianna.'' At the soft sound of protest from the girl, Lady Lavinia added, "You will be in a position to learn more from the inside than from without.''

Marianna could see the wisdom of this, and nodded, while dubious as to how this was to be accomplished.

"What was school life like?" asked George, seeking to draw out this provoking young woman who was getting beneath his skin more than he liked.

"Following breakfast there was instruction in writing and French, then a walk to the sea. After a rather Spartan lunch came lessons in painting and needlework, music and dancing. The girls are taught all the essentials for a young lady of today." Her tone was faintly ironic, for she considered the entire effort a farce. "The young ladies delight in reading poetry, but few learn the globes or mathematical science. That is considered beyond their tender minds."

That a young woman would benefit from mastering the rudiments of ciphering so that she might better keep household accounts was ignored. Small wonder that a housekeeper was able to steal with impunity, knowing her mistress unable to detect the theft.

Lady Lavinia frowned, then asked, "The jealousy and spite? Where might that be found?"

Blushing, Marianna cast a demure look to her lap, then bravely faced them. "When I became a junior teacher, I felt I must be careful, for I was so close in years to the older girls you see, and had been good friends with a few. Still, it was difficult to totally sever that friendship with one or two."

Marianna looked away, seeking to hide the pain she still felt. "When Lady Phillida's sapphires disappeared, she insisted I was the only one who knew where she kept the jewels. I did not, contrary to what she said. She had been very good friends with another teacher before I joined the staff. That teacher may have missed the little gifts and attention from Lady Phillida. You cannot tell how others react to situations. There may have been a motive there."

George studied Marianna's bent head and thought of his aunt's prediction of possible danger. It was to be a tricky venture, with trouble that might be averted if one kept one's eyes open and remained alert. He turned to face his aunt. "And what is in your cup, Aunt?"

The wispy-haired lady stiffened slightly, dropped her gaze, and assumed a rather odd expression. ''There is a trunk in my cup. This journey I undertake will have a life-changing effect for me!''

3

Marianna stared at the dignified little woman who sat so quietly at her side as though nothing out of the ordinary had been said. Indeed, Lady Lavinia wore a bemused expression, her eyes soft and almost dreamy.

"Life-changing?" Lady Wyndham echoed in faint accents.

George placed both hands behind him, looking very much the male who is tolerating nonsense. Sir John bore a similar mien.

Only Sir Alex appeared to take Lady Lavinia seriously. "I wonder what that might be?" he mused, rubbing a well-shaped hand over his chin.

Lady Lavinia gave him an appreciative look before waving her fan in a negligent manner. "It could be some mere trifle, you know."

But Marianna, watching closely, doubted if the lady really believed that tarradiddle. No, something momentous was to happen to Lady Lavinia while on this journey. What could possibly appeal to an elderly lady? Romance? That seemed like utter silliness, and Marianna smiled, in spite of herself. But life-changing? Her gaze sought George's and they exchanged warmly amused looks.

"Well, I should think the sooner we begin this trip, the sooner we shall find out what this is all about," George said with an eye now on his volatile aunt.

"Excellent notion, George," Lady Lavinia said, turning to give Lady Wyndham a reassuring nod. "We are all very fond of your dear girl. 'Tis a monstrous thing for her to be so accused, and with no real evidence."

"Miss Chudleigh seemed only too happy to accept the word of Lady Phillida and Miss Teale. That appeared to be all she required as evidence," Marianna said, once more turning her gaze to the strange little woman at her side.

"No justice at all," huffed Sir John.

Lady Wyndham had watched the silent communication between her daughter and Viscount Barringer. Apparently satisfied at what she did or did not see, she smiled at Lady Lavinia. " 'Tis late, and we best get home so we may have a good night's rest. If Viscount Barringer is truly serious about prompt attention to this situation, we shall need to oversee packing a portmanteau. Tomorrow comes soon."

"You are wise not to say a trunk, for there would be no room on board for such, " George said. Turning to his aunt, he added, "You must do likewise, you know. And I suggest we plan to leave on the morrow."

"Dear me," said Lady Lavinia, fluttering her white fan about in the air as she rose from the sofa to join the exodus from the drawing room. "That is a task that will put my powers of planning to the test, is it not?"

"Those soft muslins you wear cannot take up all that much room, nor, for that matter, those dainty slippers. I am certain you will look all the crack, no matter that you will have a restricted wardrobe, Lady Lavinia," said a gallant Sir Alex.

"Sir Alexander, you are able to turn a very nice phrase," Lady Wyndham said with evident approval. She had apparently decided that if the viscount didn't come up to scratch, this charming young baronet would do quite nicely for her beloved daughter.

Catching sight of her dear mama, Marianna clasped her arm in a gentle manner, guiding her to the front door. Her mama had developed a very calculating expression. Marianna was all too afraid as to the meaning of it. That Lady Wyndham hoped for a good marriage was all too plain.

Arrangements were made between Sir John and George regarding the time of departure and a carriage for Marianna. George insisted that he would see to everything. Sir John smiled a bit thinly at that, but said little other than expressing his warm thanks.

During the ride to the Wyndham estate, Sir John and his lady quietly discussed the projected trip, not bothering to consult their daughter. Once she married, she would acquire more responsibility regarding plans. For now, those who were older and wiser made the decisions.

"I could wish your father might be present while your name is to be cleared," Lady Wyndham said wistfully. Nothing would convince her that her dear husband was less than perfect and able to do anything he chose. That he had not heretofore tackled the matter of Marianna's innocence she attributed to the demands of his attention elsewhere.

They entered the house in a reflective mood, going up the stairs to their rooms in near silence. Marianna was certain she would not sleep a wink. But as soon as her head touched the pillow, she drifted off amid thoughts of George arrayed in armor, fighting a fire-breathing dragon who strangely enough resembled Miss Chudleigh.

Morning brought a beehive of activity as Lady Wyndham set about supervising the packing of the one portmanteau for her daughter. Every item was scrutinized with care.

"With so little space, you must plan carefully, my dear," Lady Wyndham said sweetly.

Marianna was grateful for her support, although she would far rather have done the packing herself. For instance, her mama selected the very best of her gowns, both day and evening, to be placed within. Marianna thought that practicality demanded more simple dresses. She ventured to say as much and earned a severe frown for her effort.

"You must make the best of impressions. It is difficult to depress the pretensions of someone unless you are confident and looking your very best. It gives you an inner feeling of worth. It seems to me that Miss Chudleigh needs taking down a notch. It would be better had you a more imposing wardrobe, but there it is, you do not. What a pity your father has sustained such losses on the sale of our wool. Now that the peace has

come again, perhaps the wool market shall improve. It is to
be devoutly hoped.'' It was clear that Lady Wyndham had
visions of refurbishing her wardrobe, and possibly the manor
house as well, with the change in the international scene.

''One can only pray that Corsican will remain on Elba. I
believe 1814 promises to be a good year for us and for our
country,'' Marianna said with a decided firmness in her voice.

Her fond mama gave her a concerned look. ''You do not
believe Napoleon will be able to escape from the island where
he is being held, do you?''

''Of course not, Mama. He is there until he dies. Rest assured
our navy will keep a weather eye on him,'' Marianna declared
stoutly.

It wasn't long before the portmanteau was neatly filled with
gowns and slippers plus the other assorted basic items a young
lady required for an indefinite journey.

''When you reach Lowestoft, you must find a maid to care
for your things, my dear. You will hardly have time for washing
and such.'' Lady Wyndham inspected a shawl with a critical
eye, then placed it atop the other garments before gesturing for
the maid to close the case.

Marianna nodded. She followed her mother down the stairs,
her maid trailing behind with the portmanteau, which was
heavier than it looked.

The breeze blew from the sea this morning, Marianna noted
as the family gathered before the house to bid her farewell. The
carriage from Mayne Court had arrived to fetch her. She was
disappointed that George had not seen fit to come along, but
hid her pique well.

Handing her daughter a little posy of roses, Lady Wyndham
placed a soft kiss on her cheek. ''Do take care, dear. I am not
totally convinced this trip is without danger, in spite of Viscount
Barringer's assurances.''

''Yes, Mama,'' she said dutifully, eager to be gone. She
smiled at her mama's persistent use of George's title. He had
chosen for so long to ignore it, but never her mama. ''But I
believe there is little cause for worry.''

Sir John stepped forward to place a very heavy though small cloth sack into Marianna's hands, along with his instructions. "Here is some money. We cannot expect the viscount to bear all the expenses of this expedition. Give it to him when you are under way, if you please."

Dropping the sack into her reticule, Marianna stepped forward to place a kiss on her father's cheek. "I shall be careful and very good, Papa," she said, then turned to enter the carriage.

She waved at them once before settling back against the squabs, facing forward and toward the sea. A journey with hope, this time. How crushed she had been when she had come home from Lowestoft not so long ago. A yearning rose within her, a desire for a home and a good husband. Then she grinned a bit ruefully and shook her head. Silly thoughts at this point in time. Better to clear her name first.

That she never once considered Sir Alex as a potential husband did not occur to her. Always when the word came to mind, it was George's image that appeared.

Lady Lavinia was bustling about the entry to Mayne Court when Marianna was ushered inside the house. Several portmanteaus sat near the door. Marianna watched as hers was added to the row.

"Good. George will be pleased to know you are here and ready to depart. This is vastly diverting, is it not, dear child?" The floating white draperies settled about her slender frame as Lady Lavinia paused to consider her words. "Dear, me, that did not sound quite right, did it? But I am sure you know what I mean. To be setting off on any journey that goes farther than Scarborough must command a certain sense of expectation."

"Especially when one considers that it is to have a life-changing effect on you." Marianna smiled at the rosy tint that crept over the elderly lady's face. How delightful that the spinster could still reveal her sensibilities.

"Yes, well, that is true, I suppose." Lavinia waved a white

handkerchief at the neat row of cases, looking at Peters while she next spoke. "See that these are placed in the landau so that we need not delay my nephew when he has gathered the maps and whatever else it is that he intends to carry along with him."

"Where is George this morning?" Marianna looked about the spacious entry as though expecting to see him pop out of the woodwork.

"In his library. Why do you not seek him out? I doubt if Peters has had time to let him know you are come. I shall check on the food."

"The food?" Marianna paused on her way to the library to glance back at Lady Lavinia.

"Merely provisions for the first day. George thought we might have a picnic."

Marianna watched a moment as Lavinia hurried in the direction of the kitchen, while behind her Peters marshaled the cases toward the landau.

Continuing along the hall, the young woman found the library door ajar. Pausing in the entry, she saw George and Sir Alex bent over a stack of maps on the desk. "Good morning?"

Glancing up from his perusal of the coastal map from Scarborough to Bridlington, George nodded. "And so it is. I gather you are prepared to depart?"

"Indeed. But are you?" She drifted over to the desk, peering down at the map. "Problems?" George had been frowning when she had paused at the doorway. That usually meant difficulties, in her experience.

"No, no, nothing for you to worry about."

Marianna hated the avuncular tone in his voice. Why did men persist in believing a woman was incapable of facing a dilemma without fading away? Had she not coped with her dismissal and removal all by herself? But then, she mused, she hadn't done all that well.

"Shall we get this project under way? Alex, will you roll up the maps? I shall check our other necessary supplies." George waited by his desk.

Sir Alex inserted the maps in the case, then picked it up and walked toward the door.

Project! This was merely another project George had thrown himself into with his usual fervor. Marianna ignored the fact that her ire was out of proportion to the matter. That was all she was to him—a project? How utterly lowering! She was coming to believe he preferred projects to people. Why else had he remained unmarried until his advanced age of . . . twenty-nine, wasn't it? She stalked out the door. As a gesture it failed miserably, for her slippered feet made little sound.

Sir Alex observed the pique of his companion. "He'll join us in a few minutes. No doubt he had to get into his safe for sufficient of the ready, you know. Journeys can be full of the unexpected."

"Papa sent some money along, which I am to hand over to his lordship when he finally appears," snapped Marianna, her feelings sorely tried. Did George suspect she might steal the contents of his safe? In that case, why bother to clear her name? Then she recalled that Sir Alex had been dismissed as well, and she calmed down.

At last the four were seated in the landau and on their way to the shore where Marianna had first seen George emerge from the sea. It had been but two days, she reflected, yet how much had occurred!

Her thoughts strayed to the "fortune" in her teacup. A vulture that meant loss and theft as well as jealousy and spite. Even though the warm summer sun shone down gently upon her, she shivered a little. Spite? She knew one who qualified, perhaps. Although she hated to believe such about anyone she had known and liked. That went for jealousy too. Her eyes slid to George, seated across from her. He would be the one to avert the trouble, but what of the hidden danger that was to be revealed?

The ride took about two hours, during which the conversation was casual and did not involve the prospects of the journey. Except Sir Alex did manage to question where they were to spend the night.

·We shall have to see where we are at the time," George replied with a supreme indifference to the problems of a proper inn suitable for ladies.

Aunt Lavinia flashed him a withering look, of which he took no notice in the least.

Marianna was braver. Her pride still smarted from the idea of being considered nothing more than a project to him. She knew something of the inns along the coast. Her father had talked about them not long before while neighbors were visiting. "I trust they shall be more than sailor's lodgings or havens for smugglers," she said tartly.

George said nothing at first, but fastened a narrow look upon her while he appeared to consider what she had said. At last he spoke. "While it is true I have not inspected every inn along the route we take, I trust we shall not be reduced to sleeping in a barn."

Turning her gaze to the view beyond the carriage, Marianna wondered precisely where they would sleep. This could possibly be a most interesting journey. George had been annoyed with her words. Pity. She had made up her mind not to be a spineless creature, bowing to his every command, or whatever the captain of a vessel issued to a passenger.

She held the posy of roses to her nose, sniffing the delicate scent while contemplating the man across from her. Sir Alex she ignored.

"I trust you will not prove to be a contumacious female," George said, with a hint of testiness in his voice as they rolled through the last of the villages before the shore.

"I am never contrary," she declared with an obstinate look in her eyes.

"Indeed," muttered a totally unconvinced George.

Sir Alex handed Lady Lavinia from the carriage after they had drawn to a halt at the end of the lane. The good lady stood, dismayed at the expanse of sand and shale before her. She stared out at the diving boat, now riding a gentle sea.

"Precisely how do we get out to your boat, George? I have no desire to join the fish." The dear lady bestowed a disdainful look upon the beach and tilted her white silk parasol to better protect her delicate skin. Her white skirts fluttered about her feet in a flirtatious manner, as though teasing the breeze.

Several lads from the village had joined the procession. Together with the sailors who were to go on the diving boat, they pushed out a small dory. Aunt Lavinia stared at the little wooden boat with horror.

"I shall go out first so as to make certain everything is ready and in place for you," George said. "Naturally we had to launch the boat before boarding," he added, noticing the expression on his aunt's face. "Once I give the all-clear signal, you will be ferried out one by one." His gaze strayed to Marianna, seeming to seek some manner of acknowledgment from her.

She gave him an encouraging look and almost smiled at the relief that flickered in his eyes. What had he expected her to do? Throw a tantrum?

Aunt Lavinia was only slightly aghast at being carried across the sand in the arms of a stalwart young fisherman. She bore the trip by dory in long-suffering silence, seeming to be quelled only when it came time to grab the railing and climb up, then down into the dim interior of the boat.

Sir Alex gallantly handed Marianna into the dory for her trip. She observed that the little boat reeked of fish and wondered it didn't sink, for the wood looked a fair way to rotting. Fortunately the sea was relatively calm and there was little trouble in coming alongside the diving boat. Marianna grasped the metal rail to pull herself up onto the deck, then crossed to look down into the hole that was the entrance to area belowdeck. The interior seemed rather dim, and she could see nothing much but the floor. Her heart really wasn't in this trip, she decided as she glanced back to where Sir Alex now made to come aboard.

The climb down was a bit scary. Her foot touched the bottom, her half-boots making only a faint sound on the metal. A small oil lamp hung on the wall and she watched as George lit it, brightening up the interior considerably. Once her eyes became adjusted to the light, she smiled.

Off to one side, Lady Lavinia sat on a keg, looking for all the world as though she was in her sitting room at Mayne Court. Her traveling dress was not as sturdy as the one Marianna had chosen. Somehow a sturdy navy-blue cambric gown with a spencer of blue-and-white-striped merino, even with a small bonnet of the same material, was no match for Lavinia's elegance in fine white-figured muslin. Although Marianna's bonnet did sport a curled ostrich feather.

'' 'Tis rather dismal in here, is it not?'' said Lady Lavinia.

Marianna suddenly wished they were on a regular ship with regular sails and navigating in a regular manner. She had not anticipated the interior would be like this, so stark and dim, like a cave of the very worst sort. Except it was not damp. Sending thanks for the snug dryness, she wondered what she was to do next.

George merely glanced at her. "Sit down," he ordered while neatly stowing the various bundles and portmanteaus in compartments.

Marianna handed him the sack of money as instructed by her father, then sat. So much for her decision not to be a spineless creature.

George gave her a quizzing look, hefted the sack, then stowed it in a safe place.

There were two crewmen on deck who set up the sail and shortly the diving boat was under way. Marianna missed the sight of the shore passing by. This was not her idea of a lovely way to travel. Then she reflected she was being most ungracious. After all, George was doing all this to clear her good name. She did appreciate his efforts, truly she did. It was just that business about being a project that still rankled. Since there was little chance George might alter his attitude, she had best settle down and behave herself.

"Once we get under way here we can go above, since we are using the sails." George brushed off his hands after seeing to Aunt Lavinia's portmanteau. Marianna had to admire that he didn't expect the sailors to do that rather than whatever was keeping them busy. "I prefer to see everything stowed away, and I do not want you ladies on deck unless Alex and I are there."

"Will we truly be in Lowestoft by tomorrow eve?" Marianna inquired with some disbelief. After all, it had taken her a week to get home, what with having to skirt around the Wash beyond Kings Lynne and ferry the Humber River. Travel by coach was enormously slower, it seemed.

"If the wind holds and we do not encounter any difficulties with the weather, we ought to make Lowestoft by then, yes. Alex has made a study of the weather and he believes it shall be fine." George checked on young Tom Crowdon, then turned back to the ladies. "Shall we go up on deck?"

"Oh, may we?" Lady Lavinia said with undisguised relief. She grasped her dainty parasol in one hand and prepared to climb the ladder. "Not that I desire the sunshine, you understand. 'Tis that is I dislike the feeling of being penned up down here."

Marianna watched the older lady spryly make her way to the deck, then she walked forward to join her. She placed one hand on the rail of the ladder, pausing when she observed George studying her in a rather disconcerting manner. "What is it, George?"

He glanced down at his hand, rubbing his thumb against his fingers as he sought the words he wished. He gave her a very direct gaze. "You look very fine today. That shade of blue becomes you."

It was so unlike what Marianna had expected to hear that she was sure her mouth must have dropped open. "T-thank you," she stammered, for once in her life unable to say more.

"Er, when we arrive at Lowestoft, I suspect we had best be rather formal. If you want to impress the headmistress, we ought to seem, well, imposing. You know how Aunt can be when she sets her mind to it. I doubt if there is anyone more capable of giving a proper set-down." He put his hands behind him as though to prevent himself from doing something he ought not. It was the warmest look Marianna had ever received from George, and she wondered a little at it.

Being a most perceptive young woman as a rule, Marianna added, "And you also wish me to address you as Lord Barringer, I imagine. I daresay your aunt will viscount you to death while we are there. Shall you mind that overmuch?" Her eyes twinkled up at him, sparkling with delightful humor.

"You know I have never wished to bother using my title in the past, but I know it pleases my father and in truth it does have its advantages." He gave her an endearing grin, and Marianna returned it before scrambling up the ladder to the deck. George was far too appealing when in this disarming mood; she had best remind herself that although she wished to make that short list for viscountess, there was very little chance she might actually do so.

Sir Alex gave her a hand as she exited the conning tower. "Off to our right you can see Flamborough Head as we round the coast toward Bridlington."

Marianna turned her head to gaze at the chalk cliffs that rose sharply from the where the sea ate at the base, carrying away the clay to the south. Gulls wheeled and soared above the clean blue of the water. She breathed in deeply, savoring the crisp tang of the air. This was far to be preferred to being closeted in the dim recesses of the diving boat.

She groped for a place to sit down, then smiled. "It is a lovely sight. I should never get tired of this sort of travel."

"You would soon enough if the weather turned bad." Sir Alex gave her a bland look before turning aside to speak with George.

Marianna sat quietly, trying to remain out of the way of the two sailors, George, and Sir Alex. Tom Crowdon had remained below. Near her, it appeared that Lady Lavinia felt the same way.

Above them a few puffy clouds drifted by and a frigate could be seen in the distance, no doubt one that had been fighting the French in the recent conflict.

"It seems incredible that we can sit here so calmly while we race along against the wind," Lady Lavinia said rather loudly, so as to be heard above the sounds of the water slapping against the boat and the wind snapping the sails.

Marianna surveyed the cliffs where the caves used by many a smuggler over the years could be found. Then she faced George's aunt with the misgivings she felt must clearly be seen on her face. "Do you have any ideas, Lady Lavinia? About confronting my former headmistress, that is?"

"Things have proceeded at such a pace I have scarce had time to think," Lavinia replied with a half-smile. "I expect we must have a council of war," she added with a more serious expression.

"War?" echoed Marianna, her heart beating more rapidly. She had not considered that redeeming her good name would come to that.

The two ladies subsided into thoughtful silence, rousing only when luncheon was brought forth to be enjoyed in the fresh sea air. It was a rude picnic, with none of the daintiness about it that Marianna associated with Lady Lavinia. But the food was nourishing and the wine refreshing, not to mention bolstering to her frayed nerves.

The wind slackened in the afternoon, bringing a frown of sizable proportions to George's brow. Marianna ventured to inquire what might be wrong.

"We are falling behind my schedule. I had hoped to make Skegness before eventide. At this rate, we shall be fortunate if we can land at Mablethorpe."

Marianna watched the coast slip past, more slowly now. She mulled over the options she had, wondering how to confront the person she suspected, or, indeed, if she dared do such a thing. When the boat headed toward land as the sun began to lower in the west, she wondered what they faced ashore. There were masses of people near the lone pier that jutted into the sea at Mablethorpe.

"Look at all those people. Let us hope that we do not end up sleeping in a barn," Lady Lavinia muttered in an aside to

Marianna as the boat neared the shore. Just then a rocket soared into the sky and exploded.

"War?" whispered Marianna, her problem still much in her mind.

4

"Hardly war, I should think," George replied, looking askance at the throng of people who spilled out onto the pier. It was difficult to tell at this distance as to what their mood might be.

"I suspect it is the unusual design of this vessel," offered Aunt Lavinia in a quiet aside to George. The deck being as small as it was, there was little need to speak up to be heard now.

For the first time since she had entered the diving boat, Marianna grew fearful. "I wish we had not been required to stop over here. Could we not sail on?" She knew even as she spoke the words that her question was pointless. The boat was small and the crew more so. There was no one to spell the men who had worked hard all day, not to mention the trial of navigating at night.

Sir Alex joined the three standing so close together. "You know how it is, anything strange will attract a crowd. Mustn't show them you are afraid of them. Just sail in like you expect a king's welcome." He grinned at George's derisive look, then shrugged his shoulders. "Do you have a better notion, my friend?"

George did not, it seemed. He stood tall, with a negligent ease, looking very much Viscount Barringer, son of the esteemed Earl of Cranswick of Mayne Court. Never mind that these country folk had not likely heard of either of them; they would know by his speech and manner that he was who he claimed to be.

The strange craft eased up alongside the pier and a dozen eager hands reached out to catch the ropes that the crew tossed up to them. George climbed up the ladder, looking about him with

47

an aloof disdain, totally unlike the usually agreeable person his family knew.

A plump man of middle years made his way through the crowd to stand before George. "Josiah Fincham, at your service, sir, mayor of Mablethorpe." He executed a polite bow.

"Viscount Barringer," George said with appropriate coolness. "I had planned to travel farther south, but since we are using the sails, the lack of wind brought us to your port. Is there an inn nearby?"

"I feel certain we can find you respectable beds." Then, giving the craft at the side of the pier a sidelong glance, Fincham added, "A different sort of boat you have there, milord." It was more like a question, but George merely nodded in agreement.

The man Sir Alex had quietly labeled a puff-guts motioned to Lavinia, Marianna, and Sir Alex, who promptly scrambled up the ladder of the pier to join George.

Marianna brushed down her skirts, wishing she had something more impressive than her plain navy gown to wear. Aunt Lavinia looked almost ethereal in her delicate white gown with the frilled parasol above her dainty bonnet.

The little group followed the mayor off the pier and along the street that fronted the beach—if you could call such a thing a street. The cobbles were dreadfully uneven and the buildings were not in the first state of preservation, looking as though it would not be long before they tumbled to the ground. Marianna and Aunt Lavinia exchanged worried glances.

They were brought to the most-disreputable-looking inn the ladies had ever imagined. Lady Lavinia paused to inhale a breath of fresh sea air before entering the building.

"Welcome to the Dog and Drake, good people," said the mayor, who, it appeared, was also the host of the inn.

George touched Sir Alex lightly on the arm to halt the speech he suspected was about to burst forth, then turned back to the mayor. "Is there a manner of festival here? Or does a stray boat bring this number of people to the pier?"

"Market day tomorrow. We have a bit of festivity as well,

my lord. Not like a regular fair, mind you. But a smallish event, much relished by the locals. This here inn will be full up later this evening,'' he declared with pride in his voice. He studied the ladies and Sir Alex with a slightly raised brow, as though wondering precisely who they were.

George understood immediately. "This is my aunt, Lady Lavinia Mayne, Miss Marianna Wyndham, and Sir Alexander Dent. Taking a bit of a trip. We require rooms and a good meal." Beyond that, George offered nothing, evidently deciding that was all the host deserved.

The mayor-turned-host was obviously torn, knowing full well that each of the gentry would expect a private room and that he could make much more blunt by renting those rooms out to as many as he could squeeze inside.

Not giving the man an opportunity to decide the question, George said, "I believe we shall stroll about the town a bit before we dine." He offered his arm to Marianna, leaving Sir Alex to do the pretty with Aunt Lavinia.

They left the inn, which was redolent of years of cooked cabbage, boiled beef, and fried fish, to walk along the unsavory street.

"George," Aunt Lavinia said in a tight voice. "I cannot like that place. I daresay none of us shall sleep a wink for the creatures already housed in the beds above and waiting for our tender skin. I fear I shall end up sleeping in a wooden chair the whole night."

"I know," George mused. "But as far as I can see, there is little alternative. The only other inn about here is in an even worse state. I believe this town is due either for a fire or for some new construction. Or both," he added when he caught sight of another shop looking the worse for the ages.

"Look! They are setting up a roundabout, so this must be closer to a real fair than Mr. Fincham said," inserted a curious Marianna as they turned a corner to a lane that seemed to lead to a better part of town.

"Well, at least the town has a circulating library," Lady Lavinia declared, peering at the surprisingly clean windows with an attractive display.

"And I perceive across the street from said library a fine-looking inn," Sir Alex added.

They all exchanged looks, then hurried across the street to an old but well-kept inn with a nicely painted sign proclaiming it to be the CROWNED HEAD.

The four delighted travelers entered the inn, and they were met with the odor of fresh-baked bread and roast beef. Aunt Lavinia smiled for the first time since they stepped foot on dry land. The common room was full of decent-looking people and there was a prosperous bustle. From the neat muslin curtains at the shining windows to the polished oak tables, there was a welcoming appearance to the place.

"I wonder if that Mr. Fincham told the truth about anything," Marianna whispered to Lady Lavinia.

George sought out the busy host of the inn, returning with a gloomy face. "No room. There is indeed a market day tomorrow."

They were standing near the front door, wondering if they could bear to return to the Dog and Drake, when an older gentleman in fine dress walked up to George and made a very nice bow. Marianna noted his bearing was quite military and judged him to be a retired officer.

"General Henry Eagleton at your service, Lord Barringer. Took the liberty of checking with the proprietor to find out who you were. I claim the privilege of knowing your papa. How is it you are stranded in this village, sir? 'Tis hardly the road to London." He smiled, making a point to include the delicate Lady Lavinia.

George explained the matter of a poor wind, then mentioned their return to the Dog and Drake.

"That never will do," said the general, shaking his head at the thought of such elegant ladies soiling their skirts with the dirt of that barely respectable inn. "You must do me the honor of spending the night in my home, longer if you can," he added with another glance at the elegant Lady Lavinia.

In the background, Sir Alex nudged Marianna, saying very softly, "The old gentleman most likely has an unmarried girl at home. Your old chum is considered a good catch by any parent, you know,'' he concluded, rather cynically for the usually agreeable baronet.

Marianna gave him a puzzled look before returning her attention to the general and George. She wished to know if George would be sensible and say yes to the offer.

Lady Lavinia solved the problem by gliding forward to place her hand upon the general's arm. She smiled fetchingly up at him. ''We are most grateful for your kind invitation, General Eagleton. I daresay I should have perished from fright to spend a night beneath that disgusting roof. Do you really know my dearest brother?''

Marianna trailed behind with Sir Alex and George. They were now followed by Tom Crowdon, who had been sent for, carrying their portmanteaus from the boat. The five trudged along to where a carriage waited.

''Would you credit your aunt, George?'' said the amused Marianna, noting that George looked as though someone had hit him over the head.

''Amazing,'' George breathed, taking another look at his aunt. True, she was about old enough to be his mother, but she had taken care of herself, no doubt benefiting from having carried no children and being cosseted by one and all. ''I had no notion she could flirt.''

''All women can flirt,'' Sir Alex muttered, again revealing a different side of his usually sunny nature.

George gave him a tolerant look, then explained to Marianna, ''Alex is always a touch cynical when it comes to matchmaking mamas . . . or papas, for that matter.''

With Tom jumping up behind the carriage, the group set off down the dusty lane with good humor and anticipation on the part of those who were now to avoid the stay in the Dog and Drake.

Their alternative was far better than they had expected. General Eagleton's home was a sprawling Tudor-style red brick house with gleaming mullioned windows and neat gardens to either side. Sparkling fresh paint on the door and window surrounds showed evidence of proper attention to preservation, a point noted by the sharp-eyed Lady Lavinia.

The plump, motherly housekeeper who showed them with a flustered smile into the drawing room was a far cry from the starched-up butler one might have envisioned. General Eagleton smiled as he seemed to guess their thoughts. "Mrs. Nesbit has taken over while my butler, who is also her husband, is laid up with a bout of ague. Very handy, that, having a couple to oversee the place while I must be gone. Can't think why more folk don't do it."

Lady Lavinia was most impressed with the thoughtfulness and gentility of their host as he saw to their refreshment. She caught at a part of his words. "You are frequently absent?"

"Indeed, good lady. With my daughter off to boarding school and duties calling me, I find I must turn over the care of the place more than I like. Mind you, I do not begrudge my service to our country. After all, there is nothing to especially draw me to home nowadays. Now, if things were a bit different . . ." He darted a glance to where Lady Lavinia sat daintily on her chair, sipping a glass of Madeira.

George studied General Eagleton while Marianna and Sir Alex exchanged mildly amused glances.

"I am sorry to learn of your bereavement, General." George inclined his head in a nice manner, just as he ought.

"My wife's been gone these many years. Died sixteen years ago when my girl was born. Until now, I have been too preoccupied, what with chasing Boney and other duties, to consider a change. This old house ought to have a lady's care, not to mention my girl. She needs more than I suspect she gets at that school in Lowestoft."

At these last words, Marianna paled. Her gaze sought George, who gave a faint nod of reassurance in return.

"Miss Chudleigh's establishment, I gather?" The viscount's voice held polite interest, yet there was an underlying hint of something the acute-eared general didn't miss.

"I am surprised a young man like you would know of the place, unless you have a sister who attends there?" The general's shrewd eyes did not fail to note the exchange of looks his remark had provoked.

"My sister is wed, sir. No, as matter of fact, we are on our

way to visit Miss Chudleigh. There is a small matter that needs
attention.'' His tone indicated to the general that the matter might
be small to some, but it was of significance to the viscount and
his party.

"It is a most unusual to travel by boat," said the general by
way of reply. He was far too polite to inquire what their business
with Miss Chudleigh might be. ''You ladies are to be congratulated on such a daring voyage.''

Lady Lavinia set her glass down on the polished surface of
the cherry-wood table with a snap, then smiled at their host.
"You do my nephew a disservice, General Eagleton. He would
never permit us to travel with him unless it was safe for us to
do so. You cannot fathom how delightful it is to sail along the
sea, thinking how tedious the same trip would be by land. I am
persuaded one ought to journey by water whenever possible.''

"And when the tranquillity of the sea is not disturbed by a
storm or rough tides,'' George added with a wry expression
shared by the other men.

"Interesting you should be going to Lowestoft. I must travel
there myself shortly. It is my duty to oversee the militia.''
Though he was looking mostly at Lady Lavinia, he did not miss
the altered expressions of the others.

"But surely," objected Lady Lavinia in a polite way, "there
is no need to drill the men, with Napoleon safely ensconced
in Elba, is there?'' She looked to Marianna, who recalled
reassuring her on this point not long ago.

The men in the room exchanged uneasy glances, George and
Sir Alex wondering precisely where General Eagleton stood on
this point of national preparedness. There were a number of
generals who took an aggressive stance, yet others who were
most sanguine about the matter.

"I realize there does not seem to be the threat of an emergency
in the air, dear lady,'' replied the general with a bow to Lavinia.
"However, it is my view that an island nation such as ours is
most foolish not to be armed and well-trained. A nation well
able to defend itself is far less vulnerable to attack by a bully.''

"And you consider the French to be bullies?'' inquired a
curious Marianna.

"Perhaps not the people, but their leader certainly has been." His voice was grim, remembering the many battles fought against the French over the past years, battles in which Napoleon had played an increasingly central part. Even though the tyrant was deposed and in exile, he was not to be trusted until dead, in Eagleton's humble opinion.

Lady Lavinia shuddered at the recollection of the threat from the little French general turned emperor, and changed the subject. "I expect you shall visit with your daughter while in Lowestoft?" It was really more of a statement than a question, although her voice did rise in inflection.

"Aye, my little Sibyl is a fetching girl, although quite young. Too young for you, my lords," he added with a smile.

He must have suspected what had been said earlier, thought Marianna. She took a deep breath and plunged ahead into what must be said. "I know your daughter, sir. I was a junior teacher at Miss Chudleigh's until recently. Before that, I attended the academy for some years." She met his inquiring gaze with a resolute look while wondering if his daughter had reported Marianna's supposed crime to him. He might be most unwilling to house a suspected criminal beneath his roof. She thought of the grim comfort of the Dog and Drake and sighed.

His eyes narrowed at this intelligence, then he nodded. "I wondered why your name rang a bell in my head. She has written, telling me of the charges placed against you by young Lady Phillida, charges she does not accept, mind you. 'Tis a sad state of affairs when a young woman can be dismissed from her position without a reference on the trumped-up accusations not proved to the satisfaction of a judge or jury."

"I could not prove I did not take those jewels. They have never been found, either, as far as I know. Of course, as my father pointed out, whoever did take them has likely removed the stones for sale and melted down the gold so as to prevent identification." She turned to Lady Lavinia and added, "I know you believe them to be near the water, but that does not say as to what form they might take if they are there."

"True," Lady Lavinia replied most thoughtfully.

General Eagleton looked confused, but George decided it was

best not to enlighten him as to his aunt's peculiar gifts. Not all people were willing to accept them with a generous spirit.

The housekeeper bustled into the room, inviting them to the table now set with dinner. The general offered his arm to Lady Lavinia, leaving Marianna to follow with George and Sir Alex.

"I gather I was wrong," whispered Sir Alex in an aside. "I was certain he had a nubile daughter to spring on us."

"Ah, do you think you are such a great prize?" Marianna teased lightly.

"No, but our friend here is," Sir Alex gibed, laughing softly at the faint rise of color on George's face.

"Now, Alex," remonstrated George, a slight testiness in his voice. "Just because you have been the target of so many match-making mamas is no reason to impugn the motives of every other parent in the kingdom."

The taunting smile on Sir Alex's face faded. He said nothing more while taking his seat at the round table favored by so many who lived in the country.

George saw to Marianna, noting that her earlier nervousness had not completely disappeared in spite of the general's kind words. He turned to that good man, but was forestalled in his remarks.

"I trust you are not in any great rush to arrive in Lowestoft, are you?" The general's gaze sought out Marianna, undoubtedly suspecting she was the one who most urgently wished to get to their destination.

"We had intended to leave in the morning, sir," George replied respectfully. "We are most grateful for your generous hospitality this evening. My man informed me that the host at the Dog and Drake declared himself desolate at our absence, but 'tis doubted his grief was sincere." George shared a knowing smile with his host.

"I would that you spend the day here tomorrow. The little fair is not what you may be accustomed to in your home community, but it promises to be entertaining in its small way." While it was understood he spoke to George as the leader of the party, his face turned to Lady Lavinia.

Marianna suppressed a smile at the sight of a pink-cheeked

Lady Lavinia. She ventured a look at George, giving him a nod of acquiescence. Her personal affairs could wait another day. After all of Lady Lavinia's past sacrifice and devotion to her brother's children—although happily given, mind you—she deserved a bit of dalliance if she so wished, and it appeared the white-garbed lady did.

"On behalf of my party, I thank you for the gracious invitation," George said. "We should be most happy to break our journey with you for a day. Perhaps you may be able to give us a bit of insight on your estimation of Miss Chudleigh while we visit?" George liked the kindly general. He recalled his name mentioned in reports from the peninsula and knew he had been ordered home after a severe wound. It was good to see him recovered and in seeming good health.

The group applied themselves to the excellent meal served by Mrs. Nesbit in the absence of her husband. There was a fine soup followed by fresh-caught fish, a fricassee of chicken, veal, hare, vegetables of all kinds, with a variety of fruit as well. There were no rich cakes or pastries.

Marianna wondered how Lady Lavinia liked that, being as fond of sweets as she was. The dear lady said nothing but good about the meal, however. Not by a flicker of an eyelash did she indicate that she longed for a sweet.

The gentlemen joined the ladies immediately upon the close of the meal, General Eagleton wishing to keep the company of the charming Lady Lavinia rather than two strangers, even if he did know the father of one of them.

"Would it be possible to pay you a visit while you are in Lowestoft, dear lady?" he inquired with a gentlemanly nicety of manners.

Lashes and hands all aflutter, Lady Lavinia first looked to her nephew and then to Marianna. Seeing nothing but encouraging expressions, she nodded her permission. "By all means, do. We shall be endeavoring to assist Miss Wyndham in her efforts, but otherwise, there shall undoubtedly be a good bit of time on our hands."

"It is often pleasant to take a stroll about the square or partake of a glass of lemonade by the sea," said the general, beaming with good nature that his attentions were being so well-received.

And so he ought, thought Marianna. Lady Lavinia came from a fine old family, one that was easily traced to the days of William the Conqueror. George had no need to apologize for his ancestry. Nor had she, for that matter. Her family had always been upstanding citizens. Until her dismissal, that is. She sighed inwardly. She must see that her name was cleared of this iniquitous charge. She had never suspected Lady Phillida to be a wicked girl. Indeed, Marianna had pitied her, making a special effort to be kind to her. And see what that had brought. Grief.

The general suggested they enjoy a game of whist. "I am alone here, for the most part, you know," he said with a touch of longing in his gruff voice. It was an appeal that neither George nor Sir Alex had the heart to deny.

Marianna declared she had no head for cards at the moment, and wandered over to study the harpsichord placed against the far wall. She picked out a melody, the quaint, plucked sound softly echoing about the room. Behind her the foursome were intent on their game and did not look up. Except for George. He glanced over to study the drooping yet brave figure by the harpsichord before returning to his hand.

The game of cards did not last far into the night. Marianna had excused herself shortly and had tumbled into a clean, lavender-scented bed with relief. She had caught the sound of footsteps on the wood floor of the hall not too long after she was snuggled beneath her covers. Someone had paused outside her door and rapped gently. Not desiring conversation when she was on the verge of oblivion, Marianna had declined to answer. No doubt Lady Lavinia would give her report of the evening, come the following day—providing it was Lady Lavinia who had rapped, that is. Marianna dismissed that intriguing thought with great reluctance. Should she begin to delve into it, she might be awake half the night.

As she drifted into sleep she could not help but wonder what role General Eagleton would play in their future. That he wished to retain contact was all too evident.

She had been correct in her assumption that Lady Lavinia would enlighten her regarding the evening. When Marianna had

risen and dressed and was brushing her tangled blond hair with
many a sigh, she heard yet another rap at the door. Going to
the door, she found the good lady waiting patiently. "Do come
in," Marianna welcomed her.

"We shall have a lovely day, for see how the sun is shining,"
Lady Lavinia said with great enthusiasm.

"I gather last evening went well," Marianna teased while
arranging her hair in a neat twist at the nape of her neck. How
tempting it was to have her hair cut as was the mode according
to the London fashion journals.

"Do hurry, dear. We don't wish to keep the general waiting,
do we?" That she had not answered the question spoke volumes
for Lavinia's abstraction.

"Most certainly not," Marianna replied in a gentle voice,
liking the sweet, older lady with the generous heart. As they
left the upper floor, Marianna inquired, "Do you intend to read
the general's fortune this morning?"

"Oh, I doubt such a thing would be at all proper," declared
Lady Lavinia in an equally soft voice. "Not all people are in
agreement, you know. Some folk believe it borders on witch-
craft, and you know it is not at all that," she concluded in
horrified accents.

Breakfast was a congenial meal. No tea leaves were read,
although Marianna suspected Lavinia longed for a try. It seemed
the general drank coffee upon arising, thus no tea leaves were
available.

When they left the house, the carriage took them back to the
central part of Mablethorpe, where the little country fair was
in full swing.

The aroma of hot gingerbread wafted over the square from
a stall at one side of it. Whatever business there had been to
transact had been concluded early in the morning, before
Marianna, George, and the others made their belated appearance. Across from where they now stood, the clever roundabout
had been set up apart from the row of food stalls and the booths
selling various articles.

Marianna impetuously seized George's hand. "Do let us

watch them.'' She tugged ever so slightly and the group slowly followed as George led her to the roundabout.

"I believe I shall have a look at this lace,'' said Lady Lavinia, pausing by one of the booths to try on a lovely white lace scarf.

The general remained at her side while the others continued on their way.

There were artfully carved wooden horses upon which little boys, not to mention grown men, rode astride. Little girls sat discreetly in spindle-backed seats or, in the case or older women, inside a coach body that had been cleverly attached to the roundabout frame. A powerful-looking horse drew the contraption around and around the well-oiled center post. Marianna didn't need much persuasion to take a short ride in the "chair,'' although she gazed longingly at a fancifully painted horse. George watched her with an indulgent expression that had Sir Alex smiling to himself.

From the roundabout the trio wandered along to where a magic-lantern show had been set up and was doing a brisk business. Marianna cast it only a passing glance, preferring to study the wares displayed at nearby stalls.

"I would have thought you would enjoy that magical production,'' Sir Alex teased as Marianna gave him a repressive look.

"I was never so disappointed as when I saw one. It was so bland as to be boring,'' Marianna replied, hurrying past the booth where the magic lantern was set up.

"Ah, but this one is about Saint George,'' Sir Alex said, his eyes dancing with delight.

Neither George nor Marianna rose to that bait, much to his disappointment. They were staring at the vision of Lady Lavinia arrayed in a pretty pink shawl. Pink? Even Sir Alex turned to give a second look at the sight.

Lady Lavinia walked up to where they now stood in surprised silence. She gave George a coquettish smile, which grew a bit sheepish at his steady gaze, saying, "Is this not lovely? General Eagleton insisted it became me quite well. I could not resist parting with a few shillings for this fine silk.'' She fingered the delicate fringe while watching George before placing her hand on the general's arm and strolling toward the gingerbread booth. Nothing was said about the shawl not being white.

"I suggest we find ourselves a piece of that fine-smelling game pie and a mug of home-brewed as 'twill not be too long before lunchtime," George murmured, gazing after his aunt with disbelief in his eyes. It bothered him that Aunt Lavinia should change her taste so abruptly, and apparently with the general in mind. At her age, too!

Marianna turned her head to look at George, wondering if he was quite prepared for what probably was in store for him.

On the other side of the square a cheapjack was selling pudding basins. "Tuppence the basin," he shouted. "All-English pudding basins for your steak-and-kidney pudding. Used at the royal palace at Windsor. Who says tuppence?"

Marianna ignored the man as well as the other sellers. Lady Lavinia was wearing pink. If this was not a life-changing event, what would be?

5

Lady Lavinia was as pink as a springtime rose, Marianna decided as she followed the lady's progress around the square. And it was not merely the reflection of the lovely shawl that was gracefully draped about her neck. She sparkled and smiled as Marianna had never seen before. It would be most interesting to see what developed in that direction. Glancing over to where George and Sir Alex were negotiating for a game pie and their pints of ale, Marianna decided she preferred something else.

"Hot spice gingerbread! Ho! Come buy my hot gingerbread, smoking hot," came the singsong call from the stall on the far side of the square.

Signaling her intent to Sir Alex, Marianna set off on her own quest. The mouth-watering aroma beckoned her. Standing before the stall, she placed the coins in the outstretched, well-scrubbed hand of the cook and proprietress, then took a slab of steaming gingerbread off with her to nibble. The shade provided by a stately tree was welcome. She had nearly finished her treat when a scruffy-looking lad came running toward her, brushing against her as he passed. She felt a tug on her arm, nearly knocking her off-balance.

"Stop," cried an incensed Marianna as she felt the pull increase.

He swiftly slashed the cords of her reticule with his knife and grabbed the body of the little carry-all bag, dropping the cords to the ground.

In a flash she was after him, heedless of the impropriety of a young lady chasing across the square and into a side street. Her long legs ate up the yards in spite of the narrowness of her skirt, and shortly she had the lad by his nape, grimacing at the dirty, long hair that straggled over his faded and grimy collar. He had dark, swarthy skin, a Gypsy lad!

The voice that came over her shoulder was cool, yet revealed a tightly controlled anger. "Taken to tackling young ladies, have you, lad? Seems you picked the wrong one today." With a firm grip, George dragged the young fellow about and pushed him to where the local constable stood with the justice of the peace. The miscreant would have a speedy sentencing today.

Marianna was torn. Part of her wished that justice was not so harsh for thieves, yet she suspected that it would not be long before he committed worse crimes. Knowing there was little she might do about it one way or the other, she trailed after George. She came up to the constable to reclaim her reticule, showing the broken cords she had retrieved on her way. The lad still foolishly held on to the knife that had cut them. Too many people had observed the scene for the culprit to go free.

In spite of his crime, Marianna opened her mouth to ask for mercy. Before she could speak, she found herself pulled away from the constable and the justice of the peace. A court of piepowder had been set up to deal with all matters relating to the fair, and this swift form of justice was already in progress. George suspected they usually had little to do, what with the town being small and most folk known to one another. Even though this was not a matter between an itinerant stall-holder and a patron, punishment would be meted out. Plus the Gypsies had been far too active as of late. There was strong resentment against them and their thieving ways. The locals would demand a reckoning.

George propelled Marianna away from the site, enjoying the softness of her so close to him even as he wished to wring her neck for taking such a chance for what he suspected was a trifling amount of money.

"None of that, now," George declared in her ear as she turned her head to look back. "The lad is clearly guilty. He would have enjoyed every hard-saved farthing you have in that reticule had you not caught him." He sighed. "I suppose I ought to give you a scold for such foolish behavior, but I cannot. What your lady mother might say is beyond me.''

George felt quite at odds with himself. That Marianna had been most brave in her dash to rescue her reticule was clear. That George wished he might have been the one to perform that service for her was also evident—to him.

Marianna flashed George a tremulous smile as she considered her precipitate action. It was quite unlike her to be this bold. Where had the sedate junior teacher gone?

Now that the danger was past, she found her knees a trifle weak, and a strong desire to sit down took hold of her. As she glanced around, George placed a supporting arm about her, steadying her with his other hand. He guided her toward the table where Sir Alex now stood guard over the game pie and pints of ale.

Marianna felt a warmth creeping up her face as George assisted her to the stool where he had been sitting. Lady Lavinia and the general hurried up to join them. Within moments they were informed what had occurred.

''Truly, 'tis not safe to be alone at these fairs,'' Lady Lavinia said as she and the general stood beside George and Marianna. A scold remained unsaid.

Sir Alex ventured to speak. ''It appears to me that Miss Marianna needs a new reticule. The one in her hands is past saving, by the looks of it. Very brave action on your part, Miss Marianna.'' Those kind brown eyes were very approving, Marianna noted with relief.

George eased her to rest against him, and she was suddenly extremely grateful for the strong figure at her back. ''I believe I can mend it,'' she replied softly.

Lady Lavinia picked up the mutilated reticule, tut-tutting over the frayed cords. She also noted the worn condition of said article. Had it been new, the knife might not have had as easy a time of it.

''I saw some pretty reticules over there.'' She waved vaguely in the direction of one of the stalls. ''You rest here, dear girl, while the general and I investigate to see what is obtainable.

Knowing how carefully we all packed, I doubt if you have a replacement tucked into your portmanteau.'' She drifted off while explaining to the general the limited storage on the unique craft in which they sailed.

''Are you all right now?'' George inquired softly, bending over to speak so only she might hear him.

Marianna nodded. ''Quite, thank you. I am grateful you came so promptly. Once I had caught him, I doubt if I would have been able to deal with him as you did. He was surprisingly strong. Another minute and he would have escaped clean away.''

Sir Alex cleared his throat, then suggested, ''May I offer a wedge of this game pie and a swallow of home-brewed? I think you would be the better for it.''

Suspecting he had the right of it, Marianna took a sip from the mug George swiftly offered her, then she ate a tiny nibble from the wedge of pie Sir Alex cut for her. How lovely it was to be so cosseted and cared for like this. Would that she might always know such.

Across the table Sir Alex inspected the pair opposite him and shook his head. ''I believe Marianna requires something more suitable than a hearty game pie and this ale. Permit me to fetch her just the thing.'' He sought George's permission, not the young lady's, a fact that seemed to escape both of them.

Marianna took another bite of the game pie before nudging it to one side. ''Why do you not bring up a stool to join me at this little table? I cannot think it right for our leader to stand while I sit.'' She managed a teasing smile and George did as she suggested, although keeping a watchful eye on her lest she look faint.

In a few minutes Sir Alex returned with a paper twist in his hand. He bowed before Marianna, presenting his gift with a slight flourish, saying, ''I thought this most appropriate.''

She opened the twist of paper to reveal a pile of Saint John's Dragon Wings, those sweet, carob-flavored triangular biscuits often served when a play about Saint George and the dragon was performed. She could not conceal her delight. Crisp delicacies such as these were beyond the slim purse of a junior teacher.

"Thank you, Sir Alex. You are indeed a thoughtful man." She beamed a smile at him before taking a bite from one.

George gave his friend a dark look. "Indeed."

"I had a feeling she might find them to her liking," replied Sir Alex as he watched Lady Lavinia and General Eagleton wend their way around the square to where the trio sat.

Marianna was facing the opposite direction and so was not aware of their approach until Lady Lavinia spoke in a gay voice.

"See what we have found, dear girl." She held up a most attractive reticule in a refined tapestry weave, one that would be suitable for any number of costumes.

Marianna's heart plunged to her toes. She knew to a penny the amount of money she now carried after giving George her papa's money, and it would not permit the purchase of the reticule held by Lady Lavinia. The dainty little bag looked so very attractive, too. She began to shake her head when George intervened.

"Thoughtful as usual, Aunt." He reached over to take the reticule, placing it before Marianna. "Allow us to replace that which was lost because I failed to assure your safety. My conscience would not permit me otherwise." George sat back with an enormously pleased expression on his face.

Lady Lavinia noted the tiny glance darted toward Sir Alex by her dear—and still-unmarried—nephew, and smiled complacently. "Just the thing." Her smile then disappeared and a look of concern took its place. "George, dear, we have been hearing some disturbing things. After the culprit who tried to steal Marianna's reticule was revealed to be one of those horrid Gypsies, we heard other tales from the townspeople and the stall-holders as well."

"What the lady is trying to tell you is that the Gypsies have been more active than usual around here. I suspect it is merely the locals' prejudice against the group that speaks," said the general.

Marianna, catching what she thought to be a beseeching glance from Lady Lavinia, spoke up. "The Gypsies are sometimes a bit rough, as I have cause to know."

"Aye," the general admitted. "And they've grown more bold as late, too. I hear tell they have taken to waylaying travelers, stealing just like any highwayman."

Lady Lavinia gave the general a troubled glance, but said nothing to reveal her feelings. Rather, she gave her nephew a thoughtful look, as though speculating on something of import.

"Well," Marianna declared, having had quite enough of gloom on what was, after all, a lovely time, "I intend to see a bit more of this fair before the end of the day comes." She offered Lady Lavinia the last of the Saint John's Dragon Wings. That good lady accepted the delicacy with evident pleasure.

The viscount nodded. "Best leave here early. If this is like the fairs at home, the going can be rather tough after sundown. There, respectable people go home, come dark."

The general silently agreed with a decisive nod of his head. Marianna shook the crumbs of the crisp biscuits from her lap, then rose to follow Lady Lavinia. The ladies were shepherded along the row of canvas-sheathed stalls to inspect the offerings. If Lady Lavinia was dismayed by the knowledge of impending rough behavior, she revealed nothing of it to Marianna.

George paused at a stall of an itinerant silversmith when a small pin caught his eye. Pulling out his purse, George paid the price without haggling overmuch, a not unusual thing for him, given his normal absentminded state. But it was uncommon to see him taking note of trifles. Strolling up to catch at Marianna's sleeve, he offered her the item, now wrapped in a bit of tissue.

Marianna shook her head. "You have given me this fine reticule, Lord Barringer. Pray do not ask me to accept more from you."

George was clearly affronted by her formality. "What is this? We have known each other since childhood. Has something I've done given you a disgust of me?" He continued to hold out the tiny package. "True, I did not recognize you when first we met, but that is surely understandable. It has been a number of years, after all."

Feeling distinctly foolish, Marianna accepted the offering, unfolding the paper with increasing delight. Inside, she found a delicate silver dragon. The polished surface gleamed, the eyes of the fanciful creature seeming to wink boldly up at her. She dearly loved the little gift. Holding it close to her bosom, she flashed a smile of great pleasure at George. "Thank you, how very kind! What a charming thing of you to do, my friend." She emphasized the last word to show George her fling at formality had ceased.

The word "friend" did not appear to satisfy George either, judging from the faint frown that settled on his brow. But he nodded in acceptance of her thanks and strolled along with her at his side.

Sir Alex was left to bring up the rear, much to his amusement.

"Marianna, have you ever seen the like?" cried an excited Lady Lavinia.

Placing her special gift safely in the bottom of her new and sturdier reticule, then clasping said item close to her waist, Marianna turned to see what had captured the lady's interest.

At a booth near the far side of the square stood a little monkey dressed in a ruff and slowly dancing about in stately steps. Marianna was enchanted with the tiny animal. The group walked over to watch for a few minutes. After the performance, they dropped a number of coins in a basket before departing, leaving the owner looking pleased.

After a pause to watch the juggler toss his brightly colored wooden balls in the air, they found they were near the very spot where the carriage had deposited them in the morning.

Reluctant to see an end to what had been, for the most part, a lovely day, Marianna stopped to look back at the open area of the square. Here, lads were preparing to chase after a greased pig, the prize being a much-coveted pair of buckskin gloves. The young men were stripped to the waist and ready to tackle the well-larded pig, whose very tail had been docked, so as to make it more difficult to catch.

"Hardly a fit sight for a lady," Sir Alex mused with a slight grin.

Recollecting herself, Marianna gave him a reluctant smile and nodded. "Now, were it the young maidens about to run for a fine linen shift, I expect my stopping to view would be acceptable." She chuckled at the gleam in his eyes as he agreed.

"If you have seen all you wish to see, and purchased what you would, I expect we had best avail ourselves of the general's kind hospitality once again," George said, giving his good friend a hard look. Really, for a man who usually avoided respectable young ladies like a plague, he was becoming far too attentive to Marianna. She was George's particular friend, and not open to any shady dealing from Sir Alex, no matter how nicely he smiled at her. If Alex thought to make any improper overtures to Marianna, he would find he had George to deal with.

Contrite that the viscount seemed displeased with her, Marianna daringly tucked her hand in the crook of his arm, nodding at him with exceeding politeness. "I am ready whenever you think it best to depart, though I confess I enjoy the pleasures of the fair far too much for my own good."

Beaming a smile at her, George patted her hand, then escorted her to where the open carriage waited.

Lady Lavinia was already seated, and observed this rare gallantry of George's with interested eyes.

The little party left the fair as dusk began to creep over the sky. The rougher elements had begun to make themselves evident. Marianna noted the increase of Gypsies and other tough characters.

"It was a lovely time. I am happy you convinced us to remain an extra day with you, General," Lady Lavinia said with an appealing smile. "I shall have some happy memories of this day." She prudently did not permit her eyes to meet his, but fastened her gaze discreetly upon the reticule and package in her lap.

"I see you did some shopping for yourself. How nice," Marianna said, pleased that the kind lady had found a memento of the fair to bring along with her. Marianna suspected a fondness for General Eagleton was also to be carried in the lady's heart, unseen but cherished.

Lady Lavinia opened the little package to reveal a pink paper fan painted with white and red roses, plus a delicate little scrap of pink linen that Marianna supposed could be called a handkerchief. Pink, again. She raised her brows in question.

"Well, I suppose a touch of color is a good thing at my age," replied Lady Lavinia to the unasked question.

A silence drifted over the group as they drove along to the general's charming home. Each person seemed preoccupied with something he or she did not wish to share with the others.

The housekeeper bustled forth as the carriage drew up to the front of the house. She tut-tutted at the story of the nearly-stolen reticule, insisting they enter the drawing room for a bit of refreshment before sitting down to the dinner she had waiting for them.

Once inside, Aunt Lavinia pulled George to one side. He watched a glowing Marianna as she was escorted off to the drawing room at the side of his good friend, then he turned to his aunt. "How may I serve you, Aunt?" he said with impeccable courtesy, not for a second revealing his inner feelings.

His aunt clutched at her parcel and white reticule, facing him with a now-worried expression on her sweet face. "I am deeply concerned about our host." At George's questioning look, she continued. "He is to travel to Lowestoft at a time the countryside is overrun with desperate characters who are intent on robbing and heaven knows what else. He might very well be killed," she declared with horror.

"True," George replied, recalling what had been told earlier. "What can we do?"

"Since we travel to the very same place, I propose he sail with us. It would be far safer for the gentleman. And I am persuaded he may be of assistance to us once we reach that town, as he knows it well. Not only does his daughter attend the school where Marianna taught, but he often sees to the affairs of the militia there. He also mentioned helping us to locate suitable lodgings for our stay. What think you?" she concluded in a very polite and seemingly disinterested manner, quite as though she was not intent on persuading her nephew to see things her way.

George slowly shook his head while rubbing his chin in a thoughtful manner. "I do not see quite how—" he began.

"Oh, George, it is but for one day. Surely the gracious hospitality of our host deserves to be repaid in kind? Is there not some way it can be done?" Aunt Lavinia placed a gentle hand on his sleeve, her eyes pleading with him in a manner she seldom used.

"I expect I can leave one of the lads here to make his way south on another boat," George said musingly, not impervious to his aunt's wiles. " 'Twill make it difficult should the weather turn nasty, you know. I doubt the general is informed on the matter of sailing ships, what with his concern with the militia."

"I would wager he could follow instructions very well, George," his aunt replied persuasively.

"Very well, I shall put the matter before him."

"Now?" insisted his aunt.

"Now," George agreed with a sigh. He led his dear aunt to the drawing room, to be greeted with the sight of Marianna laughing at some sally from his supposed friend, Sir Alexander Dent. Really, George felt he must caution Alex regarding his behavior. Marianna was not a chit to be dallied with like some doxy.

Turning to their host, George murmured some pleasantry, and when the housekeeper returned to inform them that dinner was ready to be served, he sighed again with relief.

At the table, George decided the time was proper to approach the general regarding the journey to Lowestoft. "Sir, I have been thinking about your trip south. Surely it is a hazardous journey you contemplate at this time. Why do you not consider traveling with us? I believe it would be possible, if you do not mind chancing close quarters should the weather take a turn on us."

General Eagleton nodded, his face quite serious as he contemplated the overland trip versus the sail aboard the viscount's somewhat unorthodox vessel he had observed early this morning when he'd gone down to the pier.

Perceiving the delicate hand of Lady Lavinia in this effort, Mariana added her voice. "I do believe it would be the wisest course to take. We could not bear to think of your being set upon by rogues, perhaps injured as well as robbed."

The general nodded, not smiling at her reference to the troubles lately fallen upon the countryside. He turned to Lady Lavinia. "What do you say, dear lady?"

"I say," declared the lady in question, "that you ought to join us. I would never forgive myself if you were to be injured, or worse." She raised her lovely blue eyes to plead silently with him.

Eagleton tightened his lips, considering the proposal while he accepted a serving of turbot from his footman. "I shall do it," he said at long last. "I am not the best of sailors, but what you all say is true. And not only shall I avoid the dangers of a land journey, but I shall have the delight of good company." He bowed slightly to Lady Lavinia, then to the others in the company.

Thus it was speedily settled. The viscount explained to him what was allowed in line of baggage, suggesting that the remainder of the general's things be sent on after him on the same boat George's own man, Joe, would take later.

Not long after dinner, they all decided upon an early bedtime. The sooner they left in the morning, the better. There were likely to be fewer people about at an early hour as well, something George preferred. He detested having people hanging about when he was trying to set sail.

"You say your boat can dive as well as sail?" inquired the general as the men sauntered up the stairs to their rooms. "I find that hard to believe."

"It is submersible, true. Propulsion is by means of two screws placed at the stern ahead of the rudder. Tomorrow I shall show you just how two vertical screws force the air out of the compartment between the interior and exterior so that the boat will descend or rise at will. While above water, I use a special type of sail that can be lowered and locked into place when we dive. I prefer to remain above. I have not perfected the air-replacement system to my satisfaction."

"I took a look at the diving boat early this morning. The copper sheathing makes it look mighty strange," the general said with a smile.

"Marianna said she thought at first it was a dragon rising from the sea," George said by way of an answer, chuckling as he paused by the door to his room.

In her room, Marianna heard the sound of George's deep voice as she prepared for bed. She paused to fish out her pretty little silver pin once again. Taking it closer to the candle, she again noted the dragon's appearance of winking at her. She smiled with fond regard. She placed the pin where she might see it when she arose, then she undid the heavy coil of her hair and began to patiently brush it out, allowing the curls to fall about her shoulders. Not finding her night cap near the top of her case and not wishing to unduly disturb the neatly packed case, she permitted her hair to be free.

The house settled into night-time silence, save for a rustling sound from Lady Lavinia's room. Next door to her, Marianna wondered what was the trouble, as earlier the dear lady had been most eager to go to bed. At last Marianna went to tap lightly on the lady's door.

"Thank heaven," whispered Lady Lavinia when she inched the door open. Permitting Marianna to enter her room, Lady Lavinia, still arrayed in her gown, sank onto her bed, wringing her hands. "I am a foolish old lady, my dear."

Swiftly hurrying to her side, Marianna placed a comforting arm about her shoulders. "Never say such a thing."

"To think I am so taken with illusion I imagine an attraction from the general. And I fear I have the same sort of regard for him. Such nonsense ought not be permitted." She gave Marianna a hopeful look.

"Now, that is nonsense, to talk like that. I feel certain he has a *tendre* for you, ma'am. You are a lovely lady. Perhaps he feels he aims too high?"

"Really?" whispered a distinctly relieved Lavinia. "I shall take care to drop a hint or two regarding that nonsense, you may be certain. Only I am such in a taking, I fear I shall not sleep a wink tonight."

Marianna patted her on the shoulder. "Just slip into your nightdress and get into that comfortable-looking bed, while I see if I can find you a soothing drink. You will sleep like a babe," she promised.

Leaving the lady busily changing into her nightdress, Marianna cautiously walked down the hall to the stairs. Candles still lit the way to the lower levels. She hesitantly began her descent to the kitchen, feeling a bit strange to be wandering about the general's house in the dim light after all was so silent.

The kitchen was spotless and well-equipped with the makings of a soothing drink. Marianna brewed a cup of chamomile tea with the water still simmering on the hob.

Turning to go back upstairs, she was surprised to see the door open. "George? Whatever are you doing down here?"

"I heard a noise and I wanted to assure myself it was not one of the Gypsies come to extract vengeance." His look was steady, not revealing that he was quite attracted by the cascade of blond hair that tumbled about her shoulders in an entrancing richness. He was sorry when those lovely sea-green eyes gazed at him in alarm.

"Do you really feel there is danger? I shall not tell your aunt, or she will never sleep tonight." Marianna gestured to the still-steaming cup of tea. "I had best get this up to her before it grows cold. She had trouble settling down, you see."

"It was kind of you to take care of her." George opened the kitchen door, then walked up the stairs to the bedroom floor with Marianna.

"She is so sweet, it is a pleasure, I assure you."

"Having the general along will present an interesting challenge. In the event of foul weather, I shall see if it is possible for an untrained person to assist with the boat. This project is developing some scientific value, after all," he mused, mostly to himself.

Marianna stopped in the middle of the hall, glaring at George with disgust. "Is that all you can ever think of . . . your blessed scientific projects? Your aunt ought to come before that. My difficulty as well, for that matter."

"Marianna . . ." muttered George, hoping Alex didn't come charging out to see what caused the noise.

"Oh," she declared, quite miffed with him. She hurried to his aunt's door, entering with a decided huff.

George went to his bed with a perturbed frown.

When Lady Lavinia was at last settled and comforted, Marianna returned to her room. She finished her bedtime ritual, then slipped beneath the covers of her bed.

That George! Tears stung her eyes as she considered how little she must mean to him when all he could think about was the scientific aspect of this trip.

6

George stood in the hall as the angry figure of the young woman he had known most all her life whirled into his aunt's room. What had just happened? She of a certain had changed from the happy if somewhat shy little girl he had known in the dim past. It must be that her present problem beset her too much. Comforted by his conclusion, he wandered down the hall and into the room that had been assigned to him, closing the door with a muted snap.

He began to remove his coat, then paused. Her eyes, he decided while staring at the far wall, had the hue of a tempest-tossed sea. Magnificent. He shrugged from his coat and hung it over a chair back. Then he crossed to the bed to remove his boots, and again stared off into space. Her hair, swirling softly about those slim shoulders in a froth of shimmering gold, was most alluring. He sank down on the edge of his bed in contemplation of his young neighbor. He had wanted very much to touch that spun softness of her hair, run his hands through it to feel the silken texture, bring the delicate scent and feel of her close to him again.

He realized with odd curiosity that he would relish a taste of those lips the color of the wild strawberries that grew in sheltered nooks of the estate.

He had not failed to notice her enchanting state of dishabille. The misty white muslin robe over her night rail could not totally conceal the charms beneath. Indeed, he had been conscious of little else on their walk up the stairs. It quite shook him to perceive that he desired his young friend. "Marianna." The very name had a musical quality to it. Lilting.

He dropped his first boot to the floor, bending again to remove the second. And then her final words to him penetrated his somewhat bemused brain and he paused, straightening slightly. Was that all he ever thought of? His scientific projects? He pulled off his second boot, then rose from the bed to divest himself of the remainder of his garments while he considered her statement. Shaking his head with the utter nonsense of the very idea that he was far too absorbed in his studies and projects, he crawled into the comfortable bed and began to go over, with the trained approach of the scientist, the coming day's trials that might possibly present themselves.

The general had admitted to being a poor sailor. That was a negative item. Yet what Aunt Lavinia pointed out made sense. They could use someone with knowledge of the town, perhaps *entrée* to the best circles of society. George's modesty forbade acknowledging the plain fact of the matter: that Viscount Barringer would have precious little trouble in getting whatever he wished in the society of that small community.

Actually, George had gone about so little in society, he was scarcely aware of the impact on fluttering female hearts of a well-set peer, one who possessed a tidy fortune in addition to a handsome face and figure. His absentminded mien hid well the keen mind that analyzed a myriad of problems and solved an amazing number of them. If he took a notion to apply his brainpower to Miss Marianna Wyndham, there was little doubt he could solve her dilemma as well.

But his last thoughts after blowing out his candle and stretching out beneath the lavender-scented covers was of his diving boat and the weather due on the morrow. They might well be required to dive, and he really didn't relish that experience with three poor sailors aboard.

Marianna awoke to gray skies and a rising wind. She tugged her robe about her as she crossed to the windows to peer out on the morning mist. Yesterday had been so utterly lovely. Today looked the sort of day one spent by a cozy fire, toasting one's feet. It was scarcely the weather to make a body possessing a weak stomach contemplate a sea voyage. Her thoughts winged to the delicate Lady Lavinia. "Oh, dear," Marianna murmured in distress while she began to plait her hair to coil it about her head. She tucked the long golden plait in place with a goodly number of pins, then drew her clothes from the wardrobe.

Dressing hurriedly, she then packed her belongings back into her portmanteau and took a farewell glance at her pleasant room before departing. She had best attend Lady Lavinia, soothing her with peppermint tea, if possible. There was little one might do to ease the discomfort brought on by a tempestuous sea. Today's journey did not promise to be the delightful trip traveled two days past.

The group that met in the breakfast room wore most sober faces. The general looked at Lady Lavinia with consternation when she requested that peppermint tea be brought.

"Dear lady, I fear my desire that you remain a day to join in our little fair has brought problems for you."

Her protest did little to reassure him, for he looked quite dejected. The general ate sparingly of the repast set out on the sideboard, apparently deciding that the less he ate, the less there would be to disturb his stomach later.

"I shall be fine, I am sure," Lady Lavinia said dubiously. "I wish I might be a better sort of seaman, or seawoman, as the case might be," she concluded in an abstracted manner. When the pot of tea was set beside her teacup and saucer by Mrs. Nesbit, Lady Lavinia poured and sipped while not seeming aware of her actions. Between sips of hot tea she nibbled on triangles of toast with dabs of red-currant jelly on top of them.

"I could hope it will go well with you," the general persisted.

Lady Lavinia gave a dissatisfied look at the dregs of the mint leaves in her cup. "Fie, sir, 'tis a caution, nothing more." She placed the cup on its saucer with an annoyed click.

Breakfast was consumed in haste. They departed the manor silently, the general pausing to issue last-moment instructions to his housekeeper before quitting the hall.

There were few people abroad on so inclement a morning. George was relieved, yet unhappy at the cause. He set about preparing his vessel, issuing quick orders in succession to his crew. There was no time to lose. Should a storm come upon them before they were prepared, there could be trouble.

His passengers sensed his urgency and did what little they could to be of help, most of which was confined to keeping out of the way, not to mention the path of the lads who assisted him. Tom Crowdon popped down belowdeck to check that all was in readiness, then at last the group made their way aboard.

Marianna was the last to descend from the pier, giving George a searching look to see if her parting words of last night had had any effect on him. They had bothered her a great deal. She could not believe she had spoken so thoughtlessly to the very man who was trying to help her clear her name! Talk about foolish things for one to do!

"George?" she began, trying to find a way to mend her fences. A close check, mostly at his expression while he assisted her onto the deck of his diving boat, and she ceased. How like George to be so absorbed in his project that he had not heeded a word she had uttered.

Disgruntled, yet not knowing precisely why she was so annoyed, she moved to the far side of the boat, prepared to keep out of his way.

Shortly after they left the pier, the wind began to whip up the sea about them, and it was soon evident that the passengers would have to endure the trip belowdeck. They all made their way down through the cylindrical opening with various expressions ranging from dismay to fear.

The process of actually diving was rather fascinating in a strange way. Two vertical screws let water into the special chambers on either side of the boat. Marianna fancied she could hear it rushing in, though that was probably her imagination. Tom manned one of these pumps while Sir Alex took charge of the other. George tended the propeller during the descent. Marianna looked at what Alex had told her was the bathometer and realized they were indeed going down. Then the boat leveled off and silence was broken only by quiet orders from George.

The two women kept to a small area. Lady Lavinia sniffed at her surroundings. "La, George, could you not find it possible to make it more comfortable for your passengers? I feel sorely cramped in here. Why, Marianna and I are near as like atop each other. I wonder if it would have been quite as dangerous on land, in spite of the Gypsies.'' Her querulous tone was most unlike her cheerful manner, a sure indication of her nervousness.

George spared a glance at Marianna, his thoughts at that remark concealed. He nodded, then, trying to pacify, replied, ''I was not expecting guests, Aunt.''

The general decided to make himself useful, turning out to be a better sailor than he expected.

Although light from the small hanging lamp was dim, Marianna could not fail to note the serene yet tensely preoccupied expression on George's face. It gave her great comfort to observe him, somehow certain that if there was something seriously wrong, he could not conceal his anxiety.

Marianna would have been less sanguine had she known that George was indeed apprehensive. He had not subjected his diving boat to this manner of storm with passengers on board.

The boat rose from time to time for them to take in fresh air and determine the severity of the storm.

''Are we there yet?'' Aunt Lavinia asked each occasion, to George's increasing annoyance, most diligently hidden.

Even the general had a turn at the hand-cranked propeller, declaring he felt better with something to occupy him. '' 'Twill be far better when you can obtain a safe, mechanical means of propulsion,'' he said as he wiped his brow after his first stint at the crank.

The two men then spent an agreeable time discussing what to Marianna seemed complicated and almost pointless possibilities. After all, what earthly good was the diving boat? She certainly didn't desire to travel cramped up in the bottom of one again, George notwithstanding. There were all the exposed pipes and mechanical apparatus to do with the raising and lowering of the vessel, plus the men to operate those pumps and other equipment, the most necessary being the propeller. It did not make for spacious quarters.

While they nibbled on the rolls and cold chicken sent by Mrs. Nesbit for their lunch, Marianna tried to bring up the matter facing them, since Lady Lavinia was huddled so close to her. She soon abandoned the effort. The lady appeared lost to conversation.

So they traveled south, listening to the terse commands from George to his men in the eerie silence beneath the waves. Even Sir Alex had little to say.

And then they arrived.

The turbulent waves had subsided into tranquillity. The storm had passed with no more effect on the passengers and crew of the diving boat than a faintly greenish tinge to several of them.

George gave a sigh of well-earned relief when he ordered Tom to operate the pumps that forced out the water so the boat might rise. Sir Alex went topside to release and raise the sails so the diving boat might enter the port with a more normal appearance and with greater speed. Even then, the sight of the copper-clad boat, with its peculiar shape, the odd cylindrical entrance dome, and the viewing tower, would bring questioning looks from the old sailors who hung about the pier. It would be plain to most that this was no ordinary sailboat.

The slow speed at which they had traveled meant that they reached Lowestoft at a late hour, when most of the populace were at their dinner tables, considering how early provincials dined. George could not help but feel this to be a benefit.

General Eagleton, still faintly pale but holding up remarkably well, declared, "I shall see to our transportation. Naturally you shall reside with me until a house can be arranged for you to rent. I would not consider anything less." His words brooked no opposition.

So, when the boat nudged the pier and curious hands helped them secure the ropes, it was the general who was the second person to set foot on solid wood planking. The first up was Tom Crowdon, who set about his business with practiced ease.

Marianna and Lady Lavinia were discernibly glad to be ashore. Lady Lavinia went so far as to give the pier a little pat when she reached the final step of the ladder before clambering to the wooden planks with surprising grace, accepting Sir Alex's hand with gratitude.

Marianna caught George's offered hand, gazing at him with a modest air. "I do thank you, Lord Barringer," she stated demurely as she managed the climb with a fluid grace. " 'Tis most kind of you to help me and I do appreciate it, you know."

"Marianna," George cautioned, then smiled as he caught sight of that gleam in her eyes, now dancing with sparks of green. A few years ago he would have patted her charming posterior. He must keep his inclinations to himself . . . for the moment.

Before long, the group, minus the crew, who would remain near the pier and close to the boat, set off down Lowestoft Road in a hired landau.

"Lowestoft is a nice little town," commented the general as he looked about him. "Population of a little over three thousand, so I am told. Farther along this road is the headquarters for the squadron of militia still stationed here. It is where I spend a good deal of my time when away from home. Things are much quieter around here now that the threat of invasion has passed. During the late war, the local inhabitants lived in perpetual dread of that possibility."

Lady Lavinia exchanged a glance with Marianna that said volumes concerning the subject of threatened war and the tyrant Napoleon.

In the tranquillity of twilight, the town seemed much like any other to Lady Lavinia. The rain-washed cobbled streets were lined with trees like so many soldiers marching to the rhythm of the unseen breeze. She judged there were many dignified houses in which visiting families could entertain their friends and acquaintances at fair time as well as enjoy the desirable amenities of town life. There should be no difficulty in locating a pleasant house to rent for the time they were here.

She glanced across at her nephew, then to where Marianna perched in silence. The girl looked very apprehensive, as though that awful Miss Chudleigh might jump out from behind a bush to confront her.

"We shall begin first thing in the morning," Lady Lavinia announced in a firm manner. "I trust you gentlemen to make arrangements for our comfort. The general appears to be very clever at that sort of thing. I shall approach the school and that nasty Miss Chudleigh with no delay.''

The general looked immensely pleased at the encomium from the lady he found so appealing.

Marianna looked distressed at the words. "Tomorrow?" The time for attack was upon them. Marianna's mouth was dry and her heart seemed to beat at a very fast rate. Were her feet rather chilled? No time to back away from this now. She lifted her chin a trifle. Her name would be cleared.

They supped in the nicely appointed dining room of the house the general rented, then retired to their various rooms quite early. Marianna shared a bedroom—one she suspected was used by the general's daughter when she visited here—with Lady Lavinia, while George and Sir Alex shared another. The house was not a large one, but comfortable and pleasingly decorated.

Late the following morning Lady Lavinia, arrayed in the best of the day gowns she had brought with her, sallied forth to beard the dragon, or so the general put it.

Lavinia merely smiled and said, "I hope to convince that lady that it is grossly unfair to judge our dear Marianna with so little evidence.'' That she fully intended to employ the rank of her esteemed brother, the Earl of Cranswick, as well as his son, Viscount Barringer, was unspoken, but surmised by those who remained.

Once the general, George, and Sir Alex left to seek out a tolerable place to rent, Marianna was left to fidget about on her own. It proved to be a most boring occupation.

Lady Lavinia had read her tea leaves this morning and was feeling most confident as she approached the front entrance of the school. She was not the daughter of an earl, and now the sister of one, accustomed to the normal deference due her, for nothing. Besides, the reading had told her that her day would be fruitful.

Pausing before the school, she took assessment. The three-storied building was of brick, well-built, and there appeared to be sufficient windows for good light. It seemed in fine repair, with no broken windows or shutters needing mending. Lady Lavinia suspected the parents of the girls educated therein would have paid highly for that privilege, if appearances were anything to go by.

She entered the rather drab if clean building, looking about the foyer with intently curious eyes. Her glance missed nothing, from the dull paint on the walls to the uncomfortable-looking benches placed along them. It was not a place in which to dawdle. When a young maid appeared, Lavinia turned to face her.

"Lady Lavinia Mayne to see Miss Chudleigh," Lavinia announced in awesome tones.

Any objection the maid might have had to this demand without an appointment disappeared at the effect of the slight, wispy figure, who maintained an imposing dignity in spite of her size. "Indeed, ma'am," was the quick reply. The unhappy maid sped off and in minutes Lady Lavinia was escorted to the office of the headmistress.

The woman who rose from behind her desk was a tall, thin person with no particularly outstanding characteristic, other than a nose that tended to be a bit on the prominent side. "To what do I owe this honor, milady?" inquired the obviously impressed woman, who was also obviously trying not to reveal that she was impressed.

Lady Lavinia did not make known the nature of her visit immediately. She seated herself on the small velvet-covered chair to face her opponent while sizing her up. The experienced General Eagleton could have faced an enemy with no more deliberate caution.

At last Lady Lavinia spoke. "I come as a close family friend of someone you know. My dear brother, the Earl of Cranswick, is most distressed at what has occurred here. Although he is quite indispensable at the War Ministry, he keeps well-informed on the affairs of his home community. Indeed, he is well-pleased that his son, Viscount Barringer, has chosen to escort and champion his dear friend and neighbor's daughter in her trial. Sir John Wyndham has friends in higher places than you could have possibly imagined," Lady Lavinia added at the sight of the suddenly paled countenance that faced her.

"I assume you refer to Marianna Wyndham," the woman said, her manner quite blunt as color slowly returned to her cheeks. "The girl is a thief. I do not care whose relative or friend she is, I shall not harbor her beneath my roof." Miss Chudleigh's eyes narrowed and her long nose seemed to quiver with indignation.

"And how do you know she is such a thing?" demanded Lady Lavinia, her voice quiet but her manner most intimidating.

"All indications pointed to her," Miss Chudleigh said with an increasing air of righteousness. "Lady Phillida insisted that only Miss Wyndham knew where the sapphires were concealed. Miss Teale, one of my teachers, attested that Miss Wyndham was not in her room at the hour when the jewelry disappeared. Miss Teale had intended to visit with Miss Wyndham, and that young woman was gone from her room for ample time necessary to remove the jewels. The maid informed me that Miss Wyndham's room was unoccupied for some time. I do not countenance my teachers absenting themselves in the evening, Lady Lavinia. The only teachers who leave at the end of the day are Miss de Vere, the French and needlework teacher, and the dancing master. It was hardly proper for Miss Wyndham to be gone from the school. She had left to hide the gems. Poor Lady Phillida is desolate at her loss."

That Miss Chudleigh could not afford the loss of reputation from such a theft was unspoken, but Lady Lavinia could well imagine the vexation and fear that had clutched at her heart. The headmistress would not tolerate a threat to her school.

"First of all, I wonder if Miss de Vere might not have had access to the upper floor where the girls reside. Have you considered the possibility? And then you must know I am most surprised that you would encourage a young girl to have such a valuable possession with her. Surely a sapphire necklace ought to have been locked in your safe? You do have such a safe, do you not?" Lady Lavinia tilted her head slightly, resembling a windblown bird, with her wisps of hair peeking from beneath her bonnet.

Indignant that her management of her school was called to question, the headmistress snapped back, "But of course I have a safe." She darted a glance at a rather poor painting of a tranquil cow in a green meadow that hung on the side wall before confronting Lady Lavinia again. "As far as Miss de Vere is concerned, she is far too eager to depart, come the end of her lessons. I feel sure Lady Phillida knew better, but the poor girl wished to impress her classmates, I suppose."

This was the first sign that the headmistress had something of a heart. Lady Lavinia made a mental note of it. And she was unconvinced regarding the French teacher.

"I have known Marianna Wyndham all of her life. I am closely acquainted with her family. That girl is no more a thief than I am," Lavinia fervently declared, conveniently forgetting her own habit of picking up—on occasion—something that took her fancy, even if it happened to belong to someone else. Fortunately, Miss Chudleigh had no way of knowing anything about that particular little vice.

Continuing her attack, Lady Lavinia said, "I insist you reinstate Miss Wyndham until you can prove beyond a shadow of any doubt that she actually took those sapphires. I should also like to have an opportunity to question Lady Phillida. Miss Teale and the maid as well."

There was no "if you please" in the stated request. Lady Lavinia's manner was polite—barely—and her voice quite firm, but with a hint of a threat contained in it. It served to intimidate Miss Chudleigh. That lady had visions of the earl appearing in her office to demand the closure of the school or something equally dire.

All at once that proud bearing crumpled slightly and the head-mistress picked up a bell from her desk. She rang it, the sound bringing the maid to the room with incredible speed. Lady Lavinia surmised the young miss had been listening from the other side of the door.

"Request Lady Phillida present herself here at once. And if Miss Teale or Miss de Vere is about, request they present themselves as well." The dry voice revealed nothing of her feelings.

The round-eyed maid scurried from the room and could be

heard running up the wooden flight of stairs to the upper floor of the building.

It was not long before the maid returned to announce that Lady Phillida had gone for a walk with her teachers, but that there was someone else to see Miss Chudleigh. The maid appeared quite taken aback.

"Yes, Miss Chudleigh," Marianna said from the open doorway. "I decided it was most unfair for me to remain at General Eagleton's residence while dear Lady Lavinia spoke to you on my behalf." Marianna drew closer to the desk. "I ought never have left the school after being accused of a crime I did not commit. I demand an opportunity to clear my name."

Miss Chudleigh gasped at the temerity of her junior teacher to actually speak in such a manner to her. She remained seated, staring in what was usually an intimidating manner that served to quell any upstart. It was distressing to observe the chit was not impressed in the least.

Marianna was quaking in her half-boots. She held her hands tightly lest she reveal just how badly they trembled. Yet she could not permit others to do what ought to be done by herself. She had considered the matter at great length after Lady Lavinia departed. A glance at that dear lady now fortified Marianna's resolve. She would not yield on her demand.

Lady Lavinia beamed a gracious smile at the other two women. "That sounds like an utterly admirable solution to me. The sooner Miss Wyndham resumes her position here, the better, as I see it. She can move back here in two days, I expect, can you not?" Turning to Marianna, she again smiled.

Marianna had been prepared for a battle and she found it almost disappointing to be deprived of it now. It appeared that Miss Chudleigh was being swept along with the momentum of the conversation and Lady Lavinia's direction. How that slight woman could manage events so adroitly was most admirable.

"But of course," Marianna replied smoothly. "I welcome the opportunity not only to clear my name, but as well to, it will be hoped, find the true criminal. You will not be sorry, ma'am, that you permitted my return."

The slightly bewildered Miss Chudleigh looked from Marianna to Lady Lavinia and back again. She capitulated. If this young woman did indeed have the sister of the Earl of Cranswick, a man even Miss Chudleigh had heard about, as her champion, it might be well to go along with the scheme. In her business it did not pay to aggravate anyone associated with the peerage. She looked down at her desk, then up again.

"Report to me in three days to resume your duties. You may return to your room whenever you wish." In a way, it would be a relief to have Miss Wyndham back again. The girls had been very fond of her, and no amount of explanation regarding her absence had satisfied them.

Miss Chudleigh had found that locating qualified teachers willing to work for the wages she offered was not easy. This solved a problem for her, at least for the moment. She was not one to look far into the future. Take each day as it came, was her motto.

"I am pleased you see the wisdom of finding the real thief," added Marianna. "Have you considered that when I prove my innocence, it may turn out that someone else here is guilty?"

"Yes," Lady Lavinia said. "How terrible it would be if another theft were to occur."

With that possibility hanging in the air, Marianna and Lady Lavinia took their departure.

"What a terrible woman," said Lady Lavinia as she tucked her hand in the crook of Marianna's arm. They sauntered along the path toward the house the general had rented, knowing there was no hurry. "How did you ever manage to work for her?" That it was a shocking thing for Marianna to be compelled to work at all was left unsaid.

"It was not easy, ma'am. One does what one must."

Coming toward them was a procession of girls from the school walking two by two, with a teacher in the lead, one following. Marianna said very soft, "Miss de Vere follows behind them, with Miss Teale in charge."

"The very one who intended to pay you a visit that fatal night? My, my." Lady Lavinia studied the demure woman, noting her neat but worn pelisse and dowdy bonnet.

At that moment Miss Teale looked their way and turned extremely pale. She motioned the girls to hurry, then gave another alarmed glance at Marianna before following them.

"How very interesting," Lady Lavinia observed.

7

"Which one of those young women is Lady Phillida?" Lady Lavinia inquired.

Marianna studied the line of girls while trying not to appear too obvious. "In the second pair from the end, the one with chestnut curls wearing a dark-green pelisse. She has a difficulty, you see. She limps rather badly. I fear the others are not always kind to her."

"And that is why she seeks attention by displaying her jewels? To gain sympathy and thus friendships? Poor child," exclaimed Lady Lavinia softly. Upon closer examination, she added, "Pity. She is a pretty little thing."

Then she looked away from the disappearing group of girls to study a bed of flowers along their path. Bending over, she touched one of them. "She is like a flower that has not grown properly. Sturdy and with nice petals, but deformed leaves."

Lady Lavinia shook her head while giving a comforting pat to Marianna's arm. "You may be accused of a crime you did not commit, but you are a lovely, lithesome creature, full of grace and charm. Compare your sylphlike beauty with that poor girl and you may begin to understand what could have prompted her actions."

Marianna gasped, for the moment ignoring the kind words heaped upon her head. "Do you suspect that Lady Phillida possibly hid her own jewels, then claimed they were stolen, merely to garner some attention? How utterly horrid of her, even if she is crippled." Marianna turned her head to see the last of the line of girls entering the school.

"I believe it is possible. As well, I chanced to observe that

little maid when you entered the room to confront Miss
Chudleigh. By the by, dear girl, that was very well done," said
Lavinia with another pat on Marianna's arm. "Where was I?
Oh, yes, the maid. She looked utterly terrified when you
appeared in that room to demand that you be allowed to clear
your name. I trust the chit is paid beggarly wages. Think what
those sapphires represented to her."

"The maid? Betsy? But she fears her own shadow," declared
Marianna as they turned up the path to General Eagleton's
house.

"Fears can be overcome if motivation is strong enough.
Witness our journey here beneath the sea." They paused before
the front door, and Lady Lavinia added, "And then there is
Miss Teale. Her pelisse is most shabby and that bonnet has seen
many seasons. I doubt Miss Chudleigh is a generous employer,
nor is she likely to provide any sort of pension for her teachers.
Would not Miss Teale—for after all, she grows old like the rest
of us—be apt to look to those days when she can no longer teach?
As for Miss de Vere, she may well have need of money, too."

They entered the house in silence, each mulling over what
had just been said as they walked up the stairs to the first floor.
When George emerged from the general's neat drawing room,
it was to discover two bemused women, deeply in thought.

"Did the meeting fare so badly?" he asked with a palpable
touch of concern in his voice.

Marianna would normally have been gratified at this display
of interest. Now she merely glanced at him before stripping off
her gloves and removing her bonnet, all the while explaining,
"I believed there was but one suspect. Your aunt reveals there
are four, each with an excellent motive."

"Four," echoed Sir Alex as he came to stand behind George.

Lady Lavinia swept past the group standing by the doorway
to enter the drawing room, heading for a comfortable chair.
She gracefully seated herself, then gazed at the three who had
trailed along behind her. "Yes, it is a possibility. Miss Teale,
the maid Betsy, perhaps Miss de Vere, and of course, Lady
Phillida, herself. I believe we can ignore the dancing master."

"And what is that young lady like?" Sir Alex asked, strolling over to pour out glasses of wine for himself, George, and the general. Behind them, a maid discreetly entered with a tray bearing a pot of tea, cups, and biscuits for the ladies.

"She is a pretty little bit of a girl with chestnut curls and dark eyes," Marianna replied while pouring out two cups of steaming bohea tea.

"And she has a decided limp," Lavinia added. She accepted the tea, gave an approving sip, then helped herself to a dainty ratafia biscuit.

Sir Alex curled his lip, declaring, "So, to compensate for a deformity, she makes life hell for another."

"Sir Alex," admonished Lady Lavinia, "you forget yourself. I suggest that we split up our investigation. Since you feel so strongly about that young lady's guilt, Sir Alex, I suggest you apply yourself to her. Find out, if you can, what goes on in her brainbox."

Sir Alex had the expression of one who is firmly convinced that there was probably nothing in Lady Phillida's mind to be of interest to him or anyone else.

"And Miss Teale?" George asked, as though knowing his fate in advance.

"You, I believe. Make her acquaintance while she walks the girls. If I know anything at all, she will be flattered, and perhaps you may learn something from her."

George straightened, touching his chin with a thoughtful hand before sneaking a glance at Alex. The two men exchanged unreadable looks. Like many friends of long standing, they communicated easily with a minimum of words, or perhaps nothing more than a glance.

"And Betsy?" Marianna said, annoyed that George seemed so eager to interview Miss Teale.

"Once you are again installed in your room, you might be able to gain her confidence. You can but try."

Ashamed that she had harbored unkind thoughts for even a moment of the dear people who were taking precious time from their lives to help her, Marianna nodded. "Of course. How fortunate I am that we have not only a general to marshal a place for us to live, but a generous and wise lady to lead us in splendid direction.''

"Speaking of a house, what manner of place did you men find?'' inquired Lady Lavinia, turning to face the general rather than her nephew.

"Rather imposing edifice, if I do say so. Sir Alex thought it wise to make an impression on the local society, don't you know.'' The general arched a brow while exchanging looks with Lady Lavinia. She fluttered her lashes, then bowed her head to nibble at her biscuit before glancing up again. She then bestowed an approving look on Sir Alex, the first since his remark about the cripple. The young man had a touch of cynicism when it came to young ladies. It might do him good to be required to dance attendance on Lady Phillida for a bit. If only that young woman was not a total disappointment.

"Well,'' said the general in his kind but gruff voice, "the cook has sent word that she has a particularly fine bit of John Dory for nuncheon. When fresh, there's no more tasty fish than that. I suggest we repair to our rooms to freshen up a bit, then meet again in the dining room in thirty minutes.''

Lady Lavinia gave a decisive nod, rose from her chair to gently guide Marianna along with her out of the room, much to that young woman's annoyance.

"I had thought to discuss the plans a little more,'' Marianna said, trying to conceal her sense of pique as they mounted the stairs.

"Caution, dear girl. Caution. The general will offer some excellent advice regarding how to approach the problem before us. I have no doubt he has some splendid ideas that we would do well to heed. Wiser heads and all that,'' said the good lady with a maddeningly vague manner.

When the ladies sauntered down the polished oak stairs to join the men, they were discovered in the dining room and in deep conversation. Sir Alex stood by the blue brocade draperies, George next to him. Facing them was the general, who was expounding on his theories about thievery.

Marianna saw a chance to get some help regarding her

approach to the maid. She strolled over to General Eagleton to place her concern before him, so to speak. She ignored George. "Sir, since you appear to have a certain facility for this sort of intrigue, I wonder if you have a bit of advice as to how I ought to proceed with Betsy, the school maid."

"Intrigue? The man you want is Barringer. With his father in the War Office, he's a natural, I shouldn't wonder." The general shot a sly glance at George before taking himself off to escort Lady Lavinia to the table, where he placed her next to him.

"George?" Good heavens, that was a laugh, given his usual abstracted manner. It would be amazing if he noted what time of day it was . . . unless his stomach complained and he remembered it was time to eat. Marianna could not help it if a tiny smile escaped.

"You needn't look so surprised," said a clearly affronted George. "A scientific mind can be applied to any problem, you know."

"And this is quite definitely another project," replied Marianna, feeling as though she would very much like to stamp her foot, preferably on George's, while wearing her riding boots.

"You could give me a chance to prove myself," George said, a twinkle creeping into his eyes. "What sort of hero would I be if I neglected to find a solution to your dilemma?"

"I fear I was unaware that you were a hero," replied Marianna, a matching gleam entering her own sea-green eyes. A smile tilted up the corners of her pretty mouth before she continued. "Do forgive me, Lord Barringer. Henceforth, I shall try to remember your exalted mind."

"Marianna," George said in a soft and exceedingly low voice, "I shall strangle you without compunction if you do that again."

"*Moi*?" She fluttered a hand up to rest against her bosom, extremely conscious of her rapidly beating heart beneath the delicate muslin of her gown. "I shall take the utmost care, in that case, never to upset you . . . unduly. I had no idea you could react this way." She sought a light smile and found it most difficult.

George paused in the act of ushering her to the table to softly growl, "But, then, you have little knowledge of how I react in many instances, don't you?"

With those highly disturbing words lingering in her ear, he nudged her toward her place. Marianna sank onto the blue satin cushion of the mahogany chair in a state of utter confusion. Consequently, she was startled when Lady Lavinia mentioned her name.

"The next step in our plan is for each of us to get close to our targets. Marianna, dear, do pay attention. I believe you shall have to wait until you move your belongings over to the school tomorrow. By the by, I suggest you and I do a bit of shopping today. You shall need a few more things than you were able to fit into that portmanteau, you know."

"Yes, ma'am," said a subdued Marianna, devoutly hoping the unpredictable Lady Lavinia would not reveal precisely what the shopping list contained just now.

"And, George, contrive to plant yourself, along with Sir Alex, in the path of those females as they make their way to the park. When should they venture out, Marianna?"

Displeased at the thought of George chasing after Miss Teale, Marianna replied sharply. "Late each morning, ma'am."

Miss Eloisa Teale had hidden charm concealed beneath that drab exterior, if truth be told. Marianna had seen her with the older girls, diverting them with a lively tale upon occasion.

Sir Alex chuckled in what Marianna deemed a rather nasty manner, and she shot him a dark look before catching herself up in her silly notions. How utterly ridiculous to entertain any thoughts of George, one way or another. He was merely here to help her as a neighborly gesture, most likely due to his aunt's influence. He had scarcely noticed Marianna in the past few days. She must have drifted past his nose dozens of times and had been totally ignored. The knowledge was dampening on her spirits. How lowering to realize and accept that she was so easily overlooked.

The others chattered on about the immediate future, the general giving interesting details of the house George was to rent for their stay in Lowestoft. It seemed that one of the upper citizens of the town had taken himself and family off to London and the house was available for a short while. The owner was not above making a bit of profit while absent.

Knowing how expensive a Season in London might be, Marianna could sympathize with the man. Her dear mother had been so unhappy when the means for Marianna to make her come-out in London had slipped away. Marianna wasn't all that certain it was so bad a thing. At least this way, she had a chance to confront George, for whom, she was coming to see, she had nurtured an affection all these years. Dratted man. Her chances with him, even should her name be cleared, were about as real as the likelihood of a peony surviving without water, once cut.

The meal drew to a close. The fish had been excellent, Marianna reflected. It was a pity she had not been more aware of what she had consumed while seated next to the increasingly disturbing George.

Shortly thereafter Marianna and Lady Lavinia strolled from the house, to wander along the central area of Lowestoft, gazing into shop windows until they found a modiste.

"Ah, I suspected they might have such here," said Lady Lavinia to Marianna, who was totally in the dark as to what was meant.

It turned out that what Lady Lavinia had suspected was that there was a charming little French émigrée located here who had set up shop with the latest in imported silks and muslins. In addition, she combined current Parisian modes with a clever sense of design, so terribly French and chic.

Marianna felt like the veriest dowd.

"I believe you need two day dresses and at least one evening dress for the time being. Once Madame has your measurements, we can always order more later, even though you are otherwise occupied." Lady Lavinia gave Marianna a look that defied her to say one word in protest.

"But, ma'am," objected Marianna, ignoring the look from Lady Lavinia, "I shall be at the school . . . ." She didn't mention her lack of money to pay for the gowns; her friend knew the state of the family finances as well as did Marianna.

"Not to worry. My brother has settled a handsome sum upon

me, you know. I have a very nice competence. And I should like to do this. Call it an investment of sorts,'' she said in that frequently obscure manner that drove Marianna to exasperation more than once.

Yielding to the lure of lustrous silk the color of foam on a stormy sea and a delicate muslin print echoing the blue of a sunlit sky, Marianna allowed herself to be measured, then pinned into several lovely lengths of fabric. Lady Lavinia selected for her a fine muslin the color of ripe raspberries to be trimmed in blond lace. When Marianna protested, Lady Lavinia simply murmured something about George liking fruit, as though that had anything to do with the matter.

Marianna was slightly appeased when Lady Lavinia treated herself to several new gowns. Although white was the main color, one had a border of embroidered pink roses, another a tracery of pink print, the third swags of pink satin around the hem and edging prettily puffed sleeves. The pink was vastly becoming, and Marianna lost no time in exclaiming over the fact.

"How sweet of you to say such," murmured the gratified lady as she fingered a pink satin reticule.

Other little fripperies were found: slippers to match the various gowns, another reticule of attractive design for Marianna, and a bonnet surely created with Marianna's wealth of gorgeous blond hair in mind were added to the growing number of parcels.

As the tired but exceedingly pleased ladies wended their way back to the general's house, Marianna wondered aloud. "When do you remove to the rented house?"

"I expect our things are there now. We shall have dinner with General Eagleton, then go over later." The ladies waited for the butler to open the general's door, taking care that none of the bundles dropped.

Marianna observed—only to herself, mind you—that it must be lovely to always have servants to do for you rather than be compelled to do all for yourself.

"Lady Lavinia," exclaimed the general in horror as he saw

their parcel-laden arms, "had I known you needed assistance, I would have sent one of my footmen with you."

"Precisely why we said nothing. I prefer not to keep anyone waiting about while I browse among the shops." She bestowed a fond look in his direction, thus removing any sting from her words.

Marianna gave the lady a sharp look to see if anything had come along with them for which the shopkeeper had not been paid. That Lady Lavinia might be accused of taking what did not belong to her was a nightmare Marianna had no desire to witness.

She encountered an intent gaze from George. It was likely he knew of his aunt's peculiar habit, from what his sister had confided. Well, Marianna would check each package later. If there was a problem, she could consult with George . . . Viscount Barringer, she reminded herself testily. Better not to forget his station, nor hers, either.

Following the early dinner, they, as Lady Lavinia had predicted, removed themselves to the house George and the general had found to rent for an entire month, this because no one knew how long it would take to solve the problem of the missing sapphires. Marianna bestowed an appreciative smile on the house. A neat railing bordered the miniuscule lawn and the pink-and-white *bellis perennis* that dotted it.

"Quite charming," Lady Lavinia declared with approval as she marched up to the front door of the pleasant stone town house, which strongly resembled the drawings she had seen of ones executed by Busby in Brighton and Hove.

Inside, they discovered the place quite in the latest fashion. On the ground floor, they found in the dining room a sideboard fitted with pedestal cupboards that the general believed to be a Robert Adam's design. The large table displayed brass claw feet and a highly polished rosewood surface. The chairs were the latest in design, with bold curves and a wide cresting rail.

Marianna exclaimed over the dumbwaiter, saying her mother would have adored the thing. It had rectangular tiers and supports of pillars and claws, and would considerably facilitate keeping hot foods hot until serving.

They straggled up the stairs to the drawing room, each person pausing to examine anything that caught his or her fancy as they went.

Lady Lavinia paused upon entering the room, slowly looking about her with faint surprise. "Impressive. Especially for Lowestoft. One might think one was in a London drawing room." She crossed the polished wood floor, dropping her reticule on a drum table on her way, to sit down in a maghogany *bergère* chair with a blue velvet cushion and sides and a back of delicate canework. "I shall like this visit," she proclaimed in a satisfied voice. "Elegant and yet comfortable."

Marianna approached the sofa with caution. It had a boldly curved headpiece, and the arms were different heights. She supposed it was more for reclining than sitting, but she certainly did not intend to drape herself across the thing with others present. She gingerly seated herself, while wondering, if these rooms were in the latest kick, just what she might find when she went to bed.

"Well," said the general with his customary hearty manner.

"Well," echoed George, looking about him as though wondering why he had agreed to this expedition.

"Tomorrow," Lady Lavinia began. "Tomorrow we shall commence with our plans. You shall return to that cubicle Miss Chudleigh refers to as your room, Marianna. I intend to view it, you may be certain."

"Oh, ma'am," protested Marianna, shrinking from the thought of what the dear lady might do when she saw the bare walls, lumpy cot, and the few hooks upon which Marianna hung her garments, "I doubt you would think it quite the thing." It was not a very prepossessing sight. Only the small desk at which Marianna could work was halfway presentable, and that was scarred with years of letter-writing on its surface.

"Do you and Miss Teale have similar rooms?" George asked.

"Eloisa Teale has been with Miss Chudleigh for a number of years, thus she gets a nicer room." It had a single bed, rather than a narrow cot, and a comfortable chair upon which to rest at the end of the day. Of a sudden Marianna felt most sorry for herself, to be returning to her bleak existence in place of residing here amid all this luxury.

"You shall join us on your days off," declared Lady Lavinia as though reading Marianna's mind.

A grin creeping across her face, Marianna replied, "That's very kind of you, ma'am, but 'tis only a half-day each week. However, I shall welcome a change, I'm sure."

Lady Lavinia was clearly scandalized that the daughter of Sir John Wyndham was reduced to such straits and said so. "Dinner at the very least, then, my girl," she declared.

Embarrassed, Marianna was grateful when George suggested they all go to bed early. She rose from what she privately considered to be a not very comfortable sofa—unless one might recline, as the design implied.

The general offered to escort Lady Lavinia on a tour of the area late the following morning, to which she readily agreed. The two chatted quite happily as she walked with him down to the entrance.

"I best prepare to do battle on the morrow," declared Sir Alex with more than a hint of sarcasm in his voice. He sauntered from the drawing room, and shortly his steps could be heard as he marched up to the next floor and his bed. They were militant steps, as though he really anticipated a battle on his hands. Knowing Lady Phillida, Marianna could not anticipate what reaction Alex might discover when he sought to make that young lady's acquaintance. The girl was as prickly as a hedgehog, and twice as difficult to know.

Marianna gathered up her reticule and prepared to leave, wondering just where she was to lay her head tonight. Carefully skirting the drum table, she made for the door, pausing to turn toward George. "Since your aunt is not here, could you tell me which room is to be mine for the night?"

Ignoring her request, George gave her a considering look, then asked, "What shall you do once your name is cleared? Return to teach for Miss Chudleigh?"

Marianna hadn't wanted to face that particular thought at the moment. In fact, she would have put it off forever, had it been possible. Toying with the cords of her reticule, she deliberated a bit before attempting a reply. "To be honest, I do not know. Precisely. Actually, it would be difficult to continue with Miss Chudleigh, knowing she felt me capable of thievery. I expect there are often teaching positions to be found in the more rural areas. I imagine that many teachers would rather locate in a larger metropolis, thus offering vacancies from year to year."

"Would you? Like the city?" George slowly sauntered across the floor until he drew close to her. He noted with satisfaction that she edged away from him, as though slightly intimidated by his presence. He hadn't felt this desire to overwhelm or impress strongly before when around a woman. But he very much desired many things with this exquisite blond beauty who stood trembling before him.

He slowly smiled, and it lit up his sherry-colored eyes with a devastating effect on her sensibilities. Marianna almost backed into a cabinet placed near the doorway, stopped only by George as he pulled her away in time. She glanced behind her to see the room reflected in the circular convex mirror that hung above the ornate piece of furniture with which she had almost collided. The drawing room was fraught with obstacles, she decided, refusing to admit that George had the power to turn any room into a pitfall.

"Thank you," she offered in a small voice while trying to ease from his grasp. "It takes time to become acquainted, does it not?" Meaning the house, of course. His hand on her arm was warm and firmly masculine, and felt far too delicious to be allowed. It was just as well no one expected anything from her at the moment, for she was certain she was not capable of coherent speech.

"True, it does," he agreed, thinking of the house not at all. He placed his other hand on her shoulder, concentrating on those sweetly curved lips such a delectable color. He inclined his head toward hers.

The kiss, Marianna decided in her haze, was gently seductive. He could have led her anyplace, anyplace at all, and she would have floated along with him, counting the rest of the world unimportant. Where was sanity? Where were all her nicely sorted scruples now?

Her knees were strangely spongelike and her hands, instead of pushing him away as was proper, clung to his elegant blue coat like a limpet to a seashell. Yet she really did not wish to leave him, or forgo the kiss. Of such were dreams made of, dreams she would cherish in the future.

The long dark fringes of her lashes rose reluctantly, or so it seemed to George as he withdrew from what he wished might be the first of dozens of kisses that night. He wanted her at his side, close to him, not up the stairs or, worse yet, streets away. Although, on second thought, the latter might be more prudent. He knew he was going to find it difficult to sleep tonight, knowing the lovely Marianna was asleep not so far away.

A sound in the hall alerted the pair to someone's approach. When Lady Lavinia entered the drawing room, it was to see George leaning against the drum table while Marianna stood poised to fly from the room near the doorway. Glancing first at one, then the other, Lady Lavinia smiled. "Nice to see you two not quarreling for once."

George and Marianna gave her blank looks, then Marianna remembered. George could never be serious about her. What was she thinking about? She was merely a project. Suddenly as cross as crabs, she turned to leave, snapping, "I shall see you in the morning."

"It is on the second floor up as you go, first room from the stair landing," said George, who then thought it a pity he hadn't sent her to his room. Town houses being what they were, usually two rooms to a floor, Alex was placed next to George's room on the next floor up. Marianna was on the topmost level of the house, her room directly above his. Lady Lavinia had the bedroom across from the drawing room.

Marianna was thankful he couldn't see the blush she felt creeping over her face. Dratted man. He was welcome to the charming Miss Teale. How fortunate Marianna possessed a sensible heart. With that thought, she sniffed back threatened tears and climbed the stairs to her room.

It was a comfort to know that tomorrow the hunt would be on in earnest. The sooner they discovered the true thief, the better.

8

"We certainly don't look like a group of conspirators, do we?" Marianna commented the following morning as the five of them gathered in the breakfast room, a cheerful little many-windowed nook behind the formal dining room. She stood overlooking the yard, which contained a fanciful sundial. Jasmine and woodbine grew along the rear of the garden, while geraniums clustered about the sundial for a bright touch of color. She turned away from the appealing sight to face the others, her face reflecting her doubts.

"We aren't, precisely," George said with a shrug of his shoulders. He was having a few misgivings this morning. After looking at Marianna, he would be willing to wager a substantial sum that that young woman had not slept any better than he had.

"Well, we had best plan carefully if we are not to make a mess of this effort," inserted Sir Alex, watching George and Marianna from his place near the door. He strolled over to reach for a third crumpet and the jam pot. It was best to fortify oneself for distasteful work.

"Indeed," Lady Lavinia agreed, turning her attention to George. "While you attempt to make the acquaintance of Miss Eloise Teale, and Sir Alex strikes up a flirtation with Lady Phillida, Marianna shall prepare to reclaim her position at the school." She looked at Marianna, continuing with her instructions for the morning. "If possible, I think it would be well if you joined the little daily excursion to the boardwalk. Inform Miss Chudleigh it is our wish."

Marianna wondered what Miss Chudleigh would say to this

outside interference, then smiled wryly as she nodded agreement. "And what of you, milady?"

"General Eagleton and I shall seek the company of his daughter, young Sibyl. I hope to gain her confidence so that she may reveal what she knows about the matter to us. I have often observed that people sometimes see things of import without realizing it."

The general nodded, smiling fondly at Lady Lavinia while appearing to acknowledge her wisdom.

A mischievous smile on his lips, Sir Alex said, "And what do the tea leaves reveal this morning, dear lady?"

The lady in question cast a wary glance at the general before making a noncommittal reply. "Nothing new, I fear." Those shrewd faded blue eyes concealed any thoughts she might have on the subject.

"I see," murmured Sir Alex, indeed appearing to see something interesting in her reaction to his innocent question.

Marianna checked the small clock on the sideboard, frowning as she noted the time. "It is best that I go first, I suspect," she said with obvious reluctance. "I shall be able to settle in my room before it is time for the students' daily walk." She crossed the room, ignoring the appetizing pastries on the table, not to mention the eggs and kidneys steaming gently in warming pans on the narrow sideboard. Although it was far better fare than she would find at the school, her interest simply could not be stirred this morning. Undoubtedly she would regret this lapse tomorrow when she faced the lumpy porridge and poor-quality marmalade for their thin slices of wheat toast. It was fortunate that the end of hostilities had brought fresh imports of wheat and prices had fallen, or she doubted she would have had this.

The general's carriage deposited her before the school not long after she had gathered her portmanteau and new bonnet and marched out the front door, leaving George and the others behind. The gowns ordered for her were to be delivered to the house George had rented. Marianna was comforted with the knowledge she would not be forgoing the sight of him altogether, although she forlornly observed that the prospect did not appear to depress him in the least. He seemed to relish the next phase of the project. She had come to detest the very word and would not mind if she never heard it again.

Young Betsy was fortuitously in the entry when Marianna let herself in the front door, having decided she preferred to enter by that means. She would not beggar herself to sneak in the back way, like some common serving girl.

"Oh, miss, you've come back to us," Betsy said, her eyes round with apprehension and her hands nervously clasping and unclasping before her.

"It does seem so, does it not?" Marianna replied lightly. "Could you give me a hand with this?" The portmanteau was not heavy, but if she lured Betsy along with her, the investigation could begin at once. Marianna desired nothing more than the speediest conclusion to this detection work.

"Aye." Betsy eagerly followed Marianna up the stairs, seeming content to assist with the reinstatement of the pleasant Miss Wyndham rather than to continue with her dusting. Or had she been listening at Miss Chudleigh's door as Lady Lavinia had implied?

It was an unsettling thought, to consider there were three people, possibly four, she must watch. To lead each one on, try to determine—as much as she was able—whether or no they could have made off with the jewels, or, in Lady Phillida's case, secreted them safely from detection.

Once the door closed behind them, she inquired of the maid, "How have things gone since I went home? Has anything else of interest occurred?" As though being accused of stealing a sapphire necklace might be compared to the cook's cat having kittens. Marianna took note of the maid's face, watching carefully the various expressions that passed over it. It was a blessing the girl seemed so transparent. Or was she? Could she not be a clever deceiver?

Wondering how she was to contrive to see this effort through, Marianna attempted to conceal her feelings.

"Naught but the usual, miss. Miss de Vere's mum's ill again. Poor Lady Phillida's been in a rare taking." Betsy shook her head. "I don' know what the lady was thinkin' of, to bring them jew'ls along with her. 'Tis askin' fer trouble, I'm thinkin'."

Wishing to encourage her to continue along this vein of conversation, Marianna murmured most sympathetically. "And you have seen nothing that might be, er, unusual in that regard?" She hoped the casual remark might catch the maid off her guard, for, indeed, she seemed inclined to chat in a most confidential manner.

Betsy's face underwent a dramatic change, assuming the blank mien of one who is concealing everything, revealing nothing. "Naught. I best go back down t'stairs again. Miss Chudleigh'll have my head if she finds I'm gone from my place."

Wondering precisely what the maid considered her place to be, Marianna smiled encouragingly, then breathed a sigh of relief when once again alone. This was going to be far more difficult than she had anticipated. How could she find out if Miss de Vere had climbed up to the top floor that fateful day, and would the maid reveal it if she knew? And Miss Teale might be extremely clever at such a thing as slipping along to Lady Phillida's room when the girl was elsewhere. And where had that young lady been when all this was going on, pray tell?

Before long Marianna had restored her possessions to their previous location and put on her pelisse in preparation for going along on the daily walk. She wondered how Miss Chudleigh would react when informed that Marianna was to participate. There would be a dark frown, at the very least.

"Best to leave, would you not agree?" George said as he checked the long-case clock in the hall for the fourth time in the past ten minutes.

Alex shrugged. "I do not relish this day's work. I suspect Lady Phillida to be a vain chit, desiring to preen her good fortune over her schoolmates. I have never been able to abide schoolroom misses, at any rate."

"I was not aware you knew that many," George mused, enjoying the flicker of humor that asserted itself in his good friend's eyes.

"Now that you mention it, I confess I have assiduously avoided them if at all possible. My sister . . ." he concluded, as though that said it all.

"Sisters are not necessarily in the same category as young ladies about to make their come-out in society," replied George with a knowing air. After all, he had seen his own sister blossom with amazing results. She had captured the heart of the Marquess of Laverstock, no less. "Something seems to come over them when they reach a certain age."

"Hmm," answered Sir Alex by way of reply, obviously not totally convinced of the matter. "I suspect this young woman will be otherwise. Else why would she resort to such a thing as to bring priceless jewels along with her to her school, of all places?"

George was unable to answer that question. Instead, he nudged his good friend out the door and down the walk. It was not far to where they intended to cross the path of the gaggle of girls, as Sir Alex persisted in calling them, likening them to silly geese.

Marianna saw the two men in the distance, and her heart began to beat in double time as they neared. She must keep her eyes downcast so as to not reveal she knew them. In her one glance, she noted their polished image, the air of the true gentlemen stamped on every aspect of their mien. She waited for the next step to take place.

At her side, Miss Teale stiffened as she observed Sir Alex pause, then approach Lady Phillida, his hand outstretched with a scrap of white held in it. "Has that minx actually dared to drop her handkerchief? I tell you, Miss Wyndham, I shall be most relieved when her parents come to fetch her. London is welcome to her."

"Think you her parents will allow the matter of the necklace to be dropped then?" Marianna asked most daringly as she sensed the approach of her dearest George.

"We can only hope," Miss Teale murmured as she gazed up at the tall gentleman who seemed to desire her attention.

"I hope you will permit me to interrupt your daily walk for a moment of your time, dear lady?" He exhibited that charming and dignified manner of speech so natural to the true aristocrat.

Marianna clenched one dainty hand at the sound of that

smooth, suave voice. Never had she heard such dulcet tones directed at her. Oh, men! she thought most annoyed, trying hard to recall that George was doing this deed as a favor to her. She was not succeeding very well.

Miss Teale darted a suspicious glance at George, then hesitantly smiled. He was extremely handsome, and was smiling at her in a most coaxing manner. "Yes?"

"May I introduce myself? Viscount Barringer of Mayne Court. I am visiting Lowestoft and hoped to see a few of the local sights while here. I decided that a teacher, such as yourself, might well know the most important to be viewed. Those of historical interest, naturally. Could you take pity on a stranger and perhaps give me some direction?" George managed to stroll along with Miss Teale, who was clearly bewildered at this event to the point of forgetting to check to see what was going on behind her.

Marianna dropped behind the two, trying hard not to bore holes in George's back. He was doing this for her, she reminded herself. To help clear her good name, whatever that might be worth. Yet Marianna knew that without her reputation restored, she would have little chance of a decent marriage. Never mind the very thought of such had faded considerably. It was the best solution for her future.

George was asking questions about Miss Teale and the school, most adroitly, Marianna admitted to herself. She would not have suspected him to be capable of such, given his usual scientific inclinations.

"And what do each of you ladies teach the girls?" he inquired. One would have thought he was most interested in the education of young ladies.

Flattered to be so singled out, Miss Teale responded with enthusiasm. "Miss de Vere instructs them in French, so important for a young lady, as well as needlework. Miss Wyndham handles drawing, writing, and music. I conduct classes in English, the study of the globe, plus a smattering of arithmetic so they can cope with a tradesman's bill if necessary. Monsieur Saint-André is the local dancing master who comes three times a week to teach the vitals of dancing."

Miss Teale chuckled at the memory of the thin gentleman with the elegant mustache who despaired each of those days at the clumsy daughters of local merchants whose fond parents desired to become like peeresses. What a pity the one titled girl in the school had no use for his lessons.

George nodded. "Most excellent. It would seem I have sought out a most proper person for my quest. Would you know of any Roman ruins, perhaps?"

For the first time, Miss Teal showed true animation. "Indeed, sir. There is Burgh Castle some distance to the north of Lowestoft. I fear you would need quite some time to explore that site, however. Why, it must be all of twenty miles from here."

"A small matter." George waved his hand as though the distance was a mere trifle. "It cannot be more than an hour by boat. It would be excellent if you might assist me with my exploration. I fear that is undoubtedly asking too much of your time. However, I wonder," he mused. "Might it be possible for you, and a number of your charges, of course, to sail along with us for a pleasant day's outing? It would be most instructive to your oldest girls," he said persuasively. "Perhaps we might ask your headmistress?"

Behind them, where Marianna could just barely make out the conversation, she decided George had the makings for a gallant if he ever forgot his scientific projects long enough. She could almost believe he was truly interested in the Roman ruins and Miss Teale, not necessarily in that order.

Eloisa Teale fluttered her lashes and deliberated the generous offer. It took no great mind to see she was very desirous of agreeing to his proposal.

Farther back in the line of curious, fascinated girls, Sir Alex had been paying attention to the slender Lady Phillida Jarvis. Her chestnut curls peeped becomingly from beneath a bonnet Sir Alex knew to be last year's design. Her pelisse, while of excellent cut and fabric, was also not of the latest mode. Was the chit not interested in the current fashion, or were her parents, as Marianna had implied to him in quiet conversation, less than caring about their only daughter?

"Sir Alexander Dent, at your service, milady. I wonder if you did not accidentally drop this pretty scrap of linen?" he said in his smoothest, most admiring voice. "I would never wish so delicate a miss to be denied such an important accessory."

Lady Phillida took one look at the careless grin on that handsome face, then the laughing eyes, which impudently dared her claim to know nothing of the matter, and smiled. "I believe I do recognize the item, sir," she prevaricated with understandable pleasure.

He offered it with a flourish. "Allow me to restore it to the fair owner, in that case."

She curtsied slightly, then accepted the handkerchief, which she noted was embroidered with the letter P. Her initial. How might that be? She of a certainty did not know this elegant gentleman. Just wait, she reflected bitterly, he will evaporate shortly, as soon as I begin to walk. They always did. Even the lure of a healthy dowry could not entice a gentleman to her side for long.

"I believe your teacher has once again resumed progress back to your school. Surely you are too old to be residing there now?" His gentle inquiry was answered in an oblique way.

Lady Phillida gave a wry smile. "True." For it was, in both cases. She must again walk. Her parents had postponed taking her to London for as long as might be possible. Her mother hoped desperately to bring some financially imprudent peer up to snuff before that day. Yet they dare not dally too long.

Sir Alex offered his arm and Lady Phillida graciously accepted his assistance. Not that it would actually do much good, she reflected. She moved forward, limping noticeably.

He matched his pace carefully to hers, taking care to conceal any particular reaction on his part. It was a pity that a young lady who possessed such apparent charm should be discommoded by a limp. He wondered how she had come by it. Marianna hadn't been able to tell him of her past. He was glad he had been forewarned, however. It would have been a distinct shock, otherwise. His original antagonism toward Lady Phillida faded some.

"You are a very kind gentleman, sir," Lady Phillida wryly

observed when they drew near the school and Sir Alex yet remained at her side, seeming truly solicitous of her. "I will confess that usually my escorts fade from sight long before this point." Her smile, as her direct gaze met his, held a trace of the bitterness that never completely left her.

"May I be so bold as to inquire what happened to cause the limp?" Alex held his breath, for he well knew it was improper to ask so personal a question, especially on a first meeting. He found he really desired to know the answer, however. "Was it something that might be corrected?"

"I fell from a horse when I was a small child, Sir Alexander. My leg was badly broken and never healed properly. You can see the result. I fear my esteemed papa, the Earl of Sapsford, was less than pleased with his offspring. It is not well-done to fall with so little grace, you see. Had I been a better horse-woman, it should never have occurred."

Sir Alex frowned. "We shall see, my lady. Perhaps we can attempt a ride to put that skill to a test?" He sensed he was intruding into a painful area, yet something drove him to persist.

"To a test?" she echoed, seeming quite horrified at the very idea.

"Consider it." He glanced at George, to catch the almost imperceptible nod of his head. "But I daresay we shall meet in any event. My friend, Viscount Barringer, sought information from your instructor and apparently has been successful. I shall look forward to meeting you again. Providing you care to risk it."

The gaze from his brown eyes was not warm in the least. Lady Phillida decided it was downright challenging. How dare this presuming scoundrel, a mere baronet, speak to her thus? She was the daughter, albeit the unwanted daughter, of an earl. "We shall see, sir." For a moment she felt like a normal girl, repulsing the attentions of a too-forward gallant.

Sir Alex took her gloved hand from where it had rested on his arm and lifted it to his lips. He kissed it lightly, wondering if this young woman was not the culprit they sought. Indeed, she had motive enough. It must be damnably difficult to keep up with the others, in so many ways. He could almost feel the bitterness bottled within her, the simmering rage carefully controlled.

"And what do you do this afternoon?" he queried in an offhand manner.

She chuckled. "Normally I sit quietly to watch the others while they have their dancing lesson. Then I practice—once again—how to use my fan, how to cope with a curtsy, and how to rise and sit, for I cannot manage the most important, how to dance."

"You do not mind, then?" he asked with another dash of unaccustomed temerity.

She limped toward the first of the steps, then paused as she prepared to mount them. "Why?" Her eyes flashed with that aristocratic ability to cope, no matter what. "It does me little good to rail against my condition. I have accepted my limitations. Would that others could as well." With that remark, she turned and hobbled up the stairs to the school, perversely glad that this fine gentleman should see her at her worst.

George joined Sir Alex as they walked away from the school. Neither had dared to so much as look at Marianna, yet they each knew how she longed to know their reaction. Fortunately Aunt Lavinia had arranged that Marianna have a free time each day so she might communicate with them.

"Well, and did you reach any conclusions?" inquired George of his good friend.

"She has reason and plenty to desire attention. The chit is well-spoken, surprisingly so for a schoolgirl, but she has a toughness of spirit. I sensed a great deal of self-control within that young woman. Admirable. However, her parents appear to reject her, if what she says is true. A sapphire necklace might begin to compensate for not being able to dance, you see," Sir Alex concluded as though that explained everything.

"So she may well be the one who hid the necklace, then accused Marianna of the theft?" George said, intrigued with his friend's analysis of Lady Phillida.

"I did not precisely say that, merely that she could have had a motive." They crossed the cobbled street to the house George had rented.

"We knew that before, sapskull," said George, suddenly annoyed with Alex.

"What about your Miss Teale? Was she of assistance in your quest for knowledge of the countryside?" The reason for their approach had been carefully worked out in advance. Sir Alex had been particularly pleased with his notion of the mono-grammed handkerchief, even though it had been dashed difficult to obtain in this remote town. Fortunately Lady Lavinia had suggested that French modiste. She had been most accommodating, he reflected with a smile.

"There are the Roman remains of a castle north of here," George replied. "Miss Teale seems to believe it too far to view, being all of twenty-odd miles away. I recall thinking, when I studied the map earlier, that we might approach it by water, and I shall investigate obtaining a more suitable boat for a group. It should not take more than an hour to sail to Gorleston-on-Sea, then up past Yarmouth to the Breydon Water, and so to the site."

"What is your reaction to the teacher?" Alex thought of the proposed trip to Burgh Castle, and he looked forward to it, and discovering more of the poor child, as he considered Lady Phillida. He did not examine how his feelings had altered from antagonistic to curious.

"As far as I could tell, Miss Teale is naught but a charming though poorly situated woman. Who can say if she is a deceptive one." He entered the house after Alex, adding when they had reached the pleasant drawing room and the general's curious company, "I was informed the students intend to visit Southwold Church this afternoon. Miss de Vere ought to be along with them too."

"And you propose we ought to be there as well? Gads, what lengths I go to assist you, my good friend," Alex said in a chiding manner, though his eyes were warm as they gazed at the man who had been closest to him for years.

" 'Tis Marianna we help, not me," George reminded Alex, tolerant of his teasing. Turning to the general, he inquired, "And how did you fare today, sir?"

The general, rather than reply, walked to the doorway to greet

Lady Lavinia. He alone had heard her soft steps on the stairs.
"Perhaps you might explain to your nephew what we accomplished today, dear lady?"

Somewhat flustered at the gallant attentions of the general,
Lady Lavinia rearranged her shawl twice, then patted stray wisps
of hair, before seating herself on the high-backed sofa. She ran
a finger absently over the green brocade as she considered what
to say. At last, she gave George a tentative smile and began.

"It is not so simple as I had hoped. First of all, although Miss
de Vere does indeed go home to her mother at the conclusion
of her lessons in French and needlework, there are times when
she may give a bit of special help to a deserving student. Sibyl
recalled that on that particular day, she had requested assistance
in French. She has a bit of difficulty with the verb tenses, you
see. So it seems that, contrary to our expectations, we do indeed
have four, rather than three, suspects."

George absently noted that his aunt was dressed in the height
of fashion today, rather than her usual out-of-date white muslin.
While mostly white, this gown had trimmings of deep pink and
somehow made her look younger than the years he knew to be
in her dish.

"Well, if that is not the outside of enough," declared Sir Alex.
"The situation appears to worsen, not improve. Are you certain
we do the right thing?" He tilted his head to one side, studying
his good friend with a dispassionate eye.

George suddenly acquired a rather freezing gaze that would
make a lesser mortal tongue-tied in one glance. "Getting cold
feet, Alex? The schoolroom chit too much for you to handle?
Perhaps I ought to have found a man with more experience in
wooing the ladies, rather than running from them?"

"Unkind cut, my friend," Alex said, flushing from the direct
hit at what he knew to be the truth. He had run from women.
So what? But he was genuinely curious about this one. How
did she manage to cope with what must be a heartbreaking life?
He wanted to learn more about her. He also sensed she expected
nothing from him. She didn't flirt; indeed, she seemed to look
forward to his departure. It would be interesting to see what

she would do when he appeared once again. The trip to the Roman ruins might be an intriguing day, if it came off.

"Sorry," George said, wondering what in the world had made him flare up at his best friend in this manner.

"Do you think Miss Chudleigh will permit the expedition?" Lady Lavinia inquired.

George looked dubious while Sir Alex walked over to pull on the bell rope to summon the maid.

At her questioning look, he replied, "I believe it is time for a cup of tea."

9

When the tea was poured out and several cups had been drunk, Sir Alex performed the customary ritual with his empty teacup, then handed it to Lady Lavinia to read. He gave her an expectant look, then waited.

Clearly torn, Lady Lavinia darted an uncomfortable glance at General Eagleton, then cast a look of frustration at her nephew.

"I perceive you are a very talented lady, my dear," interposed the general. "Never tell me you are so gifted as to read the tea leaves." His eyes twinkled, for he had guessed from little comments dropped, mostly by Sir Alex, what her secret might be.

The smile that spread across Lady Lavinia's face was a delight to behold. "Indeed. I do not do this for just everyone, you must understand," she replied graciously. "Only for those who are close to me."

"I am fortunate to be included, in spite of being declared a sad rattle," said Sir Alex, grinning as Lady Lavinia playfully tapped him with her fan that had been at her side.

"Fie, sir," she said, smiling her forgiveness at his impudence.

"Have a care, Aunt," George said, fearing for the safety of the delicate china cup belonging to their landlord.

She immediately grew serious, studying Sir Alex's cup with her usual intensity. "There is money involved and a wish will be granted. This little parcel tells me you will have a surprise soon." She placed the cup on the table with a thoughtful expression on her face. "I wonder what that surprise might be?" Her gaze intercepted a look between George and Alex.

"You may as well do mine, too," George muttered, wishing, yet not wishing, to know what was in store for him.

Taking his cup, she turned it over to peer inside, then half-smiled at him. " 'Tis not so very bad, you know. There will be misunderstandings, but things will be all right, I am certain, for I see an angel, which means good luck on your new project."

Sir Alex chuckled, reminded of Marianna's expression every time the word "project" was mentioned.

"Might I be included, Lady Lavinia?" asked the general in an amused yet vastly polite manner.

Shrewd blue eyes were hidden by fluttering lashes for a moment, then she nodded agreeably at him. "I fail to see why not."

She instructed him to drain the tea from his cup as best he could without swallowing the tea leaves, then turn the cup upside down and pass it along to her. Once done, she rotated it the prescribed number of times, then tipped it up to look inside. The silence stretched out as she said nothing.

The general became concerned. "Trouble?"

She shook her head in denial. "The anchor is a hopeful sign. Near the rim of the cup as it is, it means you will have success . . . plus true love, or so I understand. A wish will come true soon for you. There are dots at the bottom of the cup, which tells me you will overcome present difficulties." She set the cup down on its saucer with a tiny clink, then raised her face to look at the general. An odd expression flashed in her eyes before she turned toward the front window with a complete change of subject. "I wonder how Marianna is progressing?"

"She seemed fine this morning while on the walk with the schoolgirls, although I could sense her eyes on my back while I spoke with Miss Teale," George replied.

"And how did you find Lady Phillida, Sir Alex?" Lady Lavinia inquired, her gaze now focused on that gentleman.

"I confess I was a little taken aback. She is not quite what I expected." With that vague remark, Alex ceased to speak, rising from his chair to stroll to the window. "I see Marianna approaching the house now. I was not sure that Miss Chudleigh would give her leave to visit us." He turned to study Lady

Lavinia, wondering how the dear lady had managed that clever trick.

Four pair of eyes were trained on the doorway, disconcerting Marianna no end when she entered the drawing room. She glanced about her, as though to see if someone else were around she hadn't immediately seen, then promptly approached George and Sir Alex with her information.

"Miss Teale spoke with Miss Chudleigh regarding the proposed trip to Burgh Castle. Eloisa is most persuasive, or else Miss Chudleigh suspected your fine hand in the matter, Lady Lavinia." Marianna gave that dear lady an appreciative look. "The expedition is suggested for three days hence. I cannot stay but a few minutes, for the girls are to explore the church in Southwold this afternoon and I must go with them."

Turning to Sir Alex, she gave him a curious look. "I do not know if you said something in particular to upset Lady Phillida, or indeed, if it is merely her nature, but she has been impossible since the morning walk. I vow, should she continue, I fear I shall be all shredded nerves." She gave them all a rueful smile, then stiffened her back as though to remind herself that true ladies did not permit themselves to succumb to the vapors or anything of that sort. "I shall no doubt see you all tomorrow."

She eyed the teapot and nicely laden tray rather wistfully, thinking of the ritual she had missed in the teachers' sitting room in order to make her little report, then marched to the doorway, where she paused as George called her.

"Marianna?"

Turning to look back at him and wondering what he desired of her now, she waited. She watched him fill a cup, pick up a biscuit, and walk toward her with an appealing grin on his handsome face. She glanced at the cup of tea in his hand, then the macaroon, a favorite treat.

"One moment, Marianna. I recall that coconut macaroons were once a weakness of yours, and these are fresh."

He held out the teacup, then the macaroon, and she succumbed, figuring that the girls would surely wait just a few minutes more. How amazing that George, the absentminded one, should recall such an odd bit of information. Fortunately the tea was not scalding hot. Rather, it was just right. She consumed it in one long swallow, a most unladylike manner, she knew. Taking the macaroon, she gave George a tentative smile, then hastily placed a daring kiss of thanks on his cheek before turning to dash from the room.

A bemused George stood in the doorway for a minute or two, teacup in hand, before seeming to collect himself. He spun about to face Alex and the general, who were standing by the sofa, from where they had watched the little scene with amused expressions. "Yes, well, I suspect we had better get ourselves over to that church in short order. Right, Alex? Can you give us directions, good sir?" he said to the general.

He set Marianna's cup on the table before Aunt Lavinia, listening with care as the general instructed him on how to find Southwold Church. It was some miles south and required mounts to get there, but he assured the two men they would have no difficulty in obtaining good horses.

As the two left the house, Alex glanced quickly at George to note his friend still seemed a bit preoccupied. Although that frown of concentration was not so very unusual, Alex suspected the project, *per se*, was not the object of interest at this moment, for a wonder. It did not take them long to find an excellent stable, and soon they were on their way south. The ride from town was accomplished in comparative silence as both men reflected on what Lady Lavinia had seen in the tea leaves and other interesting thoughts.

Back in the drawing room Lady Lavinia had picked up the cup used by Marianna and was thoughtfully peering into it.

"Can you read it as well?" inquired the general, fascinated by this most unique of ladies and her unusual talent. He plumped himself down on the sofa at her side, trying to understand what this charming lady could interpret from those peculiar blobs of soggy tea leaves.

"I believe it is clear. The sea gull tells me there are stormy times ahead for the poor girl yet. But I do believe that is a rainbow in the home area, near the handle." Glancing up at her gentleman friend, she added, "That means future happiness and prosperity in her home. How glad I am, for the dear girl is going through a rough patch just now, and it is nowhere near an end.''

Seeking to cheer his lady a little, the general offered a change of scenery. ''I wonder if you would accompany me on a drive, dear lady? 'Tis a lovely day and there are some pretty sights to be found in this area. Have you noticed the unusual serpentine walls in the local gardens as yet?'' He assisted her from the sofa, strolling from the drawing room at her side. ''The people hereabouts call them crinkle-crankles, or ribbon walls. Quite an attractive novelty, I assure you.''

Lady Lavinia smoothed down her elegant white muslin gown, then waved the pink silk handkerchief about in the air. ''I should find it most agreeable, General. Most agreeable, indeed. Permit me to put on my bonnet and I shall be ready for our outing directly.'' She walked up the stairs to her room with a thoughtful expression on her face.

Shortly the pair left the house to explore the town of Lowestoft. They stopped for a few minutes at the militia parade grounds so that Lavinia might see where the general spent a good deal of his time. She appeared most impressed, giving him warm, approving looks and commenting, ''How fortunate our country is that we can count on men such as you to guide us.''

The general felt about ten feet tall and as strong as Goliath under her delightful attention.

It was the beginning of a tranquil afternoon with a brief excursion south along the shore road. Woods straggled into the sandy commons and lonely marshes, and estuaries were full of little boats. It was a scene of great charm, possessing as much appeal to the lady as the gentleman at her side.

''Tranquillity'' was the very last word that might have been used to describe the scene at Miss Chudleigh's Academy for Young Ladies as they prepared for the outing. However, in an amazingly short time all was sorted out and the girls settled down for the ride to Southwold, mostly due to the efficient organization of Miss Teale.

She settled against the hard wood back of her seat in the

conveyance with a satisfied expression. The neat benches facing one another were affixed to the bed of the small blue wagons, built by an enterprising man in the town for just this purpose. Three such vehicles were required to transport the group from the school.

Marianna was in the second wagon, clinging to the seat as the road became bumpier. Ignoring the smothered giggles from the girls opposite, she glanced at her neighbor, the quiet Miss de Vere. "And how is your mother doing this day?"

Seeming to shrink at this notice by her fellow instructress, Miss de Vere replied in her soft voice, "Not very well, I am sorry to say. The doctor thinks she'd do better in a warmer climate. And how do I accomplish that, I ask you?" she added, mostly to herself. A bitter note had crept into her soft voice as she contemplated doing more than she could at the moment on her sparse pay.

"I am so sorry to hear that," Marianna replied, with genuine concern. Her French-born mother had never adjusted to the cold wind of winter that blew over the North Sea and across the marshes and heaths into her very bones. After her father died, Miss de Vere sought to supplement their savings, which were being rapidly depleted as her mother succumbed to one bad ague after another.

"I expect we shall come about eventually. Who knows? Perhaps we shall win a lottery, for you must know that Mother often sneaks down to buy a ticket." Miss de Vere gave Marianna a hesitant smile, then subsided into her normal shy silence.

The ride in the blue-painted wagons was completed with no further attempt at conversation as Marianna contemplated what she had just heard. If there was a person with a motive, it was Miss de Vere. To move her adored mother to a sunnier clime would be enough to push her to steal the sapphires, would it not?

The group scrambled down from the three wagons and were then called to order by a stern Miss Teale.

When they entered the fine church constructed in the mid-fifteenth century, Marianna was somehow not surprised to discover Sir Alex and George had arrived before them. The two gentlemen were wandering about the far end of the edifice, apparently admiring the very lovely and quite large expanse of stained glass. Money from the great profits enjoyed by the cloth trade near the end of the Middle Ages had resulted in a great building boom of what were called the "wool" churches, of which this was an outstanding specimen.

"Girls," announced Miss Teale in her most schoolmistressy voice, "you see before you a fine example of a church designed in the Perpendicular. The more easily executed panels and rectilinear windows of this type of construction are thought due to the shortage of workers following the Black Death." She urged her pupils along the aisle, pointing out the various features of the building, although Marianna observed that her eyes frequently strayed to the handsome pair of gentlemen on the far side. When they drew closer, Miss Teale favored the men with a smile of generous proportions.

Then Lady Phillida stumbled, hastily reaching out to place a hand against a nearby pillar. Sir Alex hurried to her side, helping her regain her balance and looking genuinely concerned for her welfare.

"La, sir, what a silly one I am, to be so clumsy." She did not simper up at him, rather gave him a direct and rather sheepish look, like she felt the veriest fool for her misstep.

"Not at all," Sir Alex denied, frowning as he looked about at the uneven paving of the church floor. "Permit me to assist you along this aisle, for 'tis obviously not made for any but the most surefooted."

Marianna thought that surely Lady Phillida would fall into one of her rages at this reference to her infirmity. She, however, merely shrugged and placed a slim, delicate hand on the firm arm offered for her support.

Sir Alex bestowed an approving smile on the upturned and most rueful countenance at her compliance with his suggestion, and he sauntered along the aisle, being most careful to take note of the state of the paving tiles before them. Any of his friends could have told you he was behaving in a decidedly uncharacteristic manner.

George's usually keen mind failed to note what Marianna

observed, merely assuming his friend was going along with the plan hatched earlier.

Her attention was drawn from Sir Alex and his care of Lady Phillida to where George now did the pretty with Miss Teale.

"I suppose you will tell me I may not stay and listen to your instruction to the young ladies," he said in a distinctly smooth voice. "I confess that I am most interested in old things, notably buildings."

The girls cast wide-eyed stares at Miss Teale when she gave a girlish laugh and shook her head in mock dismay at the bold and very handsome gentleman.

"La, sir, next you will tell me you desire to take up water-colors. I fear I shall disappoint you in that vein. Our teacher in that subject is poor Miss Wyndham." Her voice chilled as she came to mention of Marianna.

Safely behind and over a step or two, Marianna reflected on what she heard in that voice. Malice? Or perhaps spite? A touch of jealousy, maybe? She did not like to consider that a charming person such as Eloisa Teale could possess such a nature. The feeling in her voice had been quite unmistakable to one who listened closely.

Marianna wondered if such a disposition could indeed lead to theft. But why? Could she possibly desire to cast aspersions on Marianna's character merely to rid the school of Marianna's presence? It seemed like a very extreme measure, one that could easily recoil. But if that were the case, what had she done with the jewels? Where could she have hidden them, assuming that she had stolen them?

Looking from Lady Phillida—who it seemed had an excellent motive, for the theft had brought the attentions she so obviously craved—to Miss Teale—who exhibited symptons of spite—to Miss de Vere—who also had strong reasons for stealing the sapphires, Marianna could only wonder if the truth would ever be revealed. It remained only for Betsy to disclose a motive powerful enough for her to risk the theft. A maid could hang for such an offense.

Guiding Lady Phillida along the aisle, Sir Alex motioned to

the door. "I trust you have had enough of antiquities for this afternoon?"

"Heavens, yes," Lady Phillida replied, sneaking a glance back to see if her departure was observed and frowned upon. She was relieved to see the other gentleman had captured Miss Teale's attention. Only Miss Wyndham seemed aware of her escape to the sunshine and the flowers that bloomed about the church in colorful profusion.

"You do not care for your classes, I gather," Sir Alex said, wondering how much longer her parents would insist upon the young woman remaining in the school. That he had considered her a mere child before, escaped his memory. Undoubtedly they would buy a marriage with some worthy but impecunious gentleman before long, one who might find her dowry sufficient to compensate for a crippled bride. Alex found this notion rather distasteful.

"Dancing, dress, and deportment?" she answered in a wry voice. "For that is what they are, for the most part. Watercolor painting serves to remind us of our ladylike interests, as does music. Miss Wyndham is very good at that. Dancing reminds us to develop graceful gestures with our head and arms, genteel behavior, and an easy address as well. As for the remainder, well, if any of these ninny-hammers ever learn to add a column of numbers, 'twill be a miracle. And as to history, I doubt if any can recall a single thing." She exchanged an amused glance with him.

Alex thought of George, whose notable connection with the subject of history had been the mistaken notion that Charlemagne was somehow related, having referred to that esteemed gentleman as old Charlie Mayne. Alex cleared his throat, then offered, "Not all people are inclined in that direction, you know."

"A good thing, or nothing would ever get done." Lady Phillida paused, then sank down on a wooden bench placed so as to provide the best view of the church and flowers. "You know, it is most amazing how forthright I feel when I'm about you, sir. Perhaps I sense an awareness that all those missish airs we practice so assiduously would be totally lost on you. I expect you have been most set upon by fond mamas?"

He shrugged and nodded his head. "And papas." Taking courage from her outspoken words, he continued, "And you? I expect you have had a number of beaux paraded before you as well?"

"When at home, the progression never paused, but only because I made certain I walked as well. It seems no man desires an imperfect wife, sir." The glance she gave him was full of her ironic perception of life and how it had treated her.

Sir Alex joined her on the wooden bench, taking her to task for such stupid and illogical ideas.

From the door of the church Marianna watched the blooming of the odd friendship that appeared to have sprung up between two unlikely people. Then, sighing with her concerns, she turned again to the interior of the church, where Miss Teale divided her attention between her pupils and Viscount Barringer, that most elegant of gentlemen.

Standing in the shadows, Marianna studied George. Those biscuit pantaloons fit him superbly, as did that rich blue Bath cloth coat. His cravat was tied unusually well today, neat but not gaudy, which annoyed her just a bit. Why didn't he take this care everyday? And those boots of his must have taken an hour to polish to get such a high gloss to them. The landlord of the rented house was to be complimented on the selection of staff.

George was a marvelous man, tall, well-set, and so handsome as to break a girl's heart without even trying. How could she be angry at Miss Teale if she fluttered her lashes at him in that disgustingly pretty manner? To be fair, George was deliberately leading the woman on, to find out what he could from her. Never mind that it was difficult for Marianna to stand by to watch!

It was not long before the time came to depart. Miss Teale marshaled her charges into the three wagons with practiced skill. This time Marianna sat in the third conveyance, Miss de Vere in the second, while Miss Teale sat in the first. George rode a glossy chestnut by that first wagon while Sir Alex remained near Lady Phillida in the third, where she sat across from Marianna. It would have taken a woman far less aware than Marianna to fail to note the sidelong glances of a distinctly triumphant nature from Lady Phillida. Was there a trace of spite in that smile? Marianna sighed again at the very idea that two women, for very different reasons, desired her to be gone from the school.

It was rather late in the afternoon by the time they reached the school once again. The girls clambered down from the wagons, tired but happy after a day away from studies. Marianna and Miss de Vere shepherded them into the building while Miss Teale spent a few precious minutes conversing with Lord Barringer. Off to one side, Lady Phillida dared to speak with Sir Alex briefly before she climbed the steps and disappeared inside.

Marianna saw the girls to their rooms on the top floor, wondering how Lady Phillida coped with all those steps. She might be titled, but Miss Chudleigh made no concession as regarding her infirmity. Waiting at the top of the last flight, Marianna watched as Lady Phillida negotiated the final bit of stairs.

"Did you enjoy the outing, Lady Phillida?" Marianna asked. There was a wall of constraint between them, yet Marianna felt she must be civil to her former friend.

"Yes, I did, thanks to Sir Alexander Dent. Odd, he made the trip almost bearable." She paused, as though to add another remark, then changed her mind and walked to her room, the largest of the rooms for the girls. Rank did have a few privileges, even with Miss Chudleigh.

When Marianna entered her room, she discovered Betsy near the small window that looked out to the rear of the building. The girl was sniffing most dreadfully. When she turned, Marianna was appalled to see her face all blotched and red, her eyes puffy. It was clear the girl had been in tears. "Oh, miss, I am sorry. I know I ought not be here. But . . ." She subsided as Marianna noticed that the little silver dragon that George had given her was now on her bedside table. She knew it had been wrapped in tissue and placed between her handkerchiefs in the top drawer of her dresser.

"Can you explain this, Betsy?" Marianna said in a quiet voice, wishing she did not have to face this sort of thing.

"Oh, lor, miss, I cannot." At this statement, the girl reached up to wipe away a tear, and Marianna was horrified to see dark bruises on her upper arm.

"What happened while we were gone? Who did this to you?" Marianna advanced slowly so as to not frighten Betsy, then gently turned the girl, to discover more bruises on her other arm and back as well. Her indrawn breath of dismay drew a sniff from the girl, but no more tears.

Reluctant and fearful, Betsy admitted, " 'Twas Miss Chudleigh." A stray tear was gingerly wiped away, then the girl continued. "I asked her fer more pay, I did. I want ter get married . . . to the groom over at the King's Arms, y'see. I figured were I to get a few more shillings a month 'twould be soon I could leave here." Betsy edged her way toward the door, with no more than a glance at the silver pin on the bedside table.

"And Miss Chudleigh did not see it your way, I gather." Marianna felt pity for the maid, but she also realized that here was another person with a strong motive for the theft. And one who looked to be caught in the act of stealing the dragon pin Marianna prized so dearly.

"What about my pin? Were you going to steal that as well?" Marianna willed the girl to stop, for she had no desire to hold her by force. The beating Miss Chudleigh administered had done quite a thorough job; Betsy looked a fair way to fainting with the ache.

She hung her head before raising her face to meet Marianna's stern gaze. "Aye, I planned to steal somethin', I did. But I couldn't take the little pretty. I'm not a wicked girl, miss."

"What about Lady Phillida's sapphires? Did you take those?" Betsy's fright was greater at these words. "I didn't take them, honest. I don't know nothing." With those frantic words, she wrenched open the door and ran up to the attic to her cold, barren cubbyhole of a room.

Marianna slowly walked to the little table to pick up the dragon, which seemed to wink at her again as the fading light touched the gleaming silver. She held it against her breast, closing her eyes as she thought of how close she had come to losing the dear little memento.

"I shall have to wear you every day, I gather. I have no wish for another to steal you from me."

She carefully pinned the dragon to her gown, then turned to stare out the window, wondering what Betsy was looking at when Marianna had entered her room. What to do? Somehow she had no heart to report the near theft. She knew only too well the effect of an accused crime on a life. It would be far worse for the maid.

She ought not have questioned Betsy about the sapphires. Of course the girl would deny all. But the past half-hour had revealed a strong motive. How the maid must long to get away from the nasty Miss Chudleigh! Marianna knew that feeling well, for she felt the same.

The bell rang for supper and Marianna wondered how she might get away from the school to see Lady Lavinia and the others to report this latest development. Perhaps it would be best to face Miss Chudleigh rather than attempt to sneak out. She walked down the stairs with a thoughtful look on her face, missing the narrow-eyed study by two others—Miss Teale and Lady Phillida. Those two ladies followed behind, keeping watch as Marianna knocked, then entered the door leading to Miss Chudleigh's private rooms.

10

"I must see Lady Lavinia this evening, Miss Chudleigh," Marianna announced calmly, wondering why she wasn't quaking in her slippers at the very thought of facing the formidable headmistress. Then she realized she was still so angry at the beating Miss Chudleigh had given poor Betsy that she had quite forgotten to be afraid of the woman.

"I suppose you wish to report to her?" came the faintly sarcastic reply. Her eyes fairly snapped with hostility.

Marianna suspected that the headmistress was sufficiently awed by Lady Lavinia and her brother's position to overlook her usual rule that no teacher was to be allowed out in the evening.

"That is true." Marianna waited, quietly composed.

"Very well," came the reluctant assent. "See that you return at a decent hour. You recall the door is locked early and you must ring?"

Boldly, hardly daring to believe she was asking for such a thing, Marianna said, "I ought to have a key, in that case. Betsy is in no condition to answer the door." Though Marianna said nothing about the observed bruises, her eyes accused.

Miss Chudleigh pulled out a drawer in her desk, then reached inside. Scarcely able to believe her good luck, Marianna accepted the large key that would make her reticule sag with its weight. She ignored the grim expression on the woman's face.

"I shall return as soon as possible. Good evening." With that curt farewell, Marianna left the room, hurrying up the stairs to her own little cubicle to gather up her shawl and the sturdy

reticule Lady Lavinia had purchased for her while in Mablethorpe.

She knew that by her actions she had cut off all possibility
of continuing her teaching at this school, not that she desired
such. However, Miss Chudleigh would scarcely accept a teacher
who dared indulge in such bold behavior as Marianna just had.
Shortly, making sure no one was about to observe her departure,
she slipped out the front door and down the steps.

It was but a short walk to where the house George had rented
for the month stood. Marianna lifted the door knocker, twice
letting it drop with a loud noise, hoping that she had caught
them before they sat down to dinner.

The butler, whose name Marianna had never caught,
answered, ushering her to the dining room, where the others
were just sitting down to their meal.

"I do apologize for interrupting," said a most embarrassed
girl, pausing by the entry to the room. "I dared not wait any
later to get away from the school. I shall only be a few minutes.
Please do go on." Marianna hoped that she might be able to
sneak out of the school kitchen and find something to eat when
she returned. Really, that soup smelled utterly wonderful.

"I suppose you have already eaten?" Lady Lavinia hadn't
missed the yearning glance at the soup tureen.

"Do not worry about me. I must relate what happened. Young
Betsy—"

Marianna was cut off as George walked around the table to
take her firmly by the arm and guide her to a chair. "Sit. You
can tell us everything while you eat. I suspect you have not had
a thing since that bite at noon. Have you?" His voice was stern,
although his eyes held a softness Marianna totally missed in her
dismayed stare at the floor.

"It was a very filling macaroon," she said defensively.

"Hmpf," said the general. "No wonder those teachers look
underfed, if that is the sort of thing that goes on at that place."

"Well, I learned that our maid, Betsy, has a motive for
stealing the jewels," Marianna declared, as she gratefully slid
onto the chair. "She wishes to wed and sought a raise in her
pay." Turning to Lady Lavinia, Marianna added, "You were

right to suspect she might have a reason. Her wages are extremely low and Miss Chudleigh beat her most fearfully when she asked for more money. The bruises were simply frightful."

"The woman ought not have those children in her care," declared Lady Lavinia, her delicious soup neglected as she thought of battered and bruised little bodies.

"Also," Marianna continued after taking a sip of soup, "while we were on our visit to Southwold, Miss de Vere told me her mother has been most unwell again. The doctor declares a sunnier climate is most desperately needed for her. I fear there is definitely another suspect for the crime."

Marianna devoted her attention to the fragrant soup, delicately sipping, yet managing to consume the entire amount in record time without appearing greedy or unladylike. Her hunger somewhat appeased, she sat quietly while the soup plates were removed and the simple meal brought to the table. Roast beef with lashings of rich sauce, tiny garden peas, and browned potatoes. What heaven, after the unpleasant memory of meals at the school!

Inhaling the aroma of well-roasted beef, Marianna took one bite, then turned to look at Sir Alex. "Did you reach any conclusions regarding Lady Phillida?"

"The chit has had a time of it, make no doubt about that," replied Sir Alex, glancing up from his plate. "I cannot say I learned enough to declare that she concealed her own jewels. I confess I cannot like the idea very much. I suppose I feel a kinship to her, in a way." He failed to reveal what this might be.

Marianna applied herself to the excellent food while Lady Lavinia studied George from time to time. At last the lady inquired, "Well, George, are you going to relate what your reactions to the charming Miss Teale might be?"

"No. For I haven't any."

Marianna wondered if she could tell them about her feelings regarding the nuances in Miss Teale's voice when that lady had mentioned Marianna, and decided against it. Surely it would make herself appear a vain, worthless creature.

"You detected nothing during your ramble about Southwold Church?" Marianna dared to ask.

"She does not like you, but I noticed that before, so it is nothing new." George gave Marianna a darting glance, then returned to polishing off the delectable meal. Really, the owner of this house was to be congratulated on his cook. Of course, a day spent in fresh air contributed to a satisfying hunger. He glanced at Marianna, wondering how she had tolerated the life at the school all this time and not succumbed to a decline, considering what he surmised the food to be at that establishment.

"So," inserted the general, "it seems we have indeed four suspects, as Lady Lavinia thought. Now, what do you intend to do about it? How can we clear Miss Wyndham's name?" Trust a military man to get to the very heart of a matter.

"Call me Marianna, please, General Eagleton." She gave him a warm smile, then turned her gaze toward George, who, after all, was supposed to be the leader of this expedition.

The viscount motioned for the table to be cleared and the dessert to be brought in from the kitchen. The room was silent while everyone waited as the servants bustled about the table. A large nut torte was set down and slices served up to all, then coffee poured. Once the servants left the room, George spoke.

"The only thing we can do is to proceed with our plans. Tomorrow remains the same, the morning walk. Marianna will not have to go along, unless you think you might learn something more with them than remaining at the school. I think Alex and I will be elsewhere, or the suspects shall think it strange we pursue them. We will scout out a suitable boat tomorrow, instead. The trip to Burgh Castle is the day after that and we shall need to be prepared."

"But . . . what?" murmured Marianna while she savored the flavor of her last bite of the torte. She had heard a note of hesitancy in George's voice.

"Be careful if you take a notion to poke about in their rooms while they are absent." He studied the overly slim form, so willowy and graceful, as she sipped the last of her coffee. "If they believe you are merely there to resume your place, they are not as likely to be on their guard."

"There has been talk, a few questions, but no one dares to

ask outright what occurred when Miss Chudleigh spoke to me that last day before I left for home.''

Lady Lavinia signaled they were to leave the table and the men joined the ladies, knowing full well that Marianna had best return to her room at the school as soon as possible.

"May I suggest that you join us tomorrow evening, since you were able to get leave tonight?" said Lady Lavinia.

"They might get more suspicious than they are now, my lady,'' Marianna replied with a rueful shake of her head. She knew that her school meal would be sadly lacking in many ways.

George came to Marianna's side. "I shall walk you back, for it has become rather dark out, and I doubt if even Lowestoft is perfectly safe at night.''

"Quite right, my boy,'' agreed the general.

Marianna made proper thanks and farewells, then walked along at George's side in silence, wondering what to say to him. It was a soft, quiet evening, with crickets chirping and a rustle of a breeze in the treetops. Stars were shining brightly and a sliver of a moon cast a dim glow on the landscape. She listened to the clicks of his boots on the cobbles as they crossed the street.

"If possible, I would like you to examine Lady Phillida's room tomorrow while she is on the usual morning walk,'' George said with a glance at Marianna's downcast head. "Find some excuse to remain behind so there will be no question about you going along another day. Check the obvious as well as the unlikely places.''

"Just what, precisely, are the obvious, not to mention the unlikely?'' Marianna said with an ill-concealed grin.

"The obvious are the places you see when you directly walk into the room. The unlikely are the places you feel Lady Phillida would not expect anyone to check, should they dare to trespass.''

"There will be the devil to pay should anyone discover what I'm about,'' she stated flatly, not liking the idea of prowling through someone's room, poking through their possessions.

"Hope that Betsy is occupied elsewhere. Could you send her on an errand?'' he asked.

"Not likely. Miss Chudleigh is rather strict about that sort of thing." She stopped as they neared the school while in the shadow cast by a tree. "You best leave me here, lest someone see you with me, Lord Barringer."

The twinkle in her eyes as she looked up at him caught the glimmer of moonlight. George could not resist the urge that compelled him to touch her face, then gently place a light kiss on those lovely pink lips. She was so graceful and feminine, a willowy, long-limbed creature. He suspected that were he to draw her against him, she would be pliant, yielding reluctantly but beautifully to his caresses.

Odd, that, he mused as he withdrew from their kiss, then watched her run from him to the front door of the school. He hadn't really thought about such before.

When the door of the school swung shut, George strolled back to the town house. A great number of things drifted through his mind, none of which was related to any scientific project in the least.

How could he? How dared he do such a thing? Again? Marianna lightly touched one hand to her mouth, quivering with forced indignation. His previous kiss had been gently seductive, and this one even more alluring. Did he have the remotest idea what effect he had on her? Her heart still pounded, and not from the walk up the stairs. She quietly hurried up the last of the steps, then slipped down the hall to her room.

Just as she was about to enter, she heard the soft click of a door down the hall. She paused to look, but could see nothing. Whoever had watched her return, remained unknown. Marianna wondered why.

The next morning, while the girls trouped along in their usual procession, Marianna found an excuse to remain at the school. Since neither teacher seemed to care for her company, there were no questions. Miss de Vere seemed most preoccupied and Miss Teale departed with an expectant look on her face that Marianna suspected was due to a hope that she might meet the handsome lord again today. Poor Miss Teale, doomed to disappointment.

With Betsy safely occupied on the main floor, Marianna felt secure as she entered Lady Phillida's room. It was a lovely place, considering it was at school. Her linen, brought from her home, as were the other pupils' towels and sheets, was monogrammed and of high quality. Her needlework was neatly arranged on a lovely satinwood table by a comfortable-looking chair. On her dresser reposed her English and French textbooks, several music compositions for the pianoforte, and papers exhibiting her surprisingly neat handwriting. Marianna recalled Lady Phillida had a fondness for studying the globe. She didn't object to the smattering of arithmetic, either, as a few papers revealed.

But there was no sign of the sapphires. Swiftly, Marianna did a thorough search of every conceivable place and found nothing of interest. Lady Phillida was astonishingly neat, although she had the services of the maid, should she wish it.

Satisfied she had made the best attempt possible, Marianna returned to the schoolroom on the first floor. She was there well before the girls reentered the building, chattering softly to one another. From the door of the room where music and drawing was taught, Marianna observed that Miss Teale looked as though a storm cloud had settled over her head. Lady Phillida didn't appear all that pleased with the day, either.

The younger girls had a drawing lesson before nuncheon. Marianna half-expected Lady Phillida to appear at her door, an accusation on her lips, but nothing unusual happened the remainder of the day.

That evening Marianna made no request to leave. Miss Teale was actually pleasant to her, chatting about the forthcoming trip to Burgh Castle with evident pleasure. Marianna supposed Miss Teale hoped to entice Lord Barringer with her charms, of which she had many.

The following morning there was an air of expectancy throughout the school. All the older girls were up and dressed beforetimes. Marianna instructed them not to forget their drawing books and pencils, much to their obvious displeasure. Yet even that didn't last for long. Treats such as this were too few and far between.

School normally was a quiet, comfortingly dull daily routine. Little of the outside world, with the riots by the mobs of unemployed cloth-workers demanding "bread or blood," intruded. Only fewer girls from gentry no longer in funds made any impact on the numbers in attendance.

Marianna was thrilled to see how elegant Lord Barringer and Sir Alex appeared as they entered the school. Both men were dressed in restrained yet impressive clothes. She hung to the back, not wishing to call attention to herself in any manner. Rather, she marshaled the younger girls, who always obeyed her so beautifully.

They took the blue-painted wagons down to the pier, where the girls excitedly boarded the large yacht awaiting them. Marianna saw to the arrangements for them, then noticed the general and Lady Lavinia were also on board for the short trip. She gave no sign that she knew them, although she wasn't precisely certain if Miss Teale or Lady Phillida knew of the connection.

It was a perfect day for a sail along the coast. Various kinds of sea gulls wheeled and dived about the boat and kittiwakes bobbed farther out in the sea. Marianna looked at them, recalling that day—it seemed so very long ago—when she had her conversation with one, the very day she confronted George and his dragon of a boat.

The entrance to Breydon Water was, as George explained to the enthralled girls, at Gorleston-on-Sea. They would navigate up the narrow river to the broad waters of Breydon and then to the shore, from which they would walk to the castle.

George hoped all would go well. He wasn't sure how far it was to the castle from the water. Yet, knowing young people, he felt they wouldn't mind whatever the distance.

It was shortly before they made Gorleston-on-Sea that George was able to find the opportunity to speak with Marianna. She spent most of her time encouraging the pupils to sketch the shore, the birds, or the boat itself. He had caught several sketches of something that appeared to be a man, though whether it was Alex or himself he couldn't say.

"Well, what did you find? Anything?" He pretended to be seeking her advice on the students.

"Not one blessed thing that didn't belong there," she answered in a low voice. She tried not to gaze at him, fearing one of the others would see how much she cared for this man.

George sighed, rubbing the back of his neck in frustration. "Blast. I had hoped . . . Well, the next to check is Miss Teale, I expect."

"If Betsy holds to the same daily schedule, I should be able to manage that soon." Marianna looked about her, wondering what it had cost George to rent this marvelous yacht for the day. "Lord Barringer, I deeply appreciate all you have done and are doing for . . . the cause of truth." She dare not say exactly what she felt, for fear of listening ears.

Somewhat embarrassed at her thanks, George colored faintly, fortunately unobserved. The tan he had acquired on his time spent aboard the boats nicely concealed his red cheeks. "You are more than welcome, Miss Wyndham."

Drifting away to watch for the entrance to the passage into Breydon Water, Marianna hoped that no notice had been taken of the conversation. She vowed to keep her distance for the rest of the trip.

The coast between Lowestoft and Great Yarmouth included a range of low hills, grassy valleys, and sand dunes. Marianna tried to encourage the girls in their sketching by doing a bit of it herself. As she drew, she listened absently while Miss Teale explained the historical significance of Great Yarmouth to her pupils. She spoke of the Rows, the series of joined shops constructed during Tudor times. Then she talked of the remaining portions of the town walls, which dated from the Middle Ages. Marianna wondered how George fared with all this. She knew the Charlemagne story. He was no more interested in the ancient past than she was.

It was a pretty sight after they anchored near shore. The girls in their white muslin dresses and straw bonnets clambered down to a waiting dory and were rowed in to the land. Soon the sunny day was filled with giggles and laughter as the pupils skimmed across the grassy slope up toward the castle, which could be seen in the distance. Gay ribbons fluttered from below bosoms and large bonnets in the welcome breeze.

Marianna accepted the general's assistance, joining Lady Lavinia in the final load to go ashore.

"George told us that you found no sign of the jewels when you searched 'that' room last night. Do you think you will have better luck with the next?" She gave a significant look at where Miss Teale marched up the slope with several girls and Lord Barringer.

Taking note of the woman's laughing face, so full of charm and hope, Marianna shrugged. "Who can say? If she is guilty, do you believe she would have left the jewels in her room? I suspect she would be more clever than that, for she is a very clever woman." With that remark, Marianna got out of the dory and made her way up to her charges for the day.

A parasol shading her delicate skin, Lady Lavinia accepted the support of the general's arm and strolled up the path. Occasionally they looked into each other's eyes. Frequently they smiled. No one paid them any attention, which was just how the lady preferred it.

One of the younger girls made a wreath of wild nasturtium, offering to crown Marianna queen of the day.

"No, I thank you. I had best keep my bonnet on, not to mention use my parasol, in all this glorious sunshine." She smiled at them, however, liking the offer very much.

They laughed and ran gaily up the slope, and she was alone.

"Impressive, isn't it?" Sir Alex said, suddenly appearing at Marianna's elbow.

Their approach was across the gently rising flat field that faced the length of the east wall, which had to be at least six hundred feet plus. It rose perhaps fifteen feet in height now, though once it had been undoubtedly higher.

"Intimidating, I should say, or it would have been back in the fourth century when this was at its full glory. See how the flintlock is interlaced with the brick? Clever builders, those

Romans.'' Marianna looked at the narrow main gate to the former garrison, built to defend the estuary of the Yare and Bure rivers, and wondered aloud. ''What was it like then, really?'' She turned to look at her companion.

''Not too grim, I suppose, though a bit cold and damp, come the winter winds. They had a kind of central heating, or so I've read. Enjoyed life very much, I daresay. Especially on days like this. George said you found nothing in Lady Phillida's room.''

Taken aback by the sudden change in topic, Marianna could only nod.

''Good.'' Sir Alex patted her on the arm, much as one might a kitten, then strode off toward Lady Phillida.

She gave Alex a welcoming look and accepted his arm as she stumbled on a clump of grass. Marianna wondered if her accident was deliberate, then turned to observe Miss Teale.

''The main gate was called the Porter Praetoria. Little remains of the rest of this once-great fortress other than this wall.'' The schoolmistress enunciated her words clearly as she led a few of the girls with her.

Skirting the group, Marianna wandered away, to stand looking back to where the boat sat anchored off-shore. The view of the broad expanse of tranquil water, the Waveney marshes to the north, and the occasional windmill, arms slowly rotating in the wind, was unforgettable. She wished she might stand here forever . . . or at least for a long time, she amended.

George slipped away from the others to join Marianna, enjoying the sight of her soft muslin gown blowing about her slender form as she stood so silently gazing into the distance. The wind molded the fabric to her, outlining the sylphlike body most beautifully, he thought.

''Penny for them.''

''Not worth it,'' she replied, her heart suddenly racing as though she had climbed to the very top of the wall. How silly to allow this feeling to persist. A lot of good it would do her to moon over his lordship when he couldn't see her for dust. He enjoyed the challenge of projects, not necessarily the objects of such.

"Are you enjoying this day away from your classes?" He stood as close as he dared, catching the intriguing scent of her from time to time. She smelled like wild roses today.

At this query, she turned and nodded. "Oh, yes. I could wish this day might last a long, long time. 'Tis most wonderful, far better than teaching reluctant hands to draw or practice the pianoforte." She giggled at the thought of most of her pupils, who faced that instrument as though it were the guillotine rather than a means of potential pleasure.

"Have you thought more about what you shall do once we find the jewels?" He hoped she might say she would return to Yorkshire. He didn't want to lose her. Close to home, he might see her, enjoy that delicious laugh, share things with her.

"I still do not know for certain. I saw an advertisement for a teacher in a recent paper. I may apply for that, if Miss Chudleigh will give me a reference."

Stifling a sigh of disappointment, he replied, "She will have to, when you are proven innocent."

Marianna caught sight of Miss Teale looking their way. "I had best leave you now." She then extended her hand as though to thank Lord Barringer for the outing, turning and walking away from him as though it were an easy thing.

A song thrush perched on the branch of a nearby bush and trilled a gay tune. Marianna ignored it. She strove to contain her disappointment. But what, a wee voice in her head inquired, did she expect? The dratted man was so wrapped up in his various blasted projects he could scarcely see before his nose. Except, that small voice added nastily, when Miss Teale sashayed in front of him.

Marianna was jealous, she acknowledged at last. Jealous of everyone and everything that kept the man she loved from her side. And, she ruefully admitted, he was more likely to be attracted to the projects than anything else. What had he been like before he went off on this scientific binge of discovery and invention? She remembered him as a fun companion and a good son to his father and a boy who loved his home.

What would it take now to change him in his ways? Could he ever turn aside from his preoccupation of things scientific to find interest in anything else? The management of the estate? The gardens? If her senses told her the truth, Lady Lavinia might well be marrying and moving away before too long. George would be alone. For how long?

Pleasure in the day dimmed by her musings, Marianna faced the boat once again, longing for the moment when they might return to Lowestoft. She would send off that letter . . . one of these days, she assured herself.

She had a sensible heart, as Lady Lavinia had said. Resolute in her determination to see the day through, no matter what, Marianna avoided even so much as looking at George, which was a pity. George, when not attending to the desires of his guests, was casting what Lavinia decided were yearning looks toward Marianna.

It was sunny, and a lovely breeze gently cooled them all. There was a chorus of birds singing and dainty butterflies danced over the wildflowers, hovering to select precisely the right flower to light upon. Giggles and gentle chatter came from the girls as they consumed the excellent repast that the cook at the rented town house had put up for the party.

As far as Marianna was concerned, it was the dead of winter and she was in the deepest of gloom. What did her future hold for her now? No position. Certainly no money. If she did manage to see her name cleared, so what?

How she wished she had never laid eyes on George Mayne, Viscount Barringer, again. Yet that was not quite true, if she was utterly honest with herself. Not completely. Two kisses, gentle and, oh, so sweet, made a lie of that thought.

She would gallantly—her sensible heart totally intact—see the rest of the day out, return to her little room . . . and have a satisfying cry. Providing she wasn't required elsewhere and George continued to look at Miss Teale as though she owned the sapphires instead of possibly having stolen them.

11

"That is an excellent likeness of the old Roman fort. You have truly captured the mood of the place—brooding, waiting for the enemy legions to storm up the slope."

George peered over her shoulder, admiring the view of the soft sea-green muslin draped about her as much as the truly first-rate drawing of Burgh Castle. The gown's neckline was discreet, yet hinted of delectable curves. The modest amount of creamy skin revealed lured a man to desire a more expansive view. Aunt had been right when she commented on Marianna's becoming dress. He ought have noticed before how its color reflected the sea about them and caught the sparkle of her beautiful eyes. For they were beautiful. If only she would look at him once again . . . Trying to entice the spinsterish Miss Teale to reveal a secret and keep Marianna close by was deucedly difficult.

"How kind of you to say so," came the softly musical reply, so ladylike and refined. Also distant. She would not even look at him.

Marianna felt her heart beat faster and she knew her lips trembled slightly. She gently compressed her upper teeth against her lower lip, lest she say more. Yet he was her host. And he was being extremely gracious. Her good manners and lifelong training asserted themselves.

"I enjoy sketching so very much." She hazarded a glance at him, then wished she hadn't. He was gazing at her with those sherry-colored eyes, the sun picking out gold lights in that rich chestnut hair. The tenderness she thought she glimpsed was an illusion, she told herself. She was nothing more than a project. "It is fortunate that I have been able to teach something I like," she added, returning her attention to her drawing pad.

"Then this excursion has been agreeable for you?" It would be worth everything if she had taken pleasure in this day, he realized suddenly.

Startled, she looked at him again, more closely this time. Could he possibly question her reaction to this glorious day? "I cannot recall when I have enjoyed myself more, Lord Barringer. 'Tis a beautiful spot and you provided such a lovely picnic. Truly, I am quite of the opinion this is the best outing the school has ever had. A pity Miss Chudleigh had to miss it." Her eyes twinkled with amusement at the very thought of the tall, imposing woman, her nose positively quivering as she inspected the ruins of the fort.

As a compliment, it was not what George had hoped to hear, but he expected he had best be satisfied with scraps at this point. He would apply himself to the matter of persuading Marianna to return to Yorkshire once they got the matter of the sapphires out of the way. He glanced over at Alex, wondering how he fared. Then he caught sight of a frown creasing Miss Teale's forehead, and he rose from where he had crouched at Marianna's side. "Well, I had best move around a bit."

Marianna chuckled at the resigned tone in his voice. Why, he almost sounded reluctant to leave her.

When he passed the grassy knoll where Alex sat beside Lady Phillida, he overheard a scrap of what appeared a softly spoken argument.

"Allow me to remind you, sir, that your opinion was not sought," said a sweetly haughty voice. Lady Phillida glared at Sir Alex, and George had to try very hard not to laugh at his friend's chagrined expression.

"I only stated that whatever that is on your paper didn't much resemble the fort. Would you have me to lie?"

"Nooo," she drawled. "I prefer the truth, I believe."

"Why did you accuse Miss Wyndham of stealing your sapphires?" The question was sudden, sharp.

Lady Phillida froze, her eyes staring unseeingly at the paper. At last she looked at Sir Alex. His eyes did not condemn; rather, they held curiosity, nothing more. Attempting to defend her actions to him would be a challenge.

"Marianna and I were the best of friends before she found it necessary to become a junior teacher at the school. I wanted to help her, but she is so proud, she would never accept my offer. Of all the girls at the school, I liked her the best. I daresay I might have refused assistance in similar circumstances, but she did anger me. But she was the only one who knew where I kept my jewels. When they disappeared, I had to report it. They were too valuable to permit the thief to go unpunished."

"Why did you not call in an investigator?"

"Who?" she demanded quietly. "This is not London, with the Bow Street men. I did not want to believe her thievery, but I knew Marianna had need, and the knowledge." Lady Phillida found she hated to say those words, as she could see Sir Alex thought she ought to have done differently.

"How much longer do you anticipate remaining at the school?" he asked, surprising her with the change in subject. She feared his questions as much as she welcomed his attentions.

"I expect I shall return to my home at the end of this term. That will be a few weeks from now." She glanced at him in puzzlement. She knew better than to think him interested in her. He did not look to need her dowry, but then, looks could be deceiving, she well knew that.

"And the sapphires? What shall your parents say to the absence of them?"

She understood, or thought she did, his line of questions now. Slowly shaking her head, she replied, "I do not know. They shall be angry, I expect."

"What if I were able to restore them to you? What would you do then?"

"I should be most grateful to you, Sir Alex," she said, more puzzled than ever.

"Grateful enough to try something rather dangerous and most likely painful, but which could liberate you from the atrocious limp you endure?"

"Sir," she replied in harsh accents, "you go too far." She

rose from the pleasant knoll to walk away from him, her limp pronounced in her hurry.

Sir Alex followed her. "Wouldn't you like to stroll along these grounds like Marianna and the others?"

"You are a hateful man, to tease me so. Cruel and heartless!" She turned to face him when they reached the bottom of the little hill, somewhat away from the others and close to the water's edge. A hint of tears sparkled in her eyes, and her tender pink lips trembled as she glared at him.

"Not long ago I had a letter from a friend of mine who has been visiting in Scotland," Sir Alex began. "While there he discovered an unusual doctor. You see, this friend had suffered a similar injury to yours when a lad. This doctor broke the badly mended leg, then set it properly. Now it is healed and he is able to walk like a normal man, with only the faintest of limps, and that mostly when he is tired. You could try such a thing."

"No! It was horridly painful the first time, when I fell. I was in bed for months. I could not face such an ordeal again. You are cruel to even suggest such a thing." She covered her face with her hands, then glanced up as he spoke again.

"Not even if you might be free of the limp?" Sir Alex stared at her with cold eyes, accusing eyes. Lady Phillida turned from that look.

"Not even then, sir. I fear the pain, coward that I am." She moved away from his side knowing that she undoubtedly had given him every reason to dislike her.

Sir Alex watched her depart, wondering if there could be any other solution to her problem. Now, if that shorter leg could somehow be lenghtened slightly . . .

"I believe you have angered Lady Phillida, Sir Alex," Marianna said from behind him. "Whatever did you say to upset her so?"

He spared her a glance. "You can be concerned after her accusation of you?"

Marianna nodded slowly. "She looked most unhappy. We once were very good friends." A melancholy feeling crept over her and she abruptly walked away from him, to sit near the little dory that was to take them back to the yacht. Here she stared across the Breydon, not seeing much in particular.

"Ready to return?" Miss de Vere said shortly as she joined Marianna by the shore. "If I had not been so concerned about my poor mother, I would have truly enjoyed this day. It is like a day out of time, is it not? How unlike our usual hours passed in the schoolroom, trying to place some knowledge into those silly girls' heads."

"I thought you liked teaching French and needlework?" Marianna said, turning to face her fellow teacher.

"Indeed, it is better than starving, I suppose. But, had I the means, I would gladly walk from that school, never to return." The words were spoken with quiet intensity, quite as though she would do most anything to achieve her aim.

The pupils began straggling down the hill, all seeming sorry that the lovely outing was drawing to a close. The dory began ferrying them out to the boat, the young oarsman grinning at his giggling passengers.

Off to one side, supposedly supervising the transfer, Marianna was in serious thought. It certainly seemed as though Miss de Vere desired to leave the school, and she desperately wanted funds. Enough to steal?

Their sail south to Lowestoft was uneventful, much to Marianna's relief. Sir Alex stood at one end of the boat while Lady Phillida reclined on a bench at the other.

Miss de Vere attempted to show some of her charges how they might turn their sketches—the better ones—into pretty pieces of needlework. She pointed out the soft colors of the distant hills and dunes they passed. Gulls that trailed after the boat in hopes of tidbits were included in her commentary.

The only excitement was the sight of a flashing trawler limping into port with nets full of herrings. It was not possible to tell what had delayed them, but the catch appeared lively, and it was likely still salable.

"Those boats often suffer dire misfortune," George said in her ear after quietly edging up on her. "The graveyards of the parish churches of any of the seaports offer a grim commentary on our sailing. So many tombstones recall a man lost at sea.

The most dangerous part of the voyage is coming into port. Reefs, sandbanks that shift, fog, many dangers lurk hidden, unseen.''

"Then I fail to see why you must sail," Marianna said, giving him an anguished look before remembering she intended to remain aloof and not care for him.

Satisfied he had drawn a response, George went to tend to the docking of the yacht.

At the pier the girls boarded the blue wagons, more quiet and subdued now, tired from the trip and all that fresh air.

George assisted Marianna to her place in the third vehicle, wondering how to mend things between them, for he could sense all was still far from well.

"Thank you again for the glorious day, Lord Barringer," Marianna said with the nicest sort of polite manner.

"You look very lovely. My aunt was right when she said how well that color becomes you. It matches your eyes." George permitted his hand to linger on her arm before reluctantly assisting her up the steps to the wagon.

Surprise registered in her eyes as she looked down at him, and George congratulated himself that he'd been able to bring another reaction. She'd been so remote all day.

"Th-thank you," she stuttered, so unlike her normally composed self.

He stood smiling, thinking the day a success, then he turned to retrace his steps and help Miss Teale.

Marianna was able to take the key again that night. She ate her meager supper at the school first, then slipped out the back way to walk quickly to the town house, mostly to see Lady Lavinia, she assured herself.

The occupants were gathered in the drawing room when she arrived. One of the dresses she had ordered was there. She didn't take the time to try it on; that could come later.

"I am most put out you did not join us for dinner, Marianna," declared Lady Lavinia, smiling to take the sting from her words.

"Thank you, dear ma'am. I felt it best to eat with the girls tonight. To allay suspicion, if nothing else."

After some quiet conversation, she mentioned to George that

tomorrow was Miss Teale's half-day away from the school. It was the main reason she had risked leaving the school to come over.

"Where she goes and what she does have always been a mystery. She comes back late, but Miss Chudleigh says never a word to her. Miss Teale is not approachable, nor does she invite confidences, not that I desire such, mind you. However, I thought you could make use of the knowledge."

For once quick off the mark, George replied, "I trust you intend for me to follow her, find out where she goes? What transpires? Excellent notion, my dear." He gave her shoulder an avuncular pat and then crossed over to where Aunt Lavinia sat to say something quietly to her.

Sir Alex chuckled. "One never knows about those quiet sort, still waters and all that, you know."

There was little time for more. George walked Marianna back to the school as he had done before, but this time there was no gentle kiss, no tenderness. She felt the loss deeply.

Come the morning, a brisk breeze was blowing, and Marianna was glad it was not her half-day. She succumbed to the appeal of sunny skies and early-summer blooms to lead her class into the back yard of the school, where she set them to work drawing the scraggly daisies that grew there.

Frequent looks to the area beyond brought nothing to view other than the usual parade of delivery men and their carts, an occasional soldier.

At the town house Lady Lavinia joined the general in the carriage. "We shall take another ride about the town, but first I thought you might perhaps find the drill of the militia to be entertaining to watch?"

The dear lady smiled and thoughtfully agreed. He had sounded like a little boy who hoped to show off something precious to him. She hadn't the heart to refuse, and indeed, she found the idea of watching the parade rather intriguing. "Lovely! I shall enjoy that very much."

They set off down the street, her parasol of white with pink ribbons gaily twirled with youthful enthusiasm.

* * *

Shortly after the hall clock chimed noon, George slipped from the house. Walking quickly to a tree-shaded spot from where he could watch the school without being noticed, he waited patiently. It wasn't long before the figure of Eloisa Teale marched down the front steps and then headed in the direction of the sea.

She was dressed most attractively. The rose muslin trimmed with delicate lace and knots of rose riband became her well. On her head was a saucy chip-straw bonnet tied with more of the rose riband. Aunt Lavinia could have told him the bonnet was worn, and the gown at least two seasons old. She also might have wagered a guess that Miss Teale dressed to meet a man. George neither knew nor cared. The color made her easier to see, and for that he was thankful.

He followed her. It was easy enough to do, for she strolled along at an ambling pace, but with a purpose in mind, he was certain of that. She swung that reticule of hers as though it had something heavy in it, and he quickened his pace lest he lose sight of her.

She crossed over to the other side of the street, then turned at the next corner, and then turned again in a bewildering, twisting path. George was sure she hadn't seen him, nor would she expect anyone to follow her. But such an odd route to follow!

Then they arrived at the seafront. George hung back in the shadows, watching and waiting to see what might happen next.

Miss Teale strolled along the boardwalk, pausing now and again to look out to the water. She stopped to buy a glass of lemonade, then continued on her way. If she chose to spend her precious free hours doing precious little, it was nothing to him, but it was decidedly odd.

Getting bored with his tailing, George was of a mind to forget the whole idea when he espied a curious thing: Miss Teale had stopped to talk to a sailor. At least the man was dressed in the rough clothes favored by them. Yet George observed he hadn't walked with that peculiar rolling gait of a man of the sea. He had caught sight of him earlier and absently noted that inconsistency.

Most curious, George thought, and he tried to get closer to them. It was too open an area to accomplish. Miss Teale delved into her matching rose reticule, then pulled out a flat packet, handing it to the man with what appeared to be reluctance. He smiled at her, drawing her along with him into the nearby inn.

George waited until he thought he would go to sleep, when they suddenly returned. The man saluted Miss Teale, a most military farewell. Once this was accomplished, she turned away, staring out to the sea while the "sailor" left.

George waited a few minutes, then he strolled from where he had concealed himself. "Why, Miss Teale, what a surprise to see you in this area! I came down to check on my boat and thought I caught sight of you over here. Lovely day, is it not?" He appeared the picture of lordly affability and graciousness.

Miss Teale jumped as though she had been stuck with a pin. "Why, Lord Barringer, indeed 'tis a surprise, as you say. Have you been here long?" She looked worried, George noted. And her cheeks were flushed. He wondered what had occurred while she was inside the inn.

"No," George said with amiability. "Just got here, as a matter of fact. Perhaps you would do me the honor of walking along with me to where my boat is docked. I need to get a report from my man. Then we might have a light repast at an inn. Or maybe you would fancy joining my aunt and the general for tea?"

"Your aunt and the general?" she echoed faintly, the day obviously turning more to her liking with these words.

"The very thing." He placed her fluttering hand on his arm, then directed their path toward the other end of the walk, noting as they went she had cast one or two furtive looks behind them, as though fearing detection by someone. The "sailor?"

Once at the boat, he left her to wait on shore while he went out to have a talk with the clever Tom Crowdon. He gave Tom a very unusual order, then looked around to ascertain all was well with his precious boat. For some odd reason, he felt a loss of interest in the concept of diving under the water.

Miss Teale showed remarkably little curiosity in his boat, for someone who was connected in some manner with a man of the sea. They strolled along toward the town house, George wondering what on earth he would do if they arrived only to find his aunt and the general off on one of their jaunts about town. Miss Teale might get some very justifiably strange notions in her head. And George didn't know if this might be good or not.

"Is that not your aunt and General Eagleton in the carriage up ahead, Lord Barringer?" said a clearly puzzled Miss Teale.

With a relief he barely disguised, George nodded. "It certainly is." He hailed them, smiling as he looked first at Miss Teale. Then he gave his aunt a significant stare. "I thought perhaps we might all enjoy a cup of tea."

"With all the trimmings? But, of course," said a delighted Lady Lavinia, giving her parasol a gay whirl. Turning to the general, she said, "Henry, is that pretty little cake shop we just saw a good place to indulge in tea?"

He patted her gloved hand with fondness, willing to favor her with any catering to she wished. "I believe my Sibyl has commended the treats within most highly, my lady."

The general handed over the reins of the carriage to his man. Then the four sauntered along to where a brightly painted place proclaimed itself to be Miss Hattie's Tea and Bake Shoppe. Miss Teale entered with entranced eyes and an eager step. George followed.

Marianna stepped inside Miss Teale's quarters with even more reluctance than she had possessed when checking Lady Phillida's room. It was distasteful to probe through her things. But the chance had come when the girls all were gathered for a special French test by Miss de Vere.

It was much neater in here. Looking around, Marianna decided that Miss Teale was so methodical she probably put her thoughts for the day in alphabetical order. Books were lined up precisely on her one shelf. Her few dresses hung just so on the wall pegs. A pair of half-boots peeked from beneath the bed, a single size rather than the cot Marianna slept on.

Marianna checked beneath the bed, then in every other place to view, which really wasn't much, given the size of the room.

The small desk yielded nothing of great interest. Plain note paper, which in a way was odd, for whom did Miss Teale write to, anyway? Ink, quills all neatly sharpened. A bundle of old clippings and a few faded letters. Not very much.

Marianna thought she heard a noise in the hall. Slipping silently to the door, she hesitantly peeked out. No one was about in the hall, nor on the wooden stairs. After looking behind her to make sure nothing was out of place, she hurried to her room.

"I'm not meant for this work," she whispered to herself as she breathlessly leaned against the door of her room after it was safely closed. It was disappointing to find nothing in her search, but had she truly expected to uncover the jewels? She knew which person she suspected, and she longed to unmask her. But she needed more than a hunch.

What had George observed? she wondered, hardly able to wait until that evening when she would slip away to join them for dinner, wearing her pretty sea-green dress. The other gown was to be saved—for precisely what, she wasn't sure. Except that in the dim recesses of her mind she nursed a fond hope of something special.

It took great patience to wait until the others had gone down to dinner before wrapping a light muslin pelisse about her and slipping from the house. The key weighted down her reticule and she smilingly figured she could always use it to defend herself in the event of an attempted assault.

The butler, whom she now knew to be named Gadsby, ushered her into the drawing room with small ceremony.

"Marianna," cried Lady Lavinia with delight, "how well you look. I am so glad I insisted upon that shade of green, for you must know it is the same as your lovely eyes. Is it not, Sir Alex?" She turned to smile at the gentleman.

George was ignored, much to his annoyance.

Shaking her head with amusement, Marianna gently scolded, "Fie, my lady, you must not put him to the blush that way. 'Tis most unkind."

"I agree with Lady Lavinia, however. You are in first looks this evening." Sir Alex gave her a small wink as he bent over her hand.

"Never mind her looks. Did you discover anything of interest this afternoon?" George said with just a trace of testiness in his voice.

Marianna shook her head, becoming most serious. "Not anything of note. A few clippings, some old letters were the most I found."

Gadsby appeared at the door and Lady Lavinia waved her hand. "Dinner is ready. Let us remove ourselves to the dining room. We can continue to discuss this matter over our food . . . if the subject doesn't upset your appetite."

Marianna could well understand this, for she certainly did not relish the idea of further sleuthing of the same sort. When they had been served the first course, she turned to face George and asked, "And did you uncover anything of interest this afternoon? You were able to follow her with no difficulty?"

George nodded, then placed his spoon beside his empty soup bowl. "I did, but I am not sure what to make of it."

At which remark Aunt Lavinia looked up, her spoon in midair as she considered his words. "How odd. Tell us more."

He glanced at Marianna, observing that she was wearing the little dragon pin. It pleased him very much to see it on her gown, just over her heart. Then he cleared his throat, waiting a few moments until the servant left the room. "She met a man while on the boardwalk. She handed him a small flat packet, then they went into the inn for a short time. When they came out again, he sort of saluted her before they parted. He was dressed to look as though he was a sailor, but he wasn't."

"What makes you say that?" inquired the general, his ears having perked up when he heard the bit about a salute.

"He didn't walk like one," George replied, going on to explain the difference.

"She said nothing, and you couldn't very well ask, could you?" commented Marianna, feeling a bit sorry for George if he had become interested in Miss Teale, only to discover she had a male friend of one sort or another.

"You are wearing that lovely pin," said Lady Lavinia out of the blue. "Such a nice thing of George to do. But is it just the thing to wear with that gown, dear?"

"Well," replied Marianna, "Betsy was on the verge of taking it that day I returned early to find her in my room. Since then, I've kept it with me, not liking the thought of losing it, you see." She prudently neglected to reveal why she didn't wish to lose the pin.

"Ah, yes, we will have Betsy. You really ought to search her room," said Lady Lavinia, wrinkling her nose in faint distaste.

"Must I?" demanded Marianna of George.

"Yes, I rather think so, I expect it should be done."

"Her room is up in the garret, unheated and dismal. I can't think how she can bear it up there year in and year out. If I were Betsy, I'd run off with that young groom, regardless of money. There must be another way she can earn a living besides working for Miss Chudleigh," Marianna stated, glancing at Lady Lavinia, then at George.

Sir Alex spoke up. "You have carefully checked two rooms and found nothing. We shall simply have to keep looking, for I feel certain there is something, a clue."

"The strange man, perhaps?" said Lady Lavinia.

"They were by the water, were they not?"

"True. What has that to do with it?"

"But, ma'am, you yourself said the jewels were near the water."

"And," added the general, "that is where we are now."

12

It was no problem to slip up the back stairs to the top of the house where the servants slept. At this time of day they were all occupied belowstairs.

Marianna pushed open the door to Betsy's little room. Cell was more like it. Inside, she saw gray walls, bare floorboards, and a narrow iron cot with a mattress even lumpier than her own. On the far wall of the low-ceilinged room hung a spotted mirror above a washstand upon which sat a chipped basin that Marianna wagered would contain frozen water, come winter. That face flannel would be frozen as well, for there was no heat up here, no little fireplace where the chill could be warded off. Atop the battered chest of drawers was a comb lacking a few teeth taking pride of place.

Betsy was lucky in one respect: she didn't have to share her room, as did the tweeny and the kitchen maid. Nor did Cook deign to share her small quarters, better than Betsy's, Marianna was certain, if only by a few degrees.

The maid was wearing her morning dress, a print calico. On a wall peg hung the black dress she would wear in the afternoon, especially when parents were expected. In one drawer Marianna found two pairs of worn, hand-knit black stockings, a cap, a few ribands, and a night rail that looked to be a cast-off from one of the schoolgirls. In another there were two aprons, one black and of coarse fabric, the other of white cotton. As well, there was a set of underwear, handmade of unbleached calico. She pushed shut the last drawer. No jewels here. Marianna could well see why the owner of such a pitiful lot would be tempted most easily.

155

She checked the floor and walls of the little room for a hiding place, but found nothing. The only nice feature was the window, which Betsy kept shining clean. It looked down upon the garden. In the distance you could see a glimpse of the sea.

Back in the hall, Marianna went along to the attic storage, where she looked over the assortment of trunks the girls brought with them. Miss de Vere would not have one here, but Marianna located Miss Teale's. Inside, there were a few letters in a corner, little else of interest. Lady Phillida had several trunks for her belongings. They were unlocked, a thing Marianna found rather curious. Would a thief leave the hiding place open to anyone? She found nothing inside them, either.

It took only a few minutes to return to her floor and her room. How horrid she had felt, going through that poor girl's belongings. She had never considered the personal life of a maid before. How harsh and grim it must be. Small wonder Betsy yearned to be gone from here, willing to scrimp and save to marry the groom at the inn.

There was a stir in the hall and Marianna knew it was time for the noon meal, so grudingly doled out. Miss Chudleigh appeared to have the notion that if one wasn't fed, one didn't require food.

It was about an hour later that the door to her classroom opened and Miss de Vere flew inside. Her cheeks were pink and her eyes excited.

"Only see, Miss Wyndham! See! I won! I won!"

Much mystified, Marianna hurried to discover what the fuss was all about. "A list of numbers?" It hardly seemed like something to dance about.

"The lottery! I won! Now I can take my poor mother to the South of France. With this much money we can live—quite simply, mind you—for some years. I may even be able to find some sort of position there. Oh, you cannot imagine how happy I am. I depart now. Immediately. We shall be on the first boat that can take us."

She gave Marianna a hesitant look, then reached out to hug her ever so gently. "Be happy for me, please?"

"But of course, Miss de Vere. I think it is quite wonderful

that you have won your heart's desire. Can I do anything to help you?'' Class was forgotten as the students crowded around the French teacher, eager to hear the amazing news.

"I shall take my books, my needlework. That is all I care about.'' She bustled over to her classroom, removing her few books to a satchel she carried, then she stuffed in a roll of exquisite needlework, some colorful yarns, and a needle holder. She paused at the door, her eyes meeting Marianna's confounded gaze with amusement. "Good-bye, my dear. I hope you are able to accomplish what you seek to do. I trust the truth will out in the end. I never believed what I heard, you know.''

Following the French teacher to the front door, Marianna said, "You knew about the, er, loss?''

With one hand on the brass knob, Miss de Vere turned to face Marianna. "I guessed a great deal of it, but Lady Phillida whispered about her missing 'item' just before you left. I thought you foolish to flee when you did. I knew you were innocent, you don't have the necessary guile to pull off something of that sort, you know. I am glad you returned to clear your name. Good luck.'' She leaned over to place a light kiss on Marianna's cheek. And then she whirled around the corner of the entrance door and was gone.

Marianna stood stock-still for a moment until the chattering of her pupils reached her ears. Not wishing to have Miss Chudleigh leave her rooms to see what all was happening, Marianna hastily returned. The headmistress was doubtless in a fury over the defiant leavetaking of Miss de Vere. One did not disturb angry dragons.

Class was out of the question for the remainder of the afternoon. The girls could not concentrate on drawing a picture of a tree when something so wonderful and exciting had occurred. Marianna was not quite certain whether the prospect of no French or needlework classes or the incredible announcement from Miss de Vere was the more overwhelming.

Once the dinner bell had sounded, Marianna escaped to her room to slip on her pelisse. Taking her reticule, still heavy with the key she had retained, she ran lightly down the back stairs and out the door.

At the town house, Gadsby ushered her in to the drawing room. Marianna hurried past him, her face alight with her startling information.

"News, my dear?" said Lady Lavinia as she rose from her chair to join Marianna.

"Such news, ma'am. Miss de Vere rushed into the school announcing she had just won the lottery and was off with her mother to the South of France. 'Twill do her poor mother a world of good. But what a to-do! Miss de Vere gathered up her books and lovely needlework, then marched out the door. Just like that." Marianna walked along to the dining room with Lady Lavinia, scarcely aware of where she was. "I believe she scarcely paused to notify Miss Chudleigh. Do you know," Marianna continued in a wondering voice, "I did not so much as know her Christian name."

"How did Miss Teale take the news?" asked George as he escorted Marianna around to the chair she usually occupied when dining with them.

"I do not know, actually. She is always so remote, and it is difficult to tell what goes on in her mind. Needless to say, the girls were in alt. It proved an impossible task to settle them down for the rest of the afternoon."

"That gives us one fewer suspect," commented the general, who seemed to be a permanent guest at the dinner table. "I like a narrowing of the field, makes it easier, don't you know."

"Miss de Vere knew of the theft and said she was happy I had come back to clear my name," Marianna said, hardly aware she was seated at George's side.

"What do we do next?"

"Well, we can cease wondering about Miss de Vere," said Sir Alex with a frown.

"I went over poor Betsy's room this morning. She has little enough and would certainly be a likely prospect for a thief. Her room had nothing I could find, and I think I'm becoming quite good at this hunting business. I also checked the storage attic. Miss Teale's trunk had but a few letters in the bottom. Lady Phillida's trunks were unlocked and I couldn't find anything there, either."

"So," Lady Lavinia said, "what is the next thing we do?" She looked first at George, then at the general.

"My Sibyl said she has kept watch, having heard the nasty things Lady Phillida said after the sapphires went missing. Sibyl worried when you left, not knowing what had happened, precisely. She's also pleased you are here to clear your name." The general gave Marianna an approving look.

"Did everyone know?" declared Marianna in exasperation.

"Lady Phillida may have thought that if she mentioned it, someone might have a clue, you know," stated Sir Alex, the frown on his forehead even more pronounced.

"Well, I shall keep a watch on Betsy and do my best regarding Miss Teale." Eloisa so kept to herself that it was a difficult task, one made no easier by Marianna's feelings regarding the woman. "I believe Betsy knows more than we think. She has a habit of listening at keyholes and doors. Who knows what she has learned that way?"

"Interesting thought. Do you suppose most servants are guilty of such behavior?" Lady Lavinia glanced with alarm at the door.

"We have nothing to fear, Aunt. Who could make sense of what we say here?" George chuckled, hoping to allay his aunt's worries. He suspected there was little that went on in any household that the servants did not also know. Whenever he desired to find out what was going on at Mayne Court nowadays, he simply inquired of Peters. The butler was a gold mine of information.

The five spent a pleasant evening discussing the possibilities for action. Marianna was depressed. It seemed to her that those sapphires must have vanished off the face of the earth. She as much as said so.

"Odd you should comment on that," Lady Lavinia said. "I have been considering the matter at great length while the general and I have been jaunting about the town. I still feel there is that close connection to the water we must investigate."

"I have Tom Crowdon keeping an eye on the waterfront area, Aunt. If that 'sailor' Miss Teale met on her half-day is seen again, he's to let me know," George declared firmly.

Marianna gazed at George with new respect. Had George

taken on a more dashing air as of late? A more courtly mien? Perhaps he'd assumed all this from the Sir George of old, the one who rescued a fair maiden from the dragon. Although this George hardly seemed the type. Had he changed? She suspected she had altered to some degree—if for no other reason from those kisses he placed so boldly on her lips.

That wouldn't happen again. She would see to it. There was little point in arousing hope when there was no future for them together.

The clock in the hall struck the hour and Marianna suddenly realized how late it was. Miss Chudleigh was still a force to reckon with. Jumping up, she said, "I must bid you all good night. It is much later than I thought. I shall report as soon as there is anything to relay. Agreed?"

Lady Lavinia seemed to speak for all when she agreed.

Sir Alex confounded Marianna by asking her what size slipper she thought Lady Phillida wore. "Could you get me one of them? Or the outline of one?"

Giving him the sort of guarded look one bestows on people not quite in their right mind, Marianna nodded dutifully. "I shall try. Mind you, if I continue to flit in and out of these rooms, I am bound to be caught one of these days. Then I shall find myself in a pickle, to be sure."

As she left the house, she could hear Lady Lavinia quizzing Sir Alex on what he intended to do with one slipper. Turning to George, Marianna asked, "What do you think, Lord Barringer?"

"Marianna, we are not around anyone at the moment."

"Yes, I know."

They had stopped at the usual place, beneath the branches of the tree. She waited, daring him to make a move.

"Who knows what Alex will do with that slipper? Fill it with rocks, perhaps. It would be useful to hit that young lady over the head. She deserves such for maligning your name when she had no proof."

"How kind of you to keep faith in my innocence." Marianna wondered if she ought to edge away or wait. For what, she wasn't precisely certain. Hadn't she determined George was not going to kiss her again? So why did she stand here like a ninny?

"Have you given any more thought to your future? Will you return to Yorkshire?" There, he had remembered to say it. George felt rather pleased with himself. Lady Lavinia kept saying he was absentminded, but that wasn't entirely so.

"Yorkshire?" Marianna raised suddenly hopeful eyes to her dear George. Could it be that he was going to seek her hand?

"Yes. I hoped you would . . ." George broke off his train of thought as he stared into her lovely eyes. They really were beautiful. Such an interesting color in the moonlight. Her skin had a translucency that seemed to glow as though kissed with pearl dust. She was close to him, entrancingly close. He could catch a whiff of her delicate rose scent if he leaned just a bit closer to her. He did.

"George?" whispered a bewildered Marianna.

"Roses," George murmured, totally lost. "You smell like a rose garden in June." With that comment, he bent his head, glad he had so little distance to go, and kissed her again. Oh, the dear girl nestled so satisfactorily in his arms, just like she belonged there.

Nothing he had ever done before had prepared him for what he felt when he kissed Marianna Wyndham. It was a little like having the shocks from his electricity machine, one of his earlier experiments, jolt through him, only much nicer. In fact, he so completely enjoyed the experience, he gave her one chance to catch her breath, then repeated it.

He explored the satiny skin of her face, her eyes, then recaptured her mouth, finding so many facets to this kissing business, he would have been content to continue this experiment all night. His arms held her tightly against him, and he found the sensation of her slim form against his to be most agreeable.

When she surfaced for air, Marianna reluctantly gave her gallant a gentle nudge. Nothing hard, of course, but a reminder. "George, as you were saying?" she hesitantly urged.

"Saying?" George echoed, trying to recall what it was he had intended to tell her. "Oh," he remembered. The remarkable kisses had nearly driven his earlier thoughts from his mind. "I hoped you would return to your home. Then we could see each other. I do enjoy your company, Marianna.''

She listened to that husky, deep voice say the wrong words, and longed to do violence to him in some manner. Yet, best not to burn her bridges. "How nice,'' she said dryly. "I must remember that. Should I manage to return, you must stop by for a chat some time. But I may not go home, you know. It is possible I shall seek a position off in Oxford. Some school near the university wants a teacher for young ladies.'' With that remark, she patted his arm much like his aunt did, then turned to leave. "Good night, Lord Barringer.''

"Marianna!'' A wealth of frustration was in that soft cry. She heard it and kept on walking.

George saw her enter the school, then turned toward the town house. Rather than go inside, he continued strolling along in the moonlight toward the pier where his boat sat, waiting for him.

Once on board he tried to renew his enthusiasm for the concept of a diving boat. But all he could do was think of Marianna and how she had looked in the moonlight and what it had felt like to kiss her.

He did not wish to lose her to some school off in Oxford. He was coming to realize that life without that lovely girl would be unbearable.

Up in her room, Marianna thought she could not bear this much longer. She loved George with all her heart, and he, well, he seemed attracted. Things had certainly advanced, what with the intensity of his kisses and all. Her cheeks burned with chagrin as she considered her utterly wanton behavior, to allow a man she was not engaged or married to such liberties with her person.

The worst of it all was that she had enjoyed it very much. And even more terrible than that was that she most desperately hoped it would happen again. She stared out her window at the starlit sky. Was there a chance she would clear her name? And if she did, would George ever realize she was quite necessary to his life? It seemed to her she felt nothing but quiet despair, a kind of muted grief.

The following morning Marianna was struck by an admirable notion regarding the problem of Lady Phillida's slipper. She entered her classroom with a forced enthusiasm, then ordered all the girls to remove their slippers.

Lady Phillida gave Marianna a most puzzled look. "And why ought we do such a silly thing, Miss Wyndham?"

Marianna ignored the faint sneer in that voice. "We are going to draw the outline of our slippers preparatory to making, and embroidering, a new pair to take home. How impressed your parents will be with such practical demonstrations of your skill." Marianna devoutly hoped she sounded convincing. Not having taught needlework before, she had no idea if this would work, but she recalled having made her father a pair of slippers a few years back. She had used the same scheme then to get his slipper size.

The girls seemed to accept this suggestion with good will, and even Lady Phillida removed her slippers. She had difficulty and Marianna hurried to assist her in making the pattern. After it was done, she took it to the front of the room, holding it up for the others to see. "Lady Phillida has an excellent example you all would do well to follow."

A pleased Lady Phillida then offered to supervise a few others.

Somehow, the example failed to make it back to Lady Phillida. Instead, the girls got talking about fabric and yarns and how they would cut the slippers out. Marianna mentioned having a shoemaker come in to give a few hints. This idea was well-received by the chattering girls.

When the pupils all sauntered from the room, Marianna quickly made a copy of the outlines to give to Sir Alex. Then she restored the slipper pattern in with Lady Phillida's things while tucking the folded copy into her reticule. How devious she was becoming. She wasn't quite certain she approved of this aspect of her attempt to clear her name. She had been snooping, filching, and suspecting others of guilt. It would not do to acquire these traits permanently. Was this perhaps how

Lady Lavinia got started with her "borrowing," as her niece
had tactfully put it?

The remainder of her day was harried, what with having to
cover part of Miss de Vere's previous duties. Marianna thought
that Miss Chudleigh might have taken over a few of the tasks,
perhaps teaching the needlework. But then, it was possible that
Miss Chudleigh only managed and could not teach. Miss Teale
handled the French class with more expertise than Marianna
expected. She paused to listen outside the door while on her
way for supplies, and was most impressed.

Come dinnertime, Marianna gave Miss Chudleigh the look
and nod that told of her intended absence from the school. Then
she gathered up the reticule with the slipper pattern and heavy
key tucked inside to escape from the institution. She was more
than a little relieved that no one had dared to question her
regarding this almost nightly withdrawal. The girls seemed not
to care. Lady Phillida deigned not to notice; and Miss Teale
lived in her own little world, hardly paying any attention to
Marianna. It might have bothered her in the past, but now she
could only be grateful for it.

Gadsby almost smiled when he let her into the house and took
her pelisse from her. He ushered her to the drawing room, where
Sir Alex greeted her from a chair by the window.

Rising hastily, he said, "I trust you were successful? You
have that look about you of one who has done the impossible."
He sauntered across the room, all the while watching her face
most intently.

"Well," Marianna said modestly, "it turned out to be quite
simple, actually. I had all the girls remove their slippers and
draw the outlines. I used Lady Phillida's as an example, and
before restoring it to her, I traced it."

Marianna removed the folded paper from her reticule, handing
it to him with obvious curiosity. Good manners prevented her
from questioning Sir Alex, but she longed to know what he
intended to do with the information.

He unfolded the page, studied it a moment, then gave
Marianna a pleased smile. "Good girl. I am much in your debt."

He might have given her a kiss on the cheek, but for George's sudden appearance at the door to the room.

"Hullo. You are here."

"Obviously," Marianna said sweetly in reply. "I succeeded in obtaining the slipper pattern for Sir Alex and rushed it over for him. The penalty is that I must now find a shoemaker to visit the school and, it is hoped, give the girls a few suggestions regarding the cutting and sewing of slippers." Giving Sir Alex a mock glare, she went on, "See what you have brought upon my head?"

"What has the dear boy been doing now?" inquired Lavinia as she and the general entered the drawing room together.

Marianna hastily explained while observing that the lady's cheeks were a rosy pink tonight and her faded blue eyes sparkled with excitement. As well, her usually wispy hair was neatly done and covered with a marvelous turban made of pink and silver gauze. Her gown matched the turban, and was a design well-suited to her spare frame.

"How well you appear this evening, ma'am. Truly, you are in first looks."

Self-conscious glances flew between Lady Lavinia and the general. "Really?" said a flustered lady. "How kind of you to say so, dear girl."

General Eagleton looked as though he longed to open his budget, but George intervened. "I have some news to share."

Gadsby entered to signal that dinner was served, so the news perforce had to wait until the five were gathered about the table and the first course placed before them.

"Do not keep us in suspense, please, Lord Barringer," said a suddenly demure Marianna, enduring the narrow glance from George with equanimity.

"Had a report from Tom Crowdon this afternoon, late. That 'sailor,' the one Miss Teale was chatting with, has been seen. Tom trailed him, to discover he is not a sailor, as I had suspected."

"Well," urged Aunt Lavinia impatiently while George sipped his soup.

"As I stated, he is not a sailor, but a soldier. He is a sergeant in the militia under your command, General."

This announcement had the effect of a small bombshell exploding into the quiet of the dining room.

"Why do you suppose he disguises himself?" Lady Lavinia said.

"I wonder who he is?" Marianna said.

"And what does he have to do with Miss Teale?" added Sir Alex.

"Perhaps he is her brother, whom she meets to give things to, you know the sort of thing. That packet may have been mending, or some other item he requested of her," said the general with the air of one who knew about such things.

"I say it is decidedly odd," Marianna mused aloud, giving George a quizzing look.

"As do I," he replied, nodding at her with approval. "I would like you to find out what you can, at any rate, General Eagleton. How fortunate we met up with you in Mablethorpe. You are proving to be most necessary to us."

At this innocent remark, Lady Lavinia turned a delicate pink and buried her face in her napkin, as though about to cough.

When it came time for her to leave, Marianna decided that she would not allow a repetition of those delightful kisses tonight. George walked her as usual to the spot beneath the tree, then Marianna smiled up at him. "Thank you, George. I shall report to you tomorrow evening to hear what, if anything, has been learned about the mysterious sailor." With that brief remark, she took herself off quickly, lest she give in to the desire for another caress.

There was clearly no hope for George. He appeared to consider her in the light of a young woman who needed help. Nothing more. Oh, she suspected he quite enjoyed those stolen kisses. She certainly had. But she was not going to permit her heart to go into paroxysms of delight, only to be cast into depths of despair over him. No, indeed.

She slipped inside the school, feeling as though she had left that still-intact heart far behind her. With George, if truth be known.

* * *

George stood still for a few minutes, staring after Marianna until she disappeared, then at nothing in particular. He did not bother to roam down to the boat tonight. Rather, he went to the house and ordered a bottle of port to be brought to his room.

"Join me?" he asked Alex as he made his way upstairs. The general and Lady Lavinia were playing cards in the drawing room. George had no wish to join them.

Alex took a good look at his friend, then nodded. "Don't mind if I do." Better to keep an eye on George, and anyway, he was feeling rather gloomy himself. The two of them would be a matched pair tonight.

Marianna breathlessly made her way to the town house the next evening. It had been a full, harrowing day, what with trying to learn about making slippers and teach it as well. How welcome it would be to relax with friends for just a bit.

There was an air of suppressed excitement when Marianna entered the drawing room. She could feel the tension emanating from George and the general as well.

Hardly waiting for Gadsby to announce dinner, Lady Lavinia urged them all down the hall and into the room. "If I do not hear what it is you two have been concealing this past hour or more, I shall explode," she declared, glaring at George, then at her friend the general.

Once they were seated, served, and the servants had departed, George said, "I shall go first. I saw Miss Teale this afternoon." He smiled at Marianna's startled reaction to his words. So, Marianna wasn't the only one slipping away from the school!

"And?" Marianna demanded softly.

"She hurried straight to the waterfront and went for a little boat ride with her friend the 'sailor.' What do you think of that?"

"Most strange," Marianna replied. "Miss Teale has never put a foot wrong at school in the past. I can scarcely believe my ears. Why do you think they felt it necessary to take a boat ride, of all things?"

"We do not know about that . . . as yet."

General Eagleton cleared his throat, then said, "There is more. The man she meets is none other than Sergeant Rodney Teale."

"Her brother?" said an utterly absorbed Marianna, ignoring the delicious food on her plate.

"No," said the general with a sly glance at George. How these two men were enjoying their moment. "He is her husband. She is not Miss, but Mrs. Teale!"

13

"Miss Teale! Married!" Marianna dropped her fork to her plate unheeded while she absorbed this news. There was a stunned silence, then they all began to talk at once.

"What does it mean?" began Lady Lavinia.

"I cannot take it in," Marianna said, her eyes large and wondering.

"Well," added Sir Alex, "it does not mean that the woman is not guilty. I think it points the finger at her all the more." He looked at Marianna to see how she accepted this philosophy.

"You merely say that because you wish Lady Phillida to be innocent," George said with an annoyed glance at his friend. You did not allow personal feelings to intrude if you were going to be truly scientific in your approach to solving a problem.

"I shall attempt another conversation with that young woman and we shall see," Alex said with a dark look at his best of friends.

"When is your half-day, Marianna? Miss Teale had hers two days ago." George favored Marianna with a reserved glance before returning his attention to his dinner. He was still unhappy about her tearing off to the school last night. His head had felt simply awful when he arose. The effects of the port, no doubt. Yet he had somehow felt Marianna responsible for his state of ill-being this morning when he crawled from his bed.

Of course he knew she ought not spend that time alone with him, for propriety decreed otherwise. Yet he had wanted her there very much. And he hadn't stopped wanting her close to him. Right within his arms. It was a peculiar sensation and he did not quite know how to deal with it. He was so removed from society that he was not aware of what was proper. He well knew that a gently reared young lady was not to be trifled with in the least. But he found he wanted to do more than trifle. It made it difficult to look at her. Knowing that. And more.

"Things are in such a muddle. I shall be very glad when the term ends and the children can be returned to their parents, or to those who wish them returned. The others go to relatives or estates where a private tutor or governess awaits them," she explained at the confused expression on George's face. "I expect I can arrange to have my time off when I wish at this point—what with Miss de Vere gone and all. Why?"

"I may have need of you tomorrow." George gave her another cool look, one Marianna couldn't fathom in the least.

"I shall consider it. What think you, General? Do soldiers often keep marriages concealed? And do you have any theories on Sergeant Teale?" She bestowed an earnest look on him, one of faith and trust in his ability to guide.

General Eagleton gave her a kindly smile, then nodded at Lady Lavinia. "Livvy and I have been discussing it. We think they plan something soon. He intends to leave the area shortly; his serving time is nearly done. I say she has worked to earn the extra money so they can purchase a house or farm, whatever they seek to gain. I fear it does not mean she stole the sapphires, Sir Alex, much as you would like to think so."

Marianna caught the familiar name used by the general toward Lady Lavinia and also observed George was too preoccupied to take note of this closeness. A gentleman did not take that sort of liberty without the lady's permission. One of these days George was going to get an uncomfortable jolt, Marianna thought with satisfaction.

"I do not care for the woman," Sir Alex murmured in a low growl.

"What has that to do with anything?" Marianna said. "There are any number of people I do not care for, but that does not mean I consider them guilty of a crime." She tossed a significant glare at George that failed miserably, because he was not paying any attention to her.

The remainder of the dinner was spent offering arguments

pro and con regarding the remaining three suspects. Poor Betsy seemed the most favored target. While George considered Eloisa Teale capable of thievery, Sir Alex would not consider Lady Phillida culpable. So . . . they compromised on Betsy.

Marianna admitted, "Little Betsy has been looking rather guilty about something the past day or two. I should have to confess that it appears she has been involved in shady doings of some sort."

George and Alex exchanged inscrutable looks at this piece of information. Whatever passed between them was beyond Marianna to fathom.

"We saw you entering a shoemaker's this afternoon, Sir Alex," Lavinia said in an attempt to change the subject. "Are you purchasing new shoes, perhaps?" she inquired as the sweet course was brought to the table.

Marianna glanced up at this, hoping the mystery of what he wanted to do with the slipper pattern would be solved.

Sir Alex waited while strawberry sorbet was dished up before attempting an answer. "I wanted to discover something. The cobbler is a clever man, I'll grant him that. If my plan works out, I shall show you the results of my efforts, and soon."

With that vague remark, they had to be satisfied.

The following morning Marianna sought out Miss Chudleigh, requesting her half-day. It was met with a hostile expression.

"I believe it would be better were you to accompany Lady Phillida on a walk. Sir Alex has asked to escort her this afternoon. And Miss Sibyl seeks an outing with the general. All this jaunting about would never happen if the term were not about to draw to a close."

Giving the headmistress a puzzled look, Marianna replied, "She is going for tea, and I imagine Lady Lavinia will be with them. However, I shall be happy to go with Lady Phillida."

Marianna left Miss Chudleigh with a mixture of feelings. She had wanted time free for George. But perhaps this was just as well. She also desired to know what Sir Alex was up to, and what better way to find out? She sought out Lady Phillida.

Wary eyes glanced up when Marianna confronted Lady

Phillida in the schoolroom where the girls were working on the slippers. The shoemaker had come and was offering a bit of help before returning to his shop. "You wished to speak with me?"

The words in themselves were innocent, but the tone bordered on insolent.

"Miss Chudleigh has given permission for you to walk with Sir Alex this afternoon." When that piquant face lit up, Marianna added, with just a touch of satisfaction, "I shall be with you as chaperone."

It was almost comical to observe how that face fell in dismay, thought Marianna. How uncomfortable it was to be in Lady Phillida's company, knowing the girl thought her guilty of theft. Yet there was nothing Marianna might say at the moment.

"I shan't wish you to stay close to us." Those clever brown eyes danced with defiance. The chestnut curls were tossed ever so slightly as Lady Phillida turned back to her slipper with a tiny sigh.

Was she sorry she had made that accusation? wondered Marianna. The two of them had been fairly close prior to the disappearance of the sapphires. It had certainly been a shallow friendship, for it had dissolved at the first trial.

Nuncheon was quiet, as usual, for Miss Chudleigh frowned upon conversation while supposedly enjoying your food. It might have helped, Marianna reflected, to make the dreary meal more acceptable. Besides, how were these girls to learn the gentle art of conversing at the dinner table if they never practiced it? Not for the first time did she wonder at the peculiar ways of education.

Just before they were to depart, young Sibyl sought out Marianna, a shy smile on her sweet little face. She must take after her mother, for she resembled the general not at all. There was good bone structure and lovely hair, were it styled properly instead of being scraped back from her elfin features to a tight braid at her nape.

After some preliminary chatting, Sibyl got to the point. "You know Lady Lavinia, do you not?"

"Since I was a little girl. Why?" Marianna decided to ask. It saved time, she had noticed.

"Is she kind? She seems so, but ladies sometimes put on airs, you know. Would she help me with my hair and dress, and such? For you must know Papa is most serious about her. He told me he intends to wed the lady if she will have him. If she is wicked, I shall run away, for I do not desire to be under the thumb of a nasty stepmother." Wide eyes looked earnestly up at Marianna.

She couldn't refrain from a little smile. "She has the most tender of hearts and is a very wise woman for all her appearing a peagoose. You need have no fear she will turn into a jaw-me-dead once she is settled in your papa's lovely manor. I shouldn't wonder but what she would arrange a lovely come-out for you and find you a veritable prince of a husband. She has strange and wonderful gifts. It will be like having a fairy godmother rather than a crabby stepmother, I assure you."

"Gifts?" said an awed Sibyl. "You mean she is a witch?"

"Never," Marianna hastened to reassure. "But she can read the tea leaves, and quite often her readings come true."

At that young Sibyl wandered off in the direction of the front door. Marianna fervently hoped she had said the right thing. One never knew how words would be accepted once uttered.

Lady Phillida shortly joined her at the entrance. The dancing master entered, disappointing them both. He disappeared down the hall toward where Miss Chudleigh could be heard lecturing the older girls.

It was not long before Sir Alex, with George behind him, came to call. The gentleman would never have been allowed were it not close to the end of the term and Miss Chudleigh certain that the young miss would not be returning. Marianna also wondered if the headmistress was, in her own peculiar way, attempting to assist the investigation. She kept her own counsel.

Feeling much like a governess trailing behind her charge, though they were nearly of an age, Marianna followed Lady Phillida out the door. That young miss was batting those dark eyelashes at the baronet with remarkable success.

"And what think you of this fine day," Sir Alex asked.

"Girls are not taught to think, sir, for they might think differently than they ought," declared that pert miss, her chestnut curls peeking from beneath her yellow bonnet with saucy appeal.

"And I suppose you never do such a thing, or for that matter, read a novel?" teased Alex.

"Ah, no. Miss Chudleigh declares they inflame the passions of youth. She claims she must instill truth rather than stir the imagination. I suspect she picked that up from one of her books. She doesn't look to have such deep thoughts in her head, does she?" Lady Phillida giggled and limped along, for once seeming not to mind her infirmity.

"And I expect you have enough imagination not to require stirring?" He chuckled at her and hurried her along the street as though eager to reach their destination.

How entranced Lady Phillida seemed with Sir Alex. Yet only this morning Marianna had overheard her make a slighting reference to him. "He's only a mere baronet," she had said, and very coldly too. "But," the other girl had swiftly answered, "a baronet with pots and pots of money."

Money made little difference to Lady Phillida, as heir to her father's fortune and land, if not his title. But she would care about a man wanting her for that. Sensitive to her awkward limp, she had proclaimed often enough to Marianna that she hoped to marry someone who did not seek her fortune first and her last. Now it seemed she was just a young woman intent upon wringing a bit of happiness from the day.

"Quiet soul this morning," George commented, again riled that Marianna had swiftly slipped from his side last evening and rushed into the school as though someone chased her.

"Yes, well, I have a lot on my mind." She wondered if he had twigged to the upcoming nuptials between the general and Lady Lavinia yet. Perhaps women were more in tune to this sort of thing? Especially if one were inclined in that direction oneself?

"Spot anything of the maid this morning . . . anything unusual, that is?" George gave her a hopeful look, one that was wishing to make amends so they might return to their former standing, whatever that was, precisely.

"You know," Marianna said while keeping an alert eye on Lady Phillida and Sir Alex up in front of them, "I did see a curious bit. She had her arms full of stuff—said she was cleaning her room—when I came around the corner to find her going down the back stairs." Giving it a bit of thought, Marianna added, "I do believe she had everything she owned in that lot."

"Indeed," exclaimed George softly. "A most curious thing. Why did you not follow her to discover what was afoot?"

"Because a certain gentleman had as much as ordered me to get time away from school and Miss Chudleigh instructed me to trail after Lady Phillida. That's why." Marianna gave him an impudent look with those speaking sea-green eyes, tossed her lovely blond head, and then chuckled faintly at his expression. "Oh, Lord Barringer," she said with a darting glance at Lady Phillida, who was walking a shade too close to Sir Alex, "you are a wonder. I am teasing, you know."

"I suspected as much," George said wryly. "You have become a minx, I believe. Whatever shall your dear mother say to that?" He picked up her hand to place it firmly on his arm, tucked it against his side, then drew her just a bit closer to him. He could feel the sweet warmth of her body, catch that delicate rose scent of hers. This was quite definitely more like it. Whatever "it" was.

"Sir?" Marianna said, mischief dancing in her eyes.

George grinned. "I need to talk with you, and I certainly don't wish to shout to the whole world, do I?"

Marianna smiled. "True." She felt more in charity with him this morning, for it seemed the restraint of the past days had fallen away. She looked about her, suddenly realizing they were on a seldom-traveled street.

"Why are we walking down this street? Where is Sir Alex taking us? I cannot recall shopping here overmuch."

Marianna looked at the shops. There was a smithy, a cane weaver, a furniture maker, all shops devoted to practical things, not the pretty sort of frippery girls like to admire through a window—like fans and jewelry and fancy ribands.

"I expect he has his reasons. He has been deucedly closed-mouth about this business. Didn't want me along until I insisted. I figured Miss Chudleigh wouldn't let her out without a chaperone." He placed his hand over Marianna's, liking the feel of that delicately boned hand beneath his.

"I must say, 'tis a bit lowering to see myself reduced to that. How did you know I would be here rather than some maid?" She was surprised at his deduction.

The group slowed before the shoemaker's little shop and Marianna felt a surge of curiosity.

"Because you had promised to try to get off, and I knew that one way or another you would keep your promise to me. You always have," he said simply.

She flashed him a wondering smile, the sort that left him feeling like he had been hit in the stomach. "What a lovely thing for you to say."

Lady Phillida turned to Sir Alex, wonder and curiosity in her eyes. "What do we here, sir? I have no liking for shoe-shopping."

"You shall see." He ushered her into the neat little place, unusually so for a cobbler. Urging her to sit on a wooden chair, he greeted the shoemaker as one does a person one knows. "They are ready?"

From behind his back, the cobbler produced a rather odd pair of boots. One half-boot looked normal, the other had an odd piece fastened to it. Sir Alex knelt and reached for Lady Phillida's foot before she realized his intent. He removed her present half-boot, then took the built-up boot from the man. Slipping it on, he laced up the front. He performed the same task with the other half-boot.

"Stand," he commanded.

Lady Phillida gave him a stubborn look. "I do not believe I care for this."

"Phillida, for once in your life do the right thing with no argument, if you please."

Giving Sir Alex a haughty glare that would have stripped paper from a wall, she slowly rose, then stood before him, ignoring the others in the room. "Well?"

He extended his hand, a slow smile creeping across his handsome face. "Good girl. Try walking a bit."

"I cannot," she stated flatly, without making an effort to move.

He shook his head at her. "You aren't trying. Try. For me?" he coaxed, his winsome smile most pleasing.

She was not impervious to the charm in that smile. She took a step, then another, a look of wonderment coming over her face. "Most curious," she announced. "They are light as a feather, whereas I expected the one to be like deadweight."

"Aha," declared Sir Alex with satisfaction. "I got the idea from a fishing boat . . . the cork of the nets, you know. I obtained some, brought it to this excellent man, and he did the rest."

The shoemaker hazarded a small smile. "The gentleman had quite a bit more to do with them than that. Designed them himself, he did."

Lady Phillida took a few more steps, then joyously whirled about, not limping once. "How can I ever begin to thank you, sir?"

Alex gave her a sly grin. "I have already decided on that, to be sure." He paid the man, but not before placing an order for several more pair of the unusual half-boots in various colors and materials.

Leaving her old half-boots behind to be altered, the four walked on to the beach front in the general direction of Miss Hattie's Shoppe, where Sir Alex declared they were to celebrate with tea and cakes.

"You see, old chap," said Alex with a grin to George, "you are not the only inventive person about."

George glanced at Lady Phillida, then nodded. "I am quite sure that is true."

" 'Tis a beautiful day, is it not?" Lady Phillida gave a small skip of joy, seeming oblivious of any undertones in the conversation.

Marianna tried to overcome the animosity she felt toward the young woman whose allegation had done so much to create havoc in her life. What might yet occur, Marianna didn't know.

There was much implied, the threat of the constable still lingering. After her return Miss Chudleigh had told Marianna that she was being given a chance to produce the jewels before it was time to close the school. If they were not returned, she expected Marianna would face a trial.

George lagged behind the happy twosome, slowing to a near stop. "What is troubling you?"

"I fear I was thinking of Miss Chudleigh's warning. Time is running out. I must find and return those sapphires in a few days or 'twill be too late."

"You failed to pass that bit along for all that you were so eager to hand over the rest of the news." George gave a concerned look, then stared at the chestnut-haired miss ahead. In her gay yellow gown and straw bonnet, it was hard to conceive she was a dire threat to the happiness of someone George was coming to hold very dear.

"What would it accomplish?" Marianna said, wishing she had not spoken now.

"It might make us try harder." George glanced out to the harbor, frowning at what he saw.

They came to a dead stop. "Now, what?" said a puzzled Marianna.

"I believe that is someone we know." George nodded to the couple out in a little rowboat, then turned to Tom Crowdon, who had materialized at his side. "Any report?"

"I was just coming up to yer place."

"And?" came the terse reply from George.

"Mighty strange, if yer ask me. 'E takes 'er out fer a little ride, but all they do is argufy. Aye, a mighty odd couple."

"Interesting," was George's only comment to the tale. He thanked Tom, then turned to Marianna. "Is that so usual? Married couples arguing? It would seem that all is not bliss between Sergeant and Mrs. Teale."

"Depends, I suppose," replied Marianna, urging him along after the rapidly disappearing Sir Alex and Lady Phillida. It was quite plain that neither she nor George was missed in the least. "I still find it hard to accept her deception. How could they hope to keep it up?"

"I don't think they intended to do that. I believe that, once she got the sapphires, they would bide their time until you were accused publicly, then slip away from the scene of the crime, the sapphires in their bags. It would be a simple matter to dispose of the jewels later on, one at a time."

Marianna gave him a look of respect, completely forgetting the couple off in the distance. "You have thought it out very well. Where do you suppose they would hide those sapphires in the meantime?"

George shook his head in defeat. "That has me stumped. I have applied all scientific reasoning to the matter, and nothing comes to light. Did you know that the general cleverly instituted an inspection for the militia? Every item each man owned went through examination, a sort of clean-out, you know. He made some excuse for it, nothing close to the truth, so there couldn't be any suspicion from Teale. The general himself was present when Teale's stuff was checked. Nothing there. So if they have the jewels, they have hidden them most cleverly someplace none of us has considered."

Marianna saw the others had totally disappeared, and she collected her wits enough to pat George's arm to capture his attention. "We had best join Sir Alex lest Miss Chudleigh have real reason to toss me out on my ear."

George looked bewildered for a moment, then remembered why they were where they were, and set off along the walk at a fast pace. Marianna was thankful she possessed long limbs, or she undoubtedly would have found herself sailing through the air at his side.

At the tea shop, they joined Sir Alex and Lady Phillida. Both wore remarkably smug expressions.

"What kept you two?" inquired Sir Alex, though it was plain he truly didn't care about the matter.

"We spotted an unlikely couple out in a rowboat," George said, darting a glance at Lady Phillida. He desired to keep his theories regarding Mrs. Teale from the girl. He did not trust her. It was possible his own feelings about the Teales could be all wet, and Lady Phillida a clever liar. A bit of hugger-mugger would not be beyond the likes of that miss.

"I expect you have already ordered the tea. Did you find some lovely cakes as well?" Marianna said, thankful she could take a chair across the little table from Lady Phillida. She had no desire to be close to the girl.

"Yes," declared the young lady with evident satisfaction, though whether it was for the delicious cakes or for giving her chaperone the slip couldn't be told.

Sir Alex suddenly noticed the solemn expression of the two who had just joined them. He glanced to the happy face of the young woman at his side, then frowned, as though recalling something unpleasant. "And what was that particular couple doing? Merely going for an afternoon's ride?"

"Actually they were in the vicinity of the first buoy and doing nothing much other than arguing. Poor sort of way to spend an afternoon, if you ask me." George beamed a welcoming look at Miss Hattie, who chose to wait upon them herself, then applied himself to the fine tea.

Marianna was not sorry to return to the school. The strain of being polite to Lady Phillida began to tell in short order.

When she entered the door, she sensed something was amiss. Glancing about, she could see the school was not in its normal pristine condition. Quickly, she sought out the tweenie, who was cowering in the kitchen as if she might find a refuge behind the massive cook. Betsy was nowhere in sight.

"Is everything all right? I noticed the front area and stairs have not been dusted, nor have the dust bins been taken from the schoolrooms as usual. Where is Betsy?" For some odd reason she felt there was a connection between that furtive trip down the back stairs this noon and the present state of affairs.

"Ooh, miss," burst forth the tweenie. "Betsy's gone. 'E came an' got 'er, 'e did."

"Who?" demanded Marianna, taking a step toward the girl in her desire to find out the truth.

"Th' groom, from over to th' inn wot 'er's been walkin' out wi'."

Accustomed to this manner of mangled speech, Marianna

nodded in comprehension, then strode from the room, racing up the stairs in a most unladylike fashion until she got to the very top of the house. Here she entered Betsy's room, to find precisely what she had feared. "The girl has decamped, as I suspected. Why did I not take more notice of her earlier?"

It took but moments to face Miss Chudleigh, placing the facts before her in a rush. "She may be innocent, but her sneaking away from here is very suspicious. I want to try to find her. It means there will be no one to take care of my pupils. I had intended to have them do a bit of drawing."

"I shall see to them. You best chase down that impertinent maid. The nerve of the girl. She shall swing for this," declared the angry headmistress.

Marianna didn't bother to answer the obvious. The maid had taken a stupid chance to leave in the middle of the day when she was seen and could be traced. Had she the jewels in her things, she would be convicted before she could take in her breath.

Marianna ran as fast as she dared. At the stables behind the inn, she inquired politely for the groom, then went in search of him. She found him, to her great surprise. Betsy was there as well, deep in heated conversation that Marianna found barely comprehensible.

"Well?" The sound of intended intimidation worked. Betsy fell back against the stable wall, quite terrified. "I demand an explanation. And I should wish to inspect that baggage, my girl."

Normally Marianna would have shrunk from giving such an order. She had no liking for nasty people who insisted upon such intrusions. But her entire future could be in that cluster of belongings bundled neatly together as though the maid was not done yet with her flight.

Betsy, seeing she was not to be killed outright, came hesitantly forward, her hands twisting together in her fear. "Me an' Joseph, we's getting married. He's a place ter go to over in Ipswich." She knelt and opened her pitiful collection.

Marianna, hating every moment of it, also knelt and, one by

one, went through the items. Not one blessed jewel could she find. She could have wept. Instead, she sighed. "They are not here."

"What, miss?" the maid said, glancing at her groom with undisguised relief.

"Lady Phillida's sapphires. I thought, when you took flight, you had the jewels and were going to run off with them. Please forgive all this." She gestured to the clothing and precious things Betsy and the groom had managed to cadge away, now strewn about in the hay. "But why go in the middle of the day?"

"Miss Chudleigh, she locks up the place, come night. She don' pay no attention to the back stairs in the day. 'Twas the easiest thing, miss. I just walked out the door, an' that was a-that." Betsy gave her a troubled smile. "I sure am sorry about the jew'ls, miss. Be they going to hang you?"

Marianna swallowed carefully at the reminder of what happened to thieves at times, and shook her head. "I hope not." Then she gave the couple a few coins she found in the bottom of her reticule and added her blessing. Walking away a bit, she turned to find Betsy in Joseph's arms, being comforted in an age-old manner.

"Oh, drat," she murmured as she made her way back to the school. "Now what do I do?"

14

"This is certainly a mystification," declared Lady Lavinia that evening as she sat in the drawing room. The tea had just been set on the table before her. She poured out for each of the others, then herself. She absently sipped while obviously deep in thought.

"It reduces the suspects to two, does it not?" Marianna stared at the bottom of her cup, gently whirling the tea leaves about with a slight movement of her hand.

"I had been quite of the opinion that the maid was the logical one, you know. Poor thing, to run off like that. She must have been desperate," Lavinia offered with a sigh.

"Actually she looked happy, once I left them with the knowledge they were not going to be pursued." Marianna shared a small smile with her ladyship, a rather rueful one. For Lady Lavinia was not the only one who had hoped the maid was the guilty party. Marianna felt the presence of time and had hoped to put an end to this entire business. She believed Sir Alex desired to clear suspicion from Lady Phillida. And even though Eloisa Teale had turned out to be married—and Marianna was pleased at that bit—George most likely wished her name to be cleared. Why he had felt her to be innocent, Marianna didn't know. Although, come to think on it, he had presented a pretty convincing case against her while walking along to Miss Hattie's for tea and cakes. Perhaps it was merely a matter of opposing Sir Alex. Marianna had observed they indulged in a bit of rivalry from time to time.

"I believe we ought to set a trap," George said while he strolled up and down the drawing room. It made Marianna dizzy to watch him, so she returned her gaze to the rapidly cooling contents of her teacup. She took a long sip, thinking cool tea would feel good on her suddenly dry throat.

"I think that to be a sound notion, my boy," General Eagleton said. "What sort of trap?"

"Tell each of the remaining suspects that I believe I know where the jewels are concealed." George stopped his pacing, fixing his gaze on the general with the air of one who has reached a conclusion he is not willing to share at the moment.

"What will that accomplish?" Lady Lavinia said. She was willing to go along with most anything her dear nephew dreamed up, but to announce a discovery when there clearly was no such thing seemed a little foolish to her.

"Now, Livvy, George wants to frighten her. If she thinks someone has twigged to her hiding place, why, she will be apt to head straight for it, don't you know?" The general reached to place a reassuring hand over the thin one on Lady Lavinia's lap.

Watching them, Marianna wondered what had happened to the lady's inclination to snitching things that didn't belong to her. Was it as Samantha suspected, merely a ruse to bring two people together? Interesting thought. Just as long as the dear lady did not complicate life by reverting to past tendencies now. It was to be hoped the attentions from the general would prevent such a thing.

"Alex, I'll leave you to drop the word in Lady Phillida's ear," George announced, turning to give his good friend a quizzing look. "And I'll trust you to keep a watch on her, discreetly, of course. Just remember that if those jewels are not found, Miss Chudleigh has no choice but to inform the constable."

"I, for one, simply do not understand why she has not done so already. Why cast doubt, then do nothing? It seems such stupid behavior on her part," Lady Lavinia said. Then she added, as if in sudden inspiration, "Of course, I could see where she does not wish to let it be known that there is thievery in her school. A bad reputation is not to be desired; it could well bring ruin to the school and all her hopes for the future. But what will happen to our Marianna?'' she asked, a frown creasing her forehead in her concern.

"It means that Marianna could go to trial. Alex, make certainn that Lady Phillida understands the seriousness of her charge. If she is as kind and good as you insist, surely she cannot realize what the result will be for our friend. There are but a few days before Marianna's time is up. There is no real proof that Marianna took the gems, and the fact that she returned to the scene, rather than run away, must count in her favor. 'Tis Lady Phillida's claim that Marianna was the only one who knew the location of the sapphires that pins the crime to her. It could well be that others figured out where they might be kept."

Lady Lavinia had gasped at the news of the shortness of time. She turned to General Eagleton, distress plainly written on her face.

"True," added Marianna. "The room is not large and how many places can one store priceless jewels?"

"You have the right of it there. Actually, it might be one of the other schoolgirls. Have you searched the other rooms?" George demanded.

"Of course," replied Marianna. "The school was quietly gone over from top to bottom . . . by Miss Teale and Miss Chudleigh. Miss de Vere took the girls on an outing for the day while the hunt went on."

"And where were you? Were you able to protect yourself from being implicated? It would have been easy to have planted the gems in your room," Lady Lavinia said.

Marianna shook her head. "Had that been done, the thief would not have had the jewels to pawn, or whatever she desires to do with them."

"True," reflected Lady Lavinia. She searched the bottom of her cup, absently swirling the contents about, then turning the cup upside down on the saucer, before righting it again so she might read the leaves.

General Eagleton sat quietly at her side, watching the procedure with intent eyes.

"There is a swallow in the bottom of my cup," she announced.

"What does that mean, Livvy?" inquired the general.

"There will be a change for the better in every way." She looked at Marianna, who clung to her cup.

"I think not tonight," Marianna replied to the unspoken question hanging in the air. "If there is bad news, I would rather not hear it for the nonce. And if it is good, I shall enjoy the surprise." She rose from her chair, placed the cup and saucer on the tray, then turned to George. "I believe I shall depart now. Tomorrow promises to be a busy day, if rumors travel as quickly as they usually do."

Sir Alex confounded George by walking to Marianna's side. "I shall escort you this evening. George has had the pleasure of your company for too many walks, I believe." He made a faintly ironic bow in George's direction, then walked out the door with Marianna at his side.

"And what, pray tell, was the meaning of that?" she asked as they sauntered down the front steps of the house.

"George is far too sure of himself. At least, he seems complacent. I thought to shake him up a bit."

Marianna could see the flash of his grin in the faint light provided by the oil lamp at the end of the walk. They hurried along to the school, then before she ascended the steps, he said, "I imagine you harbor ill feelings for Phillida."

"What I feel is wounded, angry, perhaps frustrated that neither Lady Phillida nor Miss Chudleigh was willing to listen to me. You see, I know I am innocent. It hurts to think an old friend or someone who has known me for years would so quickly believe my guilt." She turned, preparing to walk up the steps when he detained her again.

"Remember that first reading Lady Lavinia did before we left Mayne Court? She said that there was jealousy and spite involved with the theft."

Marianna nodded. "Something like that, yes."

"Don't you see, Phillida feels no spite toward you—nor jealousy, for that matter."

"Perhaps not now, but then? Now she has your attentions to please her. Then she was limping along, teased by some, although well-enough-liked by most of the girls at the school.

At the time, it could very well have been the truth of the matter.''

"I confess I hold her dear to my heart and I do not like to think ill of her.'' Sir Alex glanced up at Marianna, and in the dim light cast by the school's lamp she could see he looked worried.

Giving him a shrewd glance, Marianna said, "If there is a flaw, 'tis best to know it beforehand. Perhaps she took a position; then, once taken, she found it difficult to back down from it. I hope so. What shall you do about her?''

"I am deliberating on that daily. I shall let you know in due time.'' With a jaunty tip of his hat, he walked away from the school.

Marianna hurried inside and up to her room. The look on George's face had been something to see, she reflected as she removed her gown and hung it up. Perhaps it was a good thing for him to be thwarted once in a while. He had gazed at Sir Alex as though his pet puppy had bitten him.

As she snuggled beneath the worn quilt on her bed, she hoped the rumor would do the trick, that the thief would show her true colors. Marianna had strong suspicions, but one needed more than that to unearth the sapphires.

"Spreading yourself about, Alex?'' George said in a low sort of growl as his friend returned to the house. The precise length of his absence had been noted. The viscount made a point of restoring his pocket time piece, then studied Alex's face.

"I wanted to speak with Marianna,'' said Sir Alex, somewhat defensively in view of George's pronounced glare. "There is no need for you to behave like a jealous dog guarding his bone.''

"Is your interest fixed elsewhere, then?'' Goerge inquired as one might about the price of tea.

"Perhaps.'' Sir Alex gave George an impatient look, clearly not wishing to discuss the state of his heart at his hour, although when in London he was frequently up much later, indeed, until dawn at times. But it was difficult to manage that in a household where so much went on in the mornings and there was nothing to do late at night.

"We shall join the young ladies for their morning walk,"
George instructed. "I will suggest we go along the sea for the
view. You will plant the information we want to spread abroad
then?"

Sir Alex glared at George. "Yes, damn it all, I shall do the
deed. I am tired. I shall see you, come morning." With that
blast, Alex flung himself from the room and was shortly heard
thundering up the steps.

"Well, well, well," was George's only reaction to the
outburst. However, he wore a pleased expression on his face.
When he strolled up the stairs to his room, he did so with a
considering look, a light step, and humming a happy little tune.

As the double line of girls paraded their way along the street
toward the sea, Lord Barringer, looking precise to a pin, and
Sir Alex, also in top form, joined them.

"Lovely day, Miss Teale." While he tipped his hat in
greeting, George had to remind himself to use the singular form
of address. The woman *was* married.

"Nice to see you again, milord." She seemed extraordinarily
glad to see him.

George glanced back to where Marianna marched along
toward the sea. The girls were like a line of lemmings, intent
on their destination, come what may.

They strolled along toward the sea-front walk, George
commenting on various sights along the way. At last the
collection of schoolgirls, gentlemen, and teachers reached the
harbor, such as it was. Clearing his throat, the viscount made
his announcement in a rather offhand manner.

"I imagine you will be pleased to know that the sapphires
believed to have been stolen have been found."

The lady at his side froze for a tiny moment, then assumed
a pleased expression. Had not George been watching with intent
eyes, he would have missed that little pause.

"I am so very happy for Miss Wyndham. She must be in alt
at being relieved of the suspicion of theft. Tell me, if you can,
where did they locate the gems?"

"I fear that is a secret for the moment. I assure you that all shall know the truth soon. Very soon," he promised.

"Miss" Teale subsided into an introspective silence, absently watching the girls as they chattered to one another.

Farther toward the rear, Sir Alex squared his shoulders and said to Lady Phillida, "You cannot have them returned to you as yet, for there are a few loose strings to tie up. But you will be pleased to know the jewels have been found."

"I am glad. Who was it? Or can you not reveal that yet either?" She spoke in low tones, her brown eyes seeking his for confirmation.

Sir Alex looked down at the delightful face that peered at him from beneath a decidedly smart bonnet, and nodded. "Correct. Like I said, there are a couple of things to clear up first before the discovery can become general knowledge. I trust you shall keep this private? Let it be a secret between us for the moment."

Lady Phillida smiled at the notion of so charming a thing as a secret between her and this elegant gentleman. "Of course I shall keep the news to myself. What fun! I adore secrets." Continuing with their walk, she gave him a thoughtful look. "You enjoy secrets, then? You are very good at them."

"Not all of the time, but there are moments when it is necessary. Phillida, one of these days there is something we must discuss." He gave her a searching look, then turned his attention to the walkway ahead of them.

"I return to my home next week, Sir Alex," she reminded him.

"I know. All will be clear before then," he murmured somewhat obscurely. "But I desire you to know that my intentions are quite honorable."

Before she could comment on that startling and most welcome remark, Lady Lavinia and General Eagleton were observed coming toward them.

"Your friends, I believe," Lady Phillida said quietly in a manner Alex could only respect. "I shall quite understand if you should wish to join them."

"No, no, they are merely out for their usual stroll."

"They seem on rather good terms," Lady Phillida said with the knowledge that comes when recognizing a lady in love while one is in that same state.

"Yes, I expect something shall come of it before too long. Poor George," he murmured as his friend walked forward to join them.

"Why do you say that?" she replied softly.

"He won't know what hit him."

Sir Alex chuckled a bit nastily, Marianna thought as she walked up to catch the last remark. She said nothing, wondering about what was to hit George by surprise when he seemed so aware, so sure of himself today.

Lady Lavinia and the general strolled along with the pupils and their teachers until they reached the school. Lady Lavinia inspected the edifice, then murmured to the general, "I shall be glad when our Marianna can leave that place. I cannot think it the best place for Sibyl, either. That dear child is near an age when she ought to make her come-out, perhaps in London." She sighed, then said, "I tried to persuade my niece to go to London. She always declared it too dangerous."

"And so it is for some, dear lady."

She gave him an arch look. "Not with the right person in charge."

George observed all this, then turned to Sir Alex, his eyebrows raised in question. "You look as though you know the answers to questions I haven't thought of, my friend. Why so smug?"

"Another day and I feel in my bones we shall have the problem of the missing sapphires solved." Sir Alex rubbed his hands together in anticipation of that happy moment.

"Really? I will do what I can to bring it about, then. I shall see all you later." With a polite nod, George left the others, who were intent upon reaching the house and the prospect of nuncheon.

Walking along at a brisk pace, George returned to the waterfront, where he stationed himself in an out-of-the-way place and waited. For what, he wasn't quite sure. Or for whom, he supposed, for he had a pretty good idea as to the what, where, and why of the matter.

The minutes ticked by at an agonizing pace. The viscount tried not to appear conspicuous, engaging another gentleman in casual conversation about the state of the nation, always a safe way to guarantee a chat.

Then he saw what he had hoped to detect. He had smoked out the woman, just as he expected. Excusing himself, he strolled to the pier edge for a better look. Positioning himself close to a shack built to hold tackle and gear, he watched as Eloisa Teale clambered into a rowboat. She slowly and most awkwardly made her way out to that first buoy. There must be something about that spot, he mused.

Keeping to the shadows, he maintained vigil while she leaned over the edge of the boat. What she was doing he couldn't see, but shortly she straightened, then turned the boat once again for shore. At the beach, she hopped out, smiling broadly as she paid the young chap for the use of his boat, then strode off in the direction of the school.

Most interesting. George found his good assistant, Tom. They looked out to where the buoy sat, then to where George's boat was located. Low conversation, fortunately overheard by no one, was followed by Tom going one way and George heading for home. He whistled a merry tune and walked with a jaunty step.

At the house, he plumped himself down for a late nuncheon, not minding that his favorite food was in short supply: the others had consumed most of it.

He ate hastily, then hurried up to his room to change into nankeen pantaloons and the jersey favored by fisherman. Dashing down the stairs in short order, he was back at the waterfront in time to greet Tom as the diving boat nudged along the side of the pier.

"Fast work, milord." Tom grinned at the sight of the most unlikely lord in the kingdom, given his attire.

"Let's go, Tom."

The boat took off from the pier in as inconspicious a manner as possible. It helped greatly that to the far end of the waterfront a band of jugglers had begun to perform, presenting a free show to one and all. There was hardly a soul paying attention to the sea or any craft going out.

Once out in the harbor, the boat slowly began to sink. Bubbles came up from around it as it disappeared from sight. George had wanted to wait until evening, knowing his unusual boat would cause comment, but he wouldn't be able to see much of anything then and it was most important that he view what was at the bottom of the buoy.

"That was a good idea to hire those jugglers. Fancy your finding them traveling through this part of the world just when we happened to have need of them." George gave Tom a wink, then they set to work.

The buoy wasn't difficult to locate. The line went snaking down to the rocky bed beneath. Attached to that line was a most curious sight. George pointed it out to Tom, then ordered the boat up once again.

On the surface, George stripped his jersey from his strong torso, pulled off his boots, then dived from the side of the boat. Tom stood watch. An occasional bubble rose to break on the slightly ruffled water. Seconds ticked by. Then George appeared once again. He was holding a sack.

"Help me aboard, will you, Tom? I have something very special in this little bag." He shook the water from his hair, then swam to the side of the boat while tightly clasping the sack in his hand.

"Gladly, milord." Tom smiled broadly, then reached out a hand to give an assist.

Once again safely on board and wrapped in the warmth of the jersey, George opened the bag to find what he had hoped to find. "They are here," he declared. "We can make for shore. I'd hate to have those jugglers finish their performance before I gain purchase of the pier and am off to the house again."

"Aye. You look a mite wet," Tom replied in an understatement of the fact.

At the pier, George pulled on a pair of dry stockings, then

his boots. The fishermen's jersey helped to blot up the moisture that clung to his body.

General Eagleton's carriage was waiting for him as planned. George hopped inside to sit on an old blanket, giving the general a triumphant look. "We were right. She knew just where to go. And so did I." He gave the sack a smug pat.

"Livvy said they were near the water, as I have been told," reminded the general.

"I told you we had to listen to her. She's a wise old lady," George said, wrapping the blanket about his thighs, which were beginning to feel the chill of the air, for the day had become cloudy.

"Oh, not so old, I think," countered the general.

"Hmm?" George said absently, planning the events for the remainder of that day as well as the next. He would conduct the rest of this project with scientific order. A plan of action would be laid out most carefully. Nothing would go amiss now . . . for he had the evidence.

The general did not answer, merely smiled to himself. The viscount was in for a surprise or two. The general tooled the carriage along to the house, then handed the reins to the groom with a complacent air.

Once he had changed from his wet pantaloons and was suitably attired, Lord Barringer sauntered down the stairs, then out the front door. He strolled along to the academy, where he requested to see Miss Chudleigh. There was a stern-looking, lean scrap of a maid who ushered him down the hall. Miss Chudleigh did not waste time in replacing her maid, he noticed.

"Good afternoon, Lord Barringer. What may I do for you?" The lady was clearly surprised, for she had not expected to see Lady Lavinia's nephew in her office.

"A simple request, nothing more." When he chose, George could be most persuasive. He had found it useful in times past with his Aunt Lavinia. Now he applied his smile and easy grace to the matter at hand. "I should like to invite Miss Wyndham, Lady Phillida Jarvis, and Miss Eagleton to our home this evening for dinner. I trust that it will present no problem? I deplore such short notice, but something urgent has come up, you see.''

The woman had thought herself immune to male charms. She learned otherwise as Lord Barringer leaned toward her, smiling in his innocently direct way. There was none of the roué about him, nothing of the rake in the least. Rather, here was a true gentleman, nicely requesting her aid. She could comply, especially since it cost her nothing to win that smile of approbation.

''I am sure that can be arranged, milord. The young ladies have nothing planned other than a bit of music. Miss Wyndham usually conducts that. I have a notion the girls will not be crushed to miss it.''

''I trust the musicale can be scheduled for another time. I shall send the carriage for them, if you will be so good as to give them these notes?'' He rose, bowed to the exact degree that was proper, then strode from the room, relieved to get that business out of the way.

When the three young women, all mystified as to why they had been summoned to Lord Barringer's house for dinner, left the carriage and entered the house, they could sense a festive air. Or perhaps it was the masses of flowers about? The drawing room looked especially nice, Marianna thought, and she told Lady Lavinia so.

That lady gave a vague smile, smoothed her gloves somewhat nervously over her hands, and nodded.''George took it into his head to have them.''

Which remark told them absolutely nothing.

Lady Phillida drifted over to stand by the window. Sibyl seated herself near Lady Lavinia, while Marianna strolled over to stand by the fireplace—now dark, as no fire was needed.

General Eagleton entered to greet Lady Lavinia, then turned to his daughter with a proper display of affection.

Sir Alex and George walked in shortly after that. George hung back a trifle. With a hint of a smile, he noted his friend's reaction to Lady Phillida's presence. Then he applied himself to the other guests, Marianna lastly.

''What are you up to now, George? Or ought I say Lord

Barringer, with all these others about?'' Her sea-green eyes teased him and a mischievous gleam crept into those delightful eyes even as he met her look. As much as he irritated her at times, she could never resist his charm for long.

"Just you wait, my dear. All will out in good time.''

They stood chatting most casually, George keeping careful track of his friend, who was rapidly recovering from the sight of Lady Phillida in the drawing room, where he didn't expect to find her.

"I vow I was most surprised to be invited here, of all places,'' whispered Lady Phillida to Sir Alex, casting a glance at Marianna, who was clearly a favorite of the house.

"I confess I knew nothing about it. I am happy to see you grace this room, my lady.'' He turned to study George, wondering what he was up to now.

Lady Lavinia smiled at the very shy Sibyl, then her dearest Henry. Very soon she would have to inform her nephew of her future plans.

Gadsby entered and announced dinner with a flourish not usually offered. He led the way, overseeing the seating in an unobtrusive manner. Then the most excellent meal commenced.

The cook had outdone himself. Everyone said so, from Lady Phillida—who really had little background, but knew good food when she tasted it—to Aunt Lavinia, who couldn't recall approving this menu in the least, but enjoyed it immensely.

Course followed course, wine flowed until they were all quite jolly and somewhat rosy. Even Sibyl was permitted a sip of delicate white wine. Another year and she would be preparing for her come-out. She best learn to judge and know good from poor.

When the last of the main courses had been removed and the butler stood stiffly at the door that led to the kitchen, George rose from his chair at the head of the table. All eyes turned to him.

He cleared his throat, then smiled his most disarming smile, directed at his dear aunt. "I believe an announcement is in order. General?''

Clearly astounded, General Eagleton slowly got to his feet,

stammered slightly before getting a reassuring pat on the hand from Lady Lavinia, then spoke. "As matter of fact, there is. I don't know how you twigged to it, but your dear aunt has seen fit to accept my offer of marriage."

There were gasps of pleasure and a coo of delight from Sibyl.

"Henry was concerned lest I not want to give up my title. The title of wife is the best I know. His wife, that is." She beamed her happiness, drawing off a glove to reveal a lovely engagement ring of diamonds and blue topaz, which the general said reflected her eyes.

Toasts were drunk and much merriment ensued. Just as they all began to chatter, the door opened and Gadsby entered with an elegant cake before him. He placed it in front of Lady Lavinia and the general. "Our compliments, milady. We all wish you happy."

"And it is only the first of such events," George murmured. Only Marianna heard his remark and wondered greatly what was going on in that surprisingly devious mind.

15

The cake was delicious. Marianna wondered how the cook had contrived to create something so special in such a short time. She detected currants and thinly sliced peel along with the taste of almond, mace, wine, and brandy. What with the sugar and spices having to be pounded and sifted, not to mention the egg whites beaten for simply ages until stiff, this had taken planning and hours of advance notice.

How had George known?

Glancing at him over her flute of champagne, another item that had to be arranged in advance, she decided George was a man of many parts. Those eyes saw more than suspected, and that brain of his, usually absorbed with things scientific, could be applied to other areas as well.

It was a most promising notion.

Her gaze shifted to where Sir Alex and Lady Phillida sat opposite her. How grateful she was that she had been placed next to Sibyl. She seemed to sense how uncomfortable Marianna was, and made an effort to smile and chat with her. It was greatly appreciated.

"A toast," urged Sir Alex, raising his glass in the air.

The others joined in the clamor until George stilled them with a raised hand, then cleared his throat.

"To the best in Christendom," George declared, giving his aunt the most fond of smiles.

"Hear, hear." The sentiment brought a tear to Marianna's eye, and she bent her head to wipe the offending drop away after drinking to the happy couple.

Lady Lavinia beamed at them all, looking, Marianna

thought, much younger than the forty-odd years in her dish.

How glad Marianna was that she had worn the raspberry gown trimmed with blond lace that had been saved for something special. Contrary to Aunt Lavinia's expectations, the color had not seemed to catch George's eye. Or had it? Marianna wasn't so sure about him anymore. He had thrown her into a complete tizzy and she did not know what to think, at least regarding him.

The champagne consumed and the cake reduced considerably in size, they pushed back their chairs and all strolled off to the drawing room. No lingering at the port for the gentlemen tonight, apparently.

Marianna found George suddenly at her side, like he had materialized out of thin air. Or had she been preoccupied?

"Miss Hattie does well with bride cakes, does she not?" His voice was low and intimate, sending flutters all through Marianna's slim body. What a mercy it was that he had no idea of the effect he had on her. How those eyes would gleam with silent laughter if he but knew.

"You were down by the waterfront this afternoon? What else did you do while there?" For some reason, perhaps the way in which he looked at her, Marianna found her hopes rising.

"That remains to be seen, my curious little bird. By the by, lest I forget to tell you later,"—he bent his head so his mouth was close to her ear, sending more of those little thrills coursing through her—"I am very fond of raspberries and cream."

She flashed him an amused look. "So am I." How pleased she was with her self-possession under this strain.

"Ah, but I have a distinct advantage there, for I can view it as well as consume." With that parting shot, he strolled from her side, leaving Marianna simmering, and not knowing why in particular.

Yes, George was certainly coming out of that absentminded shell of his, and with most amazing results!

"What a lovely gown," Sibyl whispered in a breathless but sweet voice as she joined the frustrated Marianna. "Did Lady Lavinia assist you in buying it, if I may ask something so bold?"

"Pish-tush, girl," Marianna replied, taking control of herself once more. "Don't be a peagoose. She did help me, and I suspect that when she takes you to hand, you will find yourself staring at the mirror in wonder. She has an amazing way with color for one who leans toward white herself."

"What a comfort to know. I so feared a stepmother who would hide me away, or worse. One hears stories at school, you know. Poor Lady Phillida, her parents will probably contract a marriage for her with the first likely man." Sibyl studied the chestnut-haired beauty. "She looks happier than I have ever seen her before. Would it not be lovely if Sir Alex and she were to make a match of it?"

"I must say, he cared enough to create that special half-boot for her. Look, you can see a toe peeping out from beneath her gown. She wears a boot of satin with yellow gilt buttons this evening to go with her gown. If she goes to London, she would be in high style."

Sibyl looked down at her own little foot, wearing a kind of sandal shoe laced with riband. Marianna thought the Grecian sandals vastly becoming to such a dainty girl and said so.

"Oh," Sibyl said, blushing a lovely pink, "I could not hope to outshine you or Lady Phillida, but I thank you very much."

Across the room, Lady Phillida was indeed shining—blooming, as matter of fact, thought Alex. "I trust you are enjoying the evening."

"I vow I do not know why I was included. How Miss Wyndham looks daggers at me when she thinks no one watching." Lady Phillida gave a troubled look in the direction of that person, then turned her gaze back to Alex. "When will the thief be announced? I would have my friendship with Marianna restored, for I have missed it sorely." At the skeptical reaction he could not conceal, she added, "I have been so foolish. Jealousy ill becomes one. But she is so lovely and talented and can do anything. I was so certain she was the only one who knew where I hid my sapphires. I felt it had to be her. Yet something deep inside me tells me I made a terrible mistake and I know not how to rectify it now."

His face brightened. "You are eager to have the name of the thief revealed?" As far as Alex was concerned, her attitude and words proclaimed her innocence. Why did George wait like this? And draw promises from others to keep his secret?

Removing the bowl of flowers from the clavier, George motioned to Marianna. The instrument was usually pushed to a corner, since none of the Mayne household present was in the least musical. Tonight it had been brought forward to a more prominent position.

"I believe it is more than time for us to enjoy a bit of music from our teacher." He appeared very serious, but Marianna could see his eyes dancing when she met his gaze.

Reluctantly joining him beside the clavier, she seated herself, then began to play. She was not a brilliant performer, yet she had a style and a certain delicate feeling that the listener could not help but like.

Lady Phillida tapped her foot in time, her satin boots making little sound. When the music ended, Sir Alex rose, extending his hand to one who had never danced, who had lingered in corners and behind potted palms all her school days. Over her shoulder, he requested, "A dance, Marianna. Something lively."

Her eyes large with wonder, Lady Phillida rose, then curtsied. "I should be delighted, sir." Taking his hand, she moved out into the center of the drawing room to begin the pattern of the dance. Lady Lavinia found herself drawn out and George offered to partner Sibyl.

Smiling in spite of herself, Marianna kept the tunes lively and steady, slipping from one to another as she did for the dancing master's class. Someday, she vowed, she would be out on the floor with a handsome partner rather than seated at the clavier. Although this was a handsome instrument, even if not a modern pianoforte, but well up to snuff and a joy to play.

After a number of dances, Lady Lavinia begged to catch her breath. The general looked as though he welcomed the notion of a cool drink.

George nodded to the butler, who had been stationed just outside the entrance to the room. Within minutes there was lemonade, sherry, and Madeira placed on a side table. While the general saw to the wants of his lady, George drew Sibyl to the clavier.

"I should like to partner Marianna in a dance. Sibyl, I know you have been taking lessons; give us a sample of your talent."

He gave the girl one of what Marianna considered his overwhelming sort of smiles. Sibyl melted at that look and agreed with alacrity.

Marianna glared at the man. How could he place the girl under such a strain?

Sibyl dimpled, however, and seated herself with composure. "I welcome the opportunity to show my papa how well I have learned from Miss Wyndham."

Allowing herself to be led to the center of the room, Marianna was pleased to hear Sibyl bring forth a sprightly dance tune, well played, in good meter, and with few mistakes.

"George," Marianna whispered furiously when the pattern of the dance brought him close to her, "what *are* you doing? What is going on here tonight?"

"Why, we are celebrating the engagement of my aunt and the general. What else could I possibly be up to, my dear?"

"You forget how long I've known you." Why did she bring that up? she wondered. He would be reminded of her years and that she was no longer a sweet young girl coming out in society. If she didn't know him better, she would say he was courting her. However, knowing him as she did, that was unlikely. Of course, he had been doing any number of odd things as of late. Her head in a whirl, Marianna followed his lead through a complicated dance, enjoying every moment of it.

Eyes sparkling, feet happily following Sir Alex's lead, Lady Phillida thought she had never had so good a time in her entire life.

"The boots work well?" Sir Alex whispered to her as they drew close in the pattern of the dance.

"Marvelously well. I can never thank you enough." She still wondered what he would claim as a reward for his gallantry and thoughtfulness. The ideas floating through her mind had teased and tantalized her for hours on end.

"I shall have to decide what my compensation is to be, my lady. And since you intend to depart from here soon, I suppose I must make up my mind quickly. Will you object to my choice, I wonder?"

The look in his eyes took her breath away. What would Alex

say? What did that look promise? She took a deep breath and wondered very much.

Marianna also wondered, but for more prosaic reasons. Things seemed to be drawing to a close, the girls were soon leaving for their various abodes. School was nearly over until the fall. General Eagleton and Lady Lavinia were planning a simple marriage quite soon, she suspected, if the gleam in that gentleman's eyes were any clue. And that meant her time was upon them. Or her, as the case might be.

She permitted George to guide her through an intricate step even as she wondered where on earth he had learned all these things. Indeed, he was truly a man of many parts.

At the top of the school building Mrs. Eloisa Teale paced the floor of her neat little room, not seeing any of the things she had spread out, ready to pack. Best to be prepared. That was the needful.

She hadn't been able to get word to her husband that they must meet first thing in the morning. She planned to eat her breakfast as she normally did. It would never do to call attention to herself. That stupid maid, Betsy, had done that very thing. It was as well Eloisa had nothing to hide, at least nothing serious.

In the morning, she could again bribe the delivery boy to take a note for her. He was the only one she had trusted, since he was not dependent on Miss Chudleigh.

With methodical care, she precisely folded each item, then placed it in the trunk she had herself had toted down to her room while the others sat in the drawing room with Miss Chudleigh, learning to make polite conversation.

Once her belongings were tidily stowed, she removed the last of her things, the letters from her husband, where she had kept them in the scarred little desk. Oh, for the money that would be theirs so soon. They could have a small, neat place, but the finest of interiors. The sapphires would buy the highest quality of furnishings, and Eloisa desired that very much.

Not for her the drudgery of the classroom any longer. She would move anywhere Rodney decreed, and set up housekeeping with enough of everything. He would not regret marrying her. She had promised he wouldn't. It had taken careful guile to snare the man; she didn't want him to leave her as she feared might happen were things to go against them.

She drew off her clothes, hanging her dress on the peg for the last time. Then she slipped on her night rail and crawled under the threadbare sheets and worn coverlet for her final night's sleep in this dismal place. Tomorrow loomed as an auspicious day in her life.

"I said the swallow in my cup would bring a change for the better in every way," Lady Lavinia said to the group as they assembled for a late tea.

Sibyl had played quite nicely for several dances, then begged off. Her papa had declared himself most pleased with her playing, not to mention the fine instruction she had from Marianna.

Marianna blushed and bent her head over her teacup.

Sir Alex cast a narrow, calculating glance at George. "And what about your nephew?"

Before his aunt could make any sort of disclaimer regarding his care, the viscount spoke up. "I have Peters, you know. And the housekeeper at Mayne Court has been well-trained. I trust I shall rub along tolerably well. I had the notion I might do over the gardens. Aunt has left the house in excellent repair for my father and me, so there is naught to be tended to there. What think you, Miss Wyndham? Should the gardens be redone?" His casual look revealed nothing of what might be in his mind. Really, George was most provoking this evening.

Incensed that George had the temerity to ask her something regarding his future life that undoubtedly did not include her, Marianna took a fortifying breath, then calmly replied, "I should think a sculptured garden, one of those topiary sort, would be just the thing for you, Lord Barringer. You could spend countless hours devising clever frames for an entire zoo of animals. Why, it would be the wonder of Yorkshire." She congratulated herself on the blandness of her voice. Smooth as sateen, it had been. Not for a moment could he guess she was seething inside.

"Odd, I had the notion you felt I ought to do something else. Just shows you never can tell for sure what another is thinking, can you?'' He gave her a disconcerting stare, then that slow, intimate smile that sent flutters through her.

"Quite true, my lord." She bowed her head most properly. Had she been standing, she would have given him a curtsy worthy of a court presentation. Drat the man.

Oxford seemed to loom much closer in her future than it had a week ago.

"Well, and I am sure that were George to do a garden of that sort, it would be most superior. Mayne Court has been many unusual things over the years," Aunt Lavinia said with agreeable composure.

General Eagleton removed a letter from his inside coat pocket and cleared his throat to gain attention. "I wish to give you all another piece of news this evening. 'Tis something I learned late this afternoon by post. Lady Lavinia is not the only one who shall be changing a name."

They exchanged puzzled looks with one another at this strange turn of events. "Who, dear?" Lady Lavinia ventured to say.

"I have the pleasure to announce the creation of Baron Eagleton, myself, that is. I shall be plain Henry Eagleton no more. My little Sibyl shall go to London as a baron's daughter. And Lady Lavinia shall be Lady Lavinia Eagleton. Is that well with you, my dear girl? 'Tis a reward for my years of faithful service to the crown." He bestowed a loving look upon his betrothed.

"Henry! I declare. What wondrous news you have to tell us. And you waited until now? Naughty boy. I believe that calls for more champagne"—she turned to her nephew with an anxious look in her eyes—"if we have some?"

Gadsby appeared in the door bearing a tray with said champagne and glasses, along with little thin biscuits for those who wanted something with the sparkling wine.

"I ordered some sent over, once I heard," inserted the general, now baron. "The excellent Gadsby was merely awaiting my signal."

"This evening is becoming more and more exciting. What next, I wonder?" said Lady Phillida, chuckling softly while she gazed at Sir Alex over the flute of champagne in her hand.

"And I shall have to address my letters to the Right Honorable the Lady Eagleton," teased Marianna. "My, how grand that sounds."

"I wonder how she shall address letters to you?" murmured George from where he now stood close to Marianna's side.

"Oxford, I expect," Marianna said dryly, having no illusions on her future at this point.

"I have something I wish to ask of you. Could we not draw close to the window while the others chatter over their champagne?"

She didn't miss the "of" that had been inserted. Now what was to be politely demanded of her? She had snooped, pried, chased, done about everything, all of which, she admitted, had been in effort to clearing her good name. "Yes?"

As they strolled along across the room, George tucked her free hand close to him, bending his head as though in pleasant conversation. "I want you to stick like glue to Mrs. Teale tomorrow. Do not permit her from your sight. If she becomes angry, pretend ignorance. Anything. But try your best to cling to her company."

Marianna shook her head. "You ask the impossible, sir. I told you she keeps to herself. Were I to follow her about, it would seem most peculiar."

"Can you not make some excuse? Use that clever mind of yours." He stopped before the window, examining the lovely face before him with a careful eye. The candlelight did beautiful things to her hair and skin. Almost as lovely as moonlight.

"You are the man with the inventive mind, sir. Perhaps you might think of a likely reason why I might stick to her side when we have never been close in the past."

"Ask her advice about Oxford. Tell her you wish the benefit of her experience when setting forth to a new school. Everyone likes to give advice." He looked very remote as he stared at her with that inscrutable look on his handsome face.

Nodding dumbly, Marianna heard the word "Oxford" ringing about in her head like a church bell that refused to stop clanging.

At length she replied, "I shall try. If you find me with a knife in my back, you will know the reason," she joked.

The inscrutable look vanished. "Now, see here, Marianna, you don't think she would do violence? I won't have that.'' He appeared genuinely upset.

Marianna was somewhat appeased at that display of concern. ''No, I don't actually believe she would. One never knows about other people, though.'' She gave him a considering perusal. ''They can become strangers overnight.''

''Witness Lady Phillida.''

''I know she changed overnight when the jewels disappeared, but what is strange about her now?'' Marianna wondered aloud.

''There is a nice turnabout of her attitude since Alex designed that new boot for her.''

''I have been curious. How did he know how much cork to allow for her boot?'' Marianna studied the nice little satin half-boot that could be glimpsed when Lady Phillida moved about.

George chuckled and Marianna wished with all her heart that she might have the privilege of hearing that endearing sound the rest of her life. ''He told me he paid attention to how tall she was when she stood on the right foot versus the left. He figured it out from that.''

''What a perceptive man!''

''He is not the only man who can be perceptive,'' George retorted in a low voice.

''Hah,'' Marianna teased, her heart not entirely in it. ''You see only as far as your current project.''

''Do you really believe that?'' he asked, seeming hurt by her remark.

''I do,'' she declared stoutly. ''Once this present business is finished, you will retreat to that dratted barn of yours, not to be seen other than at meals, if then. What will your next project be? I wonder. What bit of curiosity will lead you down another scientific pathway?''

Over on the far side of the room, Lady Phillida observed, ''It would appear that Lord Barringer is arguing with Miss Marianna. Odd, he seems like such an unruffled sort of man, like nothing much bothered him.''

''He's a good-enough chap,'' admitted Sir Alex. Continuing on with the thread he wished to pursue, he said, ''How do you feel regarding the general's elevation to the peerage? A baron is a notch higher than a mere baronet.''

Lady Phillida gave him a startled look. "I expect it might matter to some," she replied with care. "I believe it is more important what a friendship, or whatever relationship it might be, is like. Trust and love are of the highest value." She gave a sad glance to where Marianna stood.

"So, you could manage to care for a fellow were he not of the peerage?"

"Aye," she said thinking she much liked the turn of the conversation. "If I truly loved a gentleman, I should agree to marry him regardless of rank—if he asked me, that is." She peered up at him, the candlelight bringing darting flames into her chestnut curls.

"I perceive you catch the intent of this discussion very well," Sir Alex said, his considerable charm revealed in his smile. "Would you do me the honor of permitting me to call upon you and to seek out your father?"

"Are you asking me to marry you, Sir Alex?" she said with her usual forthright way. Her feminine wiles had never been honed due to the lack of agreeable suitors. A crippled girl does not attract the sort of gallantry an heiress usually does.

He glanced about the room, a rueful grimace curing his mouth. "This is not the proper time, nor place. But as you implied earlier, time is flying past us. I am declaring myself, my heart, fair lady."

She gave him a direct look from those soft eyes. "And I accept your offer, Sir Alex. I shall be Lady Phillida Dent, and quite happy with that, I assure you."

"We shall have lands and funds aplenty, should you wish to travel. There is nothing we can't do." His voice was soft and coaxing, and he wished he had not given his promise to George to remain silent regarding the finding of the jewels. He would have asked Phillida to marry him regardless. But would she believe it?

Glancing down to her foot, she softly replied, "I can well believe that, sir."

"Well, then, shall we?"

More perceptive than he realized, Lady Phillida had sensed undercurrents in the room that had nothing to do with the engagement or the newly acquired title. "I should like to wait a day at least to reveal our future to the others. I have no wish to steal attention from Lady Lavinia. Do you mind?''

"I can well understand that, my lady. I shall post over to your family home as soon as we are finished here to do the deed. And we shall wed promptly. None of this long-engagement business.''

"As a threat, I find it quite agreeable.'' Phillida giggled at his expression and stood smiling at him, sure she appeared as besotted as she was.

General Eagleton glanced at the clock, then spoke. "I hate to break up this delightful gathering, but Sibyl must needs return to that school lest the dragon eat her.''

Sibyl laughed. "Oh, Papa, she is nasty, but she shan't eat me when she hears my news. She shall be most impressed, I'll wager.''

"Well and good, my puss. But I believe you need your bed.'' The general, now baron, gave her a pat on the arm, then ushered her toward the door.

Lady Lavinia bestowed fond farewells on all the guests, giving Marianna an especially warm hug. Having a great liking for the dear lady and happy that her life was taking so agreeable a turn, Marianna hugged her back.

Lady Phillida walked toward the front door, smiling gently at Sibyl. "I expect we all had best consider our sleep. Tomorrow is nearly upon us.''

Glancing warily at George, Marianna concurred. "Yes, indeed. Tomorrow will be here before we know it.''

"In fact, by the time your sleepy head touches the pillow, if I make no mistake,'' George added.

He was downright scheming, decided Marianna, and she wished she knew the whole of it.

The younger ladies floated out to the waiting carriage with much laughter and giggling. George and Sir Alex took the groom's place and drove them the short distance to the school.

"Good night,'' Phillida said, mostly to Sir Alex. "It has been a most memorable evening.''

"That it has,'' Sibyl agreed with a delightful sigh. She climbed up the steps to the door; then, when Marianna had unlocked it, she slipped inside.

"I expect we shall see you all tomorrow," Marianna said to George. "I can only hope that all will go well. You know something you aren't sharing with me. And that is all right, for I am aware there are times when one thinks it is impossible to do that sort of thing. But also know that I am a person to be depended upon. I shall endeavor to shadow the lady in question tomorrow. Do your part, and I trust all shall go as you wish." She dipped a faint curtsy, then she also slipped inside the door behind Phillida.

They walked up the stairs, each totally absorbed in their own thoughts. Parting at the top, Marianna went to her room with a mind much occupied.

Lady Phillida waltzed into her room on silent feet, but feeling as though her joy had given her wings. She could walk with these special boots. She could move about like any other woman! If there were tiny doubts plaguing her this moment, she could only pray they would soon be resolved.

At the other end of the building Marianna sat on the edge of her cot, removing her slippers and stockings. What would tomorrow bring?

How delightful this evening had been, at least for Lady Lavinia and Baron Eagleton. Sibyl, as well. And for Lady Phillida to dance for the first time was truly wonderful. How happy she had seemed, glowing with what was undoubtedly love for Sir Alex. Would that it was returned and that something good came of it.

While it had been a perplexing, aggravating time for Marianna, she never did begrudge happiness for another. Perhaps she might find something, or someone, at that school near Oxford. A nice, bookish professor, maybe. She sniffed, not certain she wished to have anything to do with another absentminded-type man again. Wiping her eyes, she dropped her handkerchief on her cot.

She placed her stockings in a neat pile with the handkerchief to be washed, then remembered she ought to remove her modest jewelry from the precious raspberry-and-cream gown. She would carefully stow the pin away in tissue. It was then she made her discovery. The pin was missing.

Her dragon was gone!

16

Marianna dragged her protesting body from her bed with the greatest reluctance the next morning. She had spent far too much time searching for that precious dragon pin, worrying about where it might be, and hoping she might get the pretty little thing back.

Now it was necessary to get to work. George demanded she trail Mrs. Teale. It was hard to think of the woman as married when Marianna had called her ''miss'' for so long.

Slipping into her neat navy-blue muslin, Marianna looked longingly at the raspberry gown trimmed with blond lace that hung on the next peg. How remote last evening seemed now! It had been so lovely to dance with George, to celebrate the good fortune of Lady Lavinia and Baron Eagleton. Last night was another world, and far from the life she was most likely to find in Oxford.

Tomorrow she would write that letter, she promised herself. Tomorrow.

Mrs. Teale was just leaving her room when Marianna opened her door. She followed the other woman down the stairs to the dining room. Everything seemed normal. At least it looked normal, at any rate, if the dour expression on Mrs. Teale's face was anything to go by.

Since the older woman rarely spoke at breakfast, it was not surprising when she silently sat eating the lumpy porridge and cold toast with the thin marmalade Miss Chudleigh favored for the school. Marianna had occasion to enter Miss Chudleigh's private rooms before her dishes were cleared away, and had noted thick, heavenly-looking marmalade and the remains of creamy porridge. The cook had two different recipes, it seemed.

Deciding to make an attempt at conversation, Marianna cleared her throat. "The porridge is worse than usual this morning, is it not?"

Clearly started, Mrs. Teale glanced sharply at Marianna. "I suppose so. I merely eat it to keep from going hungry. I would not mind if I never saw the dratted stuff again as long as I lived."

Taken aback at the spate of words that had flowed from the usually taciturn woman, Marianna merely nodded in agreement. "I noticed it is rather cloudy outside. I do hope we are not expecting a storm."

These innocent words drew a surprising reaction from Mrs. Teale. She grew very pale and turned to give a worried stare out of the window.

"Is something the matter, Miss Teale?" Marianna congratulated herself that she had remembered to change her form of address.

"Matter? Not really. What do you plan to do once the school closes for the term, Miss Wyndham? Are you to seek a position elsewhere? Or do you return to the bosom of your family?"

There was an odd note in that voice that Marianna could simply not identify. But how fortunate that Mrs. Teale had brought up the subject of Marianna's future. It provided the ideal opening. "I do not know, actually. I saw an advertisement for a position at a school not far from Oxford. What do you advise? I expect you have had more experience with the teaching world than I," Marianna concluded tactfully.

How curious to see Mrs. Teale straighten and preen herself slightly. She bestowed a superior sort of smile on Marianna, saying, "That I have. I know of the school. It is quite good, actually, if one does not mind removing to that part of the country. The proximity to Oxford can only be a plus, you know. Such a fine academic community, with so many means of improving the mind."

"I had not considered that aspect. Perhaps I ought to apply, for you must know that I cannot remain here under the circumstances." Marianna surreptitiously studied the pleasant-faced woman at her side. It was most fortunate she should decide to unbend today, of all days.

"If you have the opportunity to make the change," said Mrs. Teale in that same tone as earlier.

Marianna then realized what that odd inflection had been in Mrs. Teale's voice. It had the distinct ring of spite. "Why would I not be able to seek a position at the school near Oxford?" Marianna said with some caution. It was not as though she expected the other woman to drop poison in her teacup or plunge the bread knife into her back. But there was a strange feeling that persisted, and it made Marianna uneasy.

"Who knows what might occur? Each day can bring unexpected changes to one's life." Changing her subject, she said, "Lord Barringer told me Lady Phillida's sapphires have been recovered. Is that true?" She took a precise bite from her last piece of toast, gazing at Marianna with speculative eyes.

"How would I know what Lord Barringer has found?" Marianna said carefully.

"I believe I saw you, with Lady Phillida and Miss Eagleton, go off in General Eagleton's carriage last evening. Is that not correct? Or did, perhaps, my eyes deceive me?"

"Yes. I have an acquaintance with Lady Lavinia, as she lives near my home." Then she added, as much in honesty as a desire to avoid the subject of the sapphires, "And I knew Lord Barringer as a boy. However, you must know it is no longer General Eagleton. He has been elevated to the peerage as a baron, and is now to be called Lord Eagleton. I think it a fine thing for him, and Sibyl as well. She is a sweet child and deserving of a fine marriage."

"Worthy people do not always get what they deserve. But then again, justice is served in a rare instance." This was stated in a soft musing tone that had a peculiar inflection.

Marianna felt distinctly uncomfortable. It was not the words, but the delicate insinuation that could be detected by a sensitive ear. Seeking to divert Mrs. Teale from the subject of just desserts, Marianna cleared her throat, then said with a sprightly smile, "I nearly forgot to share the best news. Lady Lavinia and the baron are to be married shortly. Miss Sibyl will have the best of help when she goes to London for her come-out.''

''How lovely. You did not have the felicity of a come-out in London. Are you not envious of Sibyl, Miss Wyndham?'' came the insinuating reply.

''Of course not, not really. I should have liked the balls and the pretty gowns and all that sort of thing, but there is little point in crying over what cannot be. Do you not agree?''

Mrs. Teale looked down her slightly thin nose at Marianna, then declared in a soft, almost-menacing tone quite at odds with her nice appearance, ''I fight to get what I want. Only the weak are satisfied with less.'' Having said her piece, she pushed back her chair from the table and left the room.

Hastily dropping her napkin beside her plate, Marianna did the same. Out in the hall, she espied Mrs. Teale going up to her room. Marianna followed.

Mrs. Teale remained there only a short time. Marianna was glad she had concealed herself when she observed Mrs. Teale exit tugging an unwieldy trunk behind her.

The furtive look cast about the deserted hallway seemed to satisfy Eloisa. She managed to tow the trunk to the back stairs, then struggled with it while going down.

Normally Marianna would have rushed to assist, or at least suggested the pot boy be brought up to help. Now she waited, listening for the thumps on an occasional step. At each landing there was a sound of the trunk being pulled along, then the occasional thump again.

In the distance was the noise of the girls, chattering as they made their way to classrooms. As she neared, the clamor of the kitchen could be heard, the maids preparing for the day to come. Marianna kept just far enough behind so as not to be seen, yet close enough so she could know what was happening.

At last the back door was reached and Mrs. Teale went out, pulling the trunk along behind her.

Marianna hurried down the last of the steps, then opened the door a crack to peek out. Eloisa Teale was standing beside a cart, ordering the trunk to be delivered to some address Marianna couldn't catch.

Pausing a few moments to watch as the cart pulled away from the back of the school, Mrs. Teale then set off in the opposite direction toward the sea. Again Marianna followed.

She wished she had on her light cotton pelisse, for the cloudy sky brought a cooler temperature. At least her navy cotton was a sensible gown, not to mention hardly one to be noticed in the early-morning light.

The rising wind tugged at Mrs. Teale's bonnet, and the woman increased her pace. Marianna hastened to catch up with her. It was difficult to trail her far enough behind so as not to be observed, yet close enough to see where Mrs. Teale was going and perhaps guess what she intended as her destination.

When they neared the pier, Marianna was glad to glimpse a sight of George to one side of an old shack. He was dressed in a peculiar rig, nankeen pantaloons, large ill-fitting boots, and that jersey so favored by fishermen. Perhaps he intended it for a disguise? Marianna would have known him anywhere, but she suddenly hoped Mrs. Teale did not. If he kept his head down, it might work, she decided.

Rather than going out on the pier, Eloisa Teale strode across to a young chap on the beach and spoke for a few moments. Never once did she cast a look in the direction of the shack. Then she got in one of the small dories. She was pushed off the shale and was soon headed for the first buoy.

How Marianna wished she had a spyglass to see what the woman was going to do. She walked briskly to the shack, still watching the figure in the boat.

"Thank you for doing as I asked," came a husky voice from behind her.

Jumping slightly, Marianna blurted out, "Well, I confess I was most curious. What is to happen now?"

"Yes, old boy. What is to happen now? We are curious as well." George and Marianna turned to discover Sir Alex and Lady Phillida standing a short distance from them. They were to the far end of the shack, where there was no possibility of Mrs. Teale seeing them.

"I shall explain later. Hide for now. If I am not mistaken, the sergeant is about to arrive." He motioned the three into the foul-smelling hut, then leaned casually against the boards of the door frame, watching.

Lady Phillida sniffed, then wrinkled her nose in distaste at the odor of fish that permeated the small space.

"What are you two doing down here at this hour of the day? And how did Lady Phillida escape Miss Chudleigh?" Marianna demanded to know. Her whispered question brought a wry grin from Sir Alex.

"We wanted to be in on the end, so to speak. I do believe our George has solved the crime and is about to come up with the evidence." He quite neglected to reveal how he had spirited Phillida away from the school, with only the new maid to witness the bold departure.

Wide-eyed and wondering why George hadn't seen fit to confide in her last evening, Marianna crept close to the door. She could not hear a thing and it was most aggravating. She picked up a pole and pried open a narrow window that had been glazed with salt spray until a misty gray and finely etched.

What she saw was quite shocking. "Oh, my goodness," she whispered in amazement.

"Can you see something? Tell us," demanded Lady Phillida.

"I do believe Mrs. Teale has slipped off her dress and is diving into the water," announced Marianna in a hushed but astounded voice.

Then the sergeant came into view. He stood near the end of the pier, watching Mrs. Teale, or rather the dory she had used and was now tied to the buoy.

Minutes dragged by. Tension mounted within the little shack while they waited for Eloisa Teale to come to the surface of the water. "I wonder if she has succumbed?" said Lady Phillida.

"No chance of that," said Sir Alex. "I'll wager this is not the first time the woman has done this sort of thing."

"I see her now," Marianna cried softly, so as to not attract attention to the shack. "She is climbing into the boat and I do believe she looks most angry. Or is it frightened she is? For I suspect she has seen her husband. Is it possible all is not as expected?"

Marianna watched as Mrs. Teale donned the plain cotton print dress she had worn at breakfast. Then the woman untied the dory and rowed to shore as fast as she could. "She certainly is in a hurry. She'll pull her arms from their sockets if she tries much harder."

"Her husband is waiting for her on the beach now. He does not appear too happy. I wonder if he thought she ought to have waited for him?" Marianna strained to see what would happen at the confrontation between them.

"Perhaps he believes she tried to get whatever was attached to that buoy only to abscond with it," Sir Alex said in a cynical tone.

"Oh, I think not. I gathered from what George said they appeared most devoted to each other," replied Marianna, sorry to see a touch of the old Sir Alex appear after being absent for so long.

"Maybe she fancies her husband has taken whatever it is," Lady Phillida offered while she clutched at Sir Alex's strong arm.

"Hush," Marianna cautioned. "They are walking out on the pier now. They will surely hear us if we do not keep our tongues still."

George shifted from his position in the shadows cast by the morning sun. He felt sure that he blended in with the scenery. No one had paid the least attention to him this past thirty minutes. He had heard the whispering within the shack and was thankful now he'd no need to rap against the wall to silence them. Nothing must happen to prevent the proper conclusion to this affair.

"I tell you," said Mrs. Teale heatedly, "it wasn't there. You think I don't know what that sack looked like? And me the one that sewed it up nice and tight?"

"Then where is it?" came the nasal voice from what Marianna presumed to be Sergeant Teale.

"I only wish I knew. Who could have known they were hidden out there?" she whined, gazing at him with a pleading expression.

"You been snoopin' about the buoy this past week?" demanded the sergeant in a rather nasty manner. He grabbed hold of Eloisa Teale as though he intended to give her a good shaking.

She looked away from him as this query. In a defensive voice, she replied, ''When I heard Lord Barringer say he had found the jewels, I had to check. And we rowed out there together, don't you forget that. Mayhap he saw us?''

''Those sapphires was our ticket to a fine house in a respectable area of Ipswich. Without them, I'll leave you behind and go my own way.''

''But you're my husband,'' she whimpered.

''An' what has that to do with the matter, I'd like to know? I don't need you anymore, Eloisa. I'll get me a younger, prettier lass who knows her way about in bed. That's another failure you can tote up on your list. No sapphires, no luck, dearie.''

He was about to walk away from her when George stepped forward, leaving the shade behind him. The sun shone down on a different man from the one who had slouched in the shadows of the shack. Even in his outrageous clothing, Lord Barringer looked precisely what he was.

To Marianna he seemed suddenly taller, stronger-looking, more intimidating than ever in the past. He was not a man to be trifled with in the least.

''I say, have you lost something? Perhaps I can be of service?'' George took another step forward.

''Lord Barringer,'' cried a dismayed Mrs. Teale.

''What have you to do with this?'' demanded the sergeant in an insolent manner. He had glanced about, had noticed that his arrogant lordship had come alone. What had the sergeant to fear from this man? The clothes he wore didn't make the lord any more powerful. Who would come to the aid of a poor sailor being tossed off the pier? Particularly if the man who tossed him was laughing like it was all a huge joke?

He took a step forward to stare at George, his eyes then catching sight of a small canvas bag in his lordship's left hand.

''What's that?'' he wanted to know.

''That's the bag I sewed for the jewels, Rodney. Grab it and we can make an escape,'' Eloisa said in a shrill voice.

''Aye,'' said the sergeant slowly. ''Who's to know that this here sailor is other than he seems? Drunk, are you, my lad?

Well, an' I know the trick to cure that. A plunge in the sea is what you need.''

He took another step forward, but George didn't move at first. Then the sergeant gave a particularly nasty laugh and used a word Marianna had never heard before. It didn't sound nice and apparently angered George.

The viscount swung with his right fist, neatly felling the sergeant in one punch.

From beside her, Sir Alex gave a small chuckle. "What would Gentleman Jackson say to that?"

Mrs. Teale crouched at her husband's side, anxiously patting his face in hope of bringing him around. Glancing up at his lordship, she demanded of him, ''Those jewels, give them to me.'' At her side, her husband stirred, then attempted to rise. Eloisa reached into her reticule to pull a small gun from its depths.

Marianna didn't know much about guns, but she suspected that even a small one could be lethal this close. "Oh, no!"

Lady Phillida ran to the door, yanking it open. "Give her the sapphires, Lord Barringer. I would not see you hurt for a mere handful of stones."

"He would not be hurt, my lady. He would be dead," Eloisa declared in a tight, hard voice, totally unlike her normal schoolteacher tone.

George reluctantly handed the sack over to Eloisa, who then pulled her husband to his feet. Still aiming the gun at his lordship, she glanced at the contents of the sack, then up at George, smiling her satisfaction. Holding the gun carefully trained on George, the couple backed off the pier.

"Did you have some plans you failed to tell me about, my man?" inquired Baron Eagleton in a cold, hard voice.

The sergeant spun about and turned so pale one would have thought him about to faint.

"In fact, I'll hazard a guess there are any number of things you have neglected to relate, are there not?" To Mrs. Teale, the baron said, "I'd like to know what is in that sack that you hold so tightly, madam."

"I'll not show you," she said in a low intense voice.

"Show me, George," ordered the implacable voice.

The trio from the shack had left those smelly confines to follow George and the Teales to where they now stood before the general and a line of men, all with guns aimed most carefully at the Teales.

Lord Barringer walked up to take the gun from Mrs. Teale's hand with slow deliberation. With the gun removed, Eloisa was merely another woman, and a pathetic one at that.

Removing the sack that had been clutched so tightly, George slowly opened it.

Behind him, Lady Phillida held her breath, clasping the hand Alex offered.

Marianna stepped forward to see the jewels that had caused such upheaval in her life.

Thrusting his hand into the sack, George withdrew it inch by inch. If intended to tease and taunt, he succeeded well. All in the cluster about him stood as if under a spell. Then it was out. Instead of sparkling sapphires, a rather plain necklace with dull blue stones—undoubtedly mere paste—came forth.

"What?" gasped Mrs. Teale. "Why, that's not what's supposed to be in there! I put the sapphires in that sack I made with my own hands. Where are they now? Decided to keep them for your own?" She began to laugh, a most shrill and chilling sound. Only when her husband struck her across the face did she stop.

"Hold your tongue, you stupid woman. Ain't you done enough damage with your blatherin' mouth?"

Behind them, Baron Eagleton motioned to one of the men. Within short order, Eloisa Teale and her husband were being marched along the street in the direction of the militia grounds, hands bound, heads bowed.

"I thought you really had found the jewels," Marianna cried in dismay, seeing her freedom once again in jeopardy.

George grinned at her, reached into a pocket of his pantaloons, and pulled forth a small linen-wrapped parcel. He held it out to Lady Phillida. "I believe this belongs to you, my lady. I always like to see a satisfactory ending to one of my projects."

Most carefully unwrapping the linen, Lady Phillida sighed

with pleasure. "My sapphires! Oh, I am so pleased. How can I begin to thank you, Lord Barringer? They were an inheritance from my maternal grandmother and I should have hated to lose them. Forgive me, Marianna." She glanced up. "Lord Barringer? Marianna?"

Rapidly disappearing across the street in the direction of the rented house was Lord Barringer. He appeared to be in pursuit of Marianna, who was sailing along as though moved by the wind.

"Whatever is going on, Sir Alex?" Phillida gave him a bewildered look from her lovely brown eyes.

"I have a very good hunch. Now, as to us, my dear. Shall we not return to the academy, gather your belongings, and drive a post chaise to your home? I most earnestly desire a conversation with your father." Sir Alex bestowed one of his famous smiles on his little love.

She would have to write to Marianna as soon as possible and hope she was of a generous and forgiving nature by then. Entirely forgetting about the puzzling Lord Barringer and Marianna, to whom she owed the most abject apology, Lady Phillida placed her hand upon his arm and meekly replied, "Yes, my dear. We most certainly shall do as you wish." Especially when it was what she wished as well.

George went tearing along the street, heedless of his rather strange appearance. "Marianna," he shouted in a manner guaranteed to raise eyebrows were there anyone about to hear him. Fortunately there was not a soul about on the increasingly cloudy day. It looked about to rain soon.

Marianna continued to march hurriedly along the walkway, ignoring the shouts, determined in her intent.

George captured her arm and impatiently drew her to a halt.

"Unhand me, sirrah." Marianna looked at the offending hand rather than face him.

George would have none of that. "I have rescued you from possible hanging and all you can do is to run away? Fine lot of thanks you give a man." Exasperation rang clear in his voice. He had felt that at the very least she might cast herself into his arms in gratitude. He had not expected flight. He positioned himself so that he could recapture her easily should she take a notion to run again.

"I give you my thanks, Lord Barringer. Now let me go," she insisted in a small, sad voice, keeping her face averted.

"At least have the goodness to tell me what is wrong." He slowly released her arm, watching lest she run again.

"Wrong? I'll tell you what is wrong. You and your blasted projects, that is what is wrong, sirrah." She scowled at him. A blond curl flopped down over her eye in a rather endearing manner. She didn't look so terribly prim or proper now. "That is all you can think about, those miserable projects. Who cares if a person can dive a boat in the water or sail a flying machine across a meadow if it absorbs all of your waking hours? And what good does it do, actually? You are so totally wrapped up in one thing or another that you forget to live."

She glared up at him, looking lost and adorable and so terribly desirable that it near made him ill with wanting her. He placed his hands on her arms once more, careful to note any tendency upon her part to kick out or whatever she might take a notion to do to free herself.

"I did this for you, you know," he said in a low growl. "I knew you were innocent of any crime. And I proved it, too. Now you are free of any shadow, free to go on with your life."

"I thank you again, sir," she said primly. "I shall post that letter to Oxford at once." She gave him a tremulous look, wishing she could run to her room and bury her face in her pillow.

"Oxford, is it?" George took a closer look at her face, then relaxed a mite. "Aye, Oxford. Shall I help you to pack? You can bring your trunk to our place until you hear word. I feel certain you cannot bear to remain at that school another day."

She compressed her lips and whirled about, marching off in the direction of the town house with ever greater determination.

At her side, George commented, "I suppose they have a milder winter in Oxford than they do in Yorkshire. It takes a strong, dedicated woman to endure those Yorkshire winters." He looked down at the averted head, its tiny chip-straw bonnet barely clinging on, what with the bouncing it was getting.

Without glancing at him, she retorted, "Your Aunt Lavinia managed well enough. My mother, too, for that matter."

"And you? Could you manage it? Could you spend long winter evenings by the hearth of your home with a husband seated across from you, children playing about your feet?"

"You paint a pretty picture, Lord Barringer." A faint sniff was heard.

She was weakening. George was sure of it.

They reached the front of the house. George gave it a puzzled look. "Why are we here? I thought you would be going to the school. Am I not to help you pack? And what about Miss Chudleigh and the students?"

"Miss Chudleigh can glue the pupils together with porridge for all I care. I have something I must do first."

He followed her up the walk and into the house, nodding absently at Gadsby as they entered. "What, my love?"

She ignored him and his fancy words, which probably meant nothing. "I want my dragon."

"Your what?" He was clearly perplexed.

"My dragon is missing. Your aunt . . ." She said no more for George, quick to twig to the problem, had turned to the butler.

"The Lady Lavinia?"

When told that lady was in the drawing room, George and Marianna continued their march into the charming room with grim determination.

"I believe you have something that doesn't belong to you. Is it possible you somehow 'picked up' the dragon pin?" George demanded of his dearest aunt in a reasonably kindly manner, given how sorely tried he was at the moment.

"Well, I couldn't imagine why Marianna would want it now. After all, what good are sad memories? I take it the sapphires are safely returned to that widgeon?"

"Yes," George replied, absently answering the question. "Why sad memories, Marianna? Has it all been so very bad?" He studied the downcast head, the bonnet now dangling by ribands and golden curls tumbling about in delightful abandon.

"I shall have no memories at all, Lord Barringer," Marianna

denied frostily. Turning to Lavinia, she said, "I did like that little pin, and if I was so foolish as to lose it here last evening, I would have it now, if you please, Lady Lavinia," she said with a deal more tact than George.

Standing behind Marianna, George gave a sideways jerk of his head in the direction of the door.

Aunt Lavinia smiled wistfully, then confessed. "I did take it. For it is so cunning, you know. He winked at me. I shall get it immediately." She rose, then silently swished from the room.

"I had thought to make a special topiary," George said in a musing, yet coaxing voice. "I got to thinking about what you said. It would be a project that would takes years and years to complete. A man could grow old working on such. Why, my children doubtless will have to finish the job."

"Congratulations," Marianna said, turning away with a deplorable sniff and wishing desperately she had a handkerchief. "I did not know you were about to take a wife."

"Neither did I," George confided, edging close to his love. "But she swept me off my feet and there is little I can do but wed the girl, lest I disgrace us all by taking her to bed without benefit of clergy."

"George!" Marianna whirled about to face him, her outrage comically clear to him. "How can you say such a thing?"

He ignored her remark. "I had thought we could plan a topiary dragon, you and I. It would be of shiny green ivy and set over that long reflecting pool at Mayne Court. Most fitting, wouldn't you say? You see, my little termagant, now that I have your full attention, I did all this because I quite fell in love with you that first time I saw you standing on the beach looking at me as though I was some sort of apparition. There you were, in some sort of green sprigged thing and so blasted lovely with that spun gold hair whipping about your head and the wind wrapping that gown so lovingly about your fine figure. I knew then that we were destined to be together eventually."

Totally astounded at these utterly incredible words of love from her scientific man, Marianna took a step forward, arms extended. "I think a topiary dragon would be a wonderful thing to create. And that,'' she promised him with her heart in her eyes, ''is not all we can create together.''

And George knew that she always kept her promises.

He had mentioned children by the hearth, and she considered that a project worthy of participation and hopefully one that might keep George as occupied as the topiary dragon.

When Lady Lavinia returned with the tiny silver dragon in her hand, she stopped by the door, putting a finger to her mouth as Gadsby neared. She closed the door very gently on the kissing couple, so tightly wrapped in each other's arms, and sighed blissfully. ''They have things to do, Gadsby. Such wonderful things.'' She gazed down at the dragon and he winked back in agreement.